THE
BESIEGED
PHARAOH

THE BESIEGED PHARAOH

BY

WILLIAM SPEIR

Progressive
RISING PHOENIX PRESS ®

Text Copyright © 2019 William Speir

All rights reserved.
Published 2019 by Progressive Rising Phoenix Press, LLC
www.progressiverisingphoenix.com

ISBN: 978-1-946329-98-1

Printed in the U.S.A.
1st Printing

Cover Photograph:
"Golden Mask of Tutankhamun" by A.M. v Sarosdy for SC Exhibitions, Germany (http://www.sc-exhibitions.com/) as part of their two touring exhibitions: *Tutankhamun - His Tomb and His Treasures* (Europe) and *The Discovery of King TUT* (United States of America). Used by permission of the owner © 2013 Semmel Concerts Entertainment GmbH.

Title Page Illustration:
Egyptian Chariot, Scanned from Nineveh and Its Palaces, by Joseph Bonomi, figure 108, 1853. This work is in the public domain in the United States because it was published (or registered with the U.S. Copyright Office) before January 1, 1923. https://commons.wikimedia.org/wiki/File:Egyptian-Chariot.png.

"Map of the Exodus" Illustration by William Speir

Book and Cover design by William Speir
Visit: http://www.williamspeir.com

ACKNOWLEDGMENTS

I want to thank all of my loyal readers, without whom I would not enjoy the creative process of writing.

Thanks to Amanda Thrasher and Jannifer Powelson at Progressive Rising Phoenix Press for believing in me and my books.

Special thanks go to my editorial team (Linda Speir, Ray Flynt, Jim Newman, Robyn Bartlett, and Gordon Napier) for their patience and their valuable contributions, suggestions, and corrections.

Deepest gratitude goes to my wife of 20 years, Lee Anne, for giving me the freedom of pursuing my passion. She is truly the love of my life. I am also grateful for my family (Sonya and Tom; and Brad, Susie, and Colten), without whom there would be no words worth writing.

To my father, William Byrd Speir, Sr., who touched the lives of so many people in ways he never knew. You are my inspiration and the standard against which I judge all of my actions.

INTRODUCTION

For decades, Ramses II ("Ramses the Great" – sometimes spelled Ramesses II) has been considered to be the Pharaoh of the Exodus (the escape of nearly two million Hebrew slaves from Egypt). I bought in to this popular myth for many years.

In 1989, the *Ramses The Great* exhibit came to Dallas, Texas. For almost nine months, I served as one of the volunteer coordinators for the exhibit. Spending hours each week surrounded by Egypt's rich treasures began my love for Egyptian history.

As I studied the history of the Pharaohs of Ancient Egypt, I happened upon a paper published in 2006 titled *Amenhotep II And The Historicity Of The Exodus-Pharaoh* by Douglas Petrovich, who serves on the faculty of Novosibirsk Biblical Theological Seminary in Novosibirsk, Russia. Petrovich presented a compelling case that Amenhotep II of the 18th Dynasty, and not Ramses II of the 19th dynasty, was actually the Pharaoh of the Exodus, placing the year of the Exodus at 1446 BC. Since reading his paper, I have found many other sources which also affirm that Amenhotep II was the Pharaoh of the Exodus.

As I studied the life and times of Amenhotep II, I discovered that the Exodus occurred in the 9th year of his reign, but he reigned for another 28 years after that. That started me wondering what those 28 years must have been like for him.

Imagine his return to his capital after the disaster at the Red Sea. The loss of the Hebrew slaves meant that there were not enough laborers to plant and harvest the crops, build buildings and temples, and tend to the needs of the Egyptians. The loss of 600 chariots at the hands of a foreign god meant that old enemies and conquered lands would sense an opportunity to exploit Egypt's newfound military weakness, and friendly nations would no longer see the appeal of having Egypt as an ally. The priests, who viewed Amenhotep II as a living god, would be humiliated by the loss of the slaves and the chariots at the hands of the god of slaves, and they would be concerned for their own positions in Egyptian society now that Pharaoh had been defeated. The people would still be mourning the loss of their firstborn children (the 10th plague on Egypt), the loss of the slaves, and the loss of the charioteers. And the various wives and concubines of Pharaoh would be plotting for their own sons to be named the next heir to Pharaoh's throne, now that Pharaoh's firstborn was among those who died from the 10th plague.

In short, Amenhotep II would be besieged on all sides by those who felt that Pharaoh had betrayed them and all of Egypt.

That's what this novel is about – the political intrigue that marked Amenhotep II's reign after the Exodus, and what he had to do to survive while restoring Egypt to its former glory before his enemies could carry out their plots against him.

William Speir
October 2018

AUTHOR'S NOTES

Egyptian Geography

The Kingdom of Egypt in the 15th Century BC centered on the River Nile and expanded very little beyond that region. Egypt's influence, though, spread across the eastern Mediterranean. Throughout this book, whenever possible, the names used at the time of Amenhotep II are used. Two notable exceptions are The Gulf of Suez and the Gulf of Aqaba. The ancient Egyptian names for these two bodies of water are lost to history, and I took the liberty of renaming them "The Gulf of Mafkat" (Suez) and "The Gulf of Reeds" (Aqaba).

Below is a table comparing the modern names to the names used in this book.

Name Used in the Book	Modern Name
The Middle Sea	The Mediterranean Sea
The Southern Sea	The Red Sea
The Gulf of Mafkat	The Gulf of Suez
The Gulf of Reeds	The Gulf of Aqaba
The Ar River	The Nile River
Lower Egypt	Northern Egypt - north of Memphis
Upper Egypt	Southern Egypt - south of Memphis

Name Used in the Book	Modern Name
City of Men-nefer Egypt's Northern Capital	Memphis (Mit Rahina, Giza, Egypt), 12 miles south of Cairo, Egypt and 120 miles south of the Mediterranean
Sakkara	The Memphis Necropolis (near Cairo, Egypt)
City of Waset Egypt's Southern Capital	Thebes (Luxor, Egypt), 500 miles south of the Mediterranean
Valley of the Kings	The Theban Necropolis, (Luxor, Egypt)
City of Peru-nefer	Naval base and port city in northern Egypt, identified with Tell el-Daba, in the Nile delta region where Avaris, the capital city of the Hyksos, once stood
Iunu	Heliopolis, Northern Religious Center of Egypt in NE Cairo, Egypt
Karnak	Southern Religious Center of Egypt in the Temple Complex of Karnak at Thebes (Luxor, Egypt)
Goshen	An area in the Nile delta 85 miles NE of Memphis just south of the Mediterranean
Red Land	The Egyptian Desert on the western edge of the Red Sea
Mafkat The Wilderness of Egypt "Country of Turquoise"	Sinai Peninsula
Kingdom of Nubia	Southern Egypt between the Nile and the Sudan
Kingdom of Kush	An ancient Nubian Kingdom in the Southern Nile Valley near the Sudan
Land of Punt	SE of Egypt in the coastal region of modern Djibouti, Eritrea, NE Ethiopia, Somalia, and Sudan
Kingdom of Mitanni	Northern Syria
Kingdom of Babylon	Mesopotamia (Iraq)

Name Used in the Book	Modern Name
Kingdom of Assyria	Upper Mesopotamia (northern Iraq, NE Syria, SE Turkey and the NW fringes of Iran)
Hittite Empire	Turkey, Syria, and Mesopotamia (Lebanon)
Kingdom of Arzawa	Area around Ephesus in Greece
Canaan	Lebanon, Israel, NW Jordan, and parts of western Syria
Anatolia	Asian Turkey
Levant Region	Eastern Mediterranean area, including Cyprus, Egypt, Iraq, Israel, Jordan, Lebanon, Palestine, Syria, and the areas of Turkey not part of Anatolia

Egyptian Calendar

The Egyptian calendar in the time of Amenhotep II was a solar calendar with a 365-day year. The year consisted of three seasons of 120 days each (organized around the annual flooding of the Nile River), plus an additional 5 days celebrated as the birthdays of the gods Osiris, Horus, Set, Isis, and Nephthys. Each of the three seasons was divided into four months of 30 days. Each month was divided into three 10-day periods known as decans. The last two days of each decan were treated as a weekend for royal craftsmen and artisans.

Seasons of the Egyptian Calendar:
- Flood (*Akhet*) – June to September
- Emergence (*Peret*) – October to January
- Low Water or Harvest (*Shemu*) – February to May

Months of the Egyptian Calendar:

Month	Egyptian Name	Season	English Name
1	Akhet Thoth	1st Month of Flood	June
2	Akhet Phaophi	2nd Month of Flood	July

Month	Egyptian Name	Season	English Name
3	Akhet Athyr	3rd Month of Flood	August
4	Akhet Choiak	4th Month of Flood	September
5	Peret Tybi	1st Month of Emergence	October
6	Peret Mechir	2nd Month of Emergence	November
7	Peret Phamenoth	3rd Month of Emergence	December
8	Peret Pharmuthi	4th Month of Emergence	January
9	Shemu Pachons	1st Month of Harvest	February
10	Shemu Payni	2nd Month of Harvest	March
11	Shemu Epiphi	3rd Month of Harvest	April
12	Shemu Mesore	4th Month of Harvest	May

Egyptian Mythology

The Gods and Goddesses of Ancient Egypt played an important part in the daily life of Pharaoh, the royal family, and the people of the kingdom. There are hundreds of deities in the Egyptian pantheon, but the following are the most important for this book.

- **Ra (Re)** – Ruler of the Egyptian gods, the primary sun god, father of every Egyptian king, the patron god of Iunu, and involved in creation and the afterlife.
- **Osiris** – The god of death and resurrection who rules the underworld and enlivens vegetation, the sun god, and deceased souls.
- **Isis** – Wife of Osiris and mother of Horus, linked with funerary rites, motherhood, protection, and magic.
- **Set** – An ambivalent god, connected with the desert and characterized by violence, chaos, and strength. Murderer of Osiris and enemy of Horus, but also a supporter of the king.
- **Nephthys** – The consort of Set who mourned Osiris alongside Isis.
- **Horus** – The son of Osiris and Isis, usually shown as a falcon or as a human child, linked with the sky, the sun, kingship, protection, and healing.
- **Ptah** – A creator deity and god of craftsmen, the patron god of Men-nefer (Memphis).

- **Amun** – A creator god, patron deity of the city of Waset, and the principal deity in Egypt during the reign of Amenhotep II.
- **Mut** – Consort of Amun, worshipped at Waset.
- **Khonsu** – A moon god, son of Amun and Mut.
- **Hathor** – One of the most important goddesses, linked with the sky, the sun, sexuality and motherhood, music and dance, foreign lands and goods, and the afterlife.
- **Anhur** – A god of war and hunting.
- **Montu** – A god of war and the sun, worshipped at Waset.
- **Khnum** – A ram god who was said to control the Nile flood and give life to gods and humans.
- **Hapi** – Personification of the Nile flood.
- **Wadj-wer** – Personification of the Middle Sea (Mediterranean Sea) or lakes of the Nile Delta.
- **Neper** – A god of grain.
- **Nepit** – A goddess of grain, female counterpart of Neper.
- **Renenutet** – An agricultural goddess.
- **Thoth** – A moon god, and a god of writing and scribes.
- **Nut** – A sky goddess.
- **Kek** – The god of Chaos and Darkness, as well as being the concept of primordial darkness.
- **Shu** – Embodiment of wind or air.
- **Sopdu** – A god of the sky and of Egypt's eastern border regions.
- **Sekhmet** – A lioness goddess, both destructive and violent, and capable of warding off disease, the protector of the pharaohs in war, and the consort of Ptah.
- **Bastet** – Goddess represented as a cat or lioness, linked with protection from evil.
- **Heket** – Frog goddess said to protect women in childbirth.
- **Maat** – Goddess who personified truth, justice, and order.
- **Anubis** – The god of embalming and protector of the dead.

The Exodus

While this is not a novel about the Exodus, the Hebrew escape from Egypt is an important event that sets the stage for what happens in this book. Given how long ago this event occurred, it should come as no surprise that, to this day, scholars still don't agree on the route of the Exodus.

Some scholars believe that the Hebrews crossed the Gulf of Mafkat (Gulf of Suez) into Mafkat (the Sinai Peninsula) and then went to Mount Sinai to worship God and receive the Ten Commandments. The principle flaw with this theory is that Mafkat was part of Egypt at the time of Amenhotep II's reign. Why would Moses lead the Hebrews through the Gulf of Mafkat on the western side of the Southern Sea (Red Sea), only to have them arrive on the other side still in Egypt? And given how long the Hebrews tarried at the base of the mountain when Moses went up to receive the Ten Commandments, it makes no sense that the mountain where they tarried was in Egypt. They would have been seen, and their presence in Egypt would have been reported to Pharaoh.

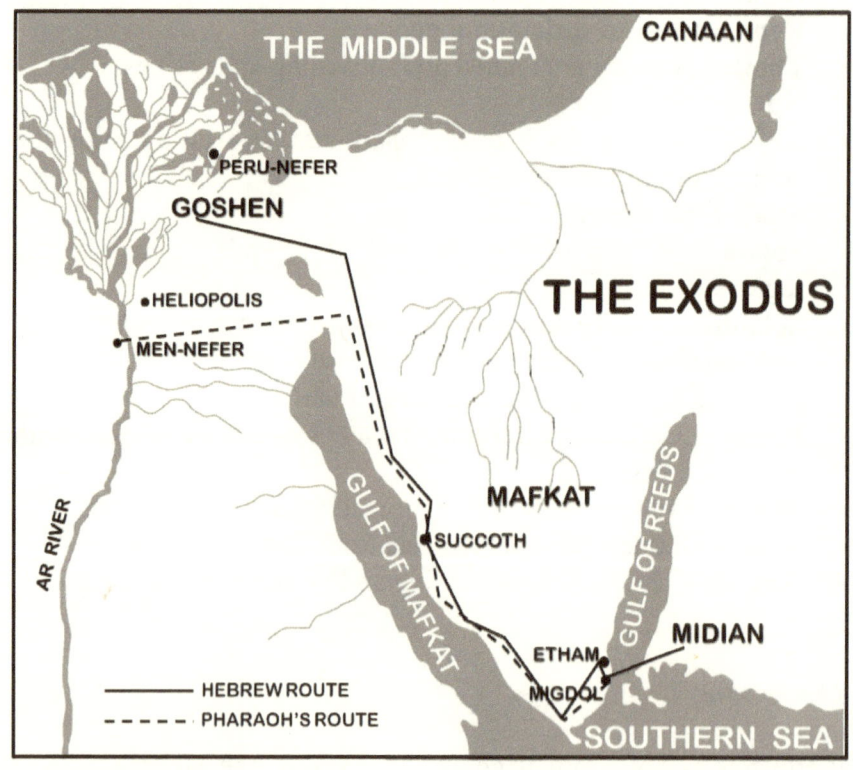

Other scholars believe that Moses led the Hebrews to the

southeastern edge of Mafkat and crossed the southern tip of the Gulf of Reeds (Gulf of Aqaba) into Midian (see map above).

There are a number of reasons why this theory makes sense from both a tactical and a logistical perspective.

1. The Children of Abraham, including the Hebrews and the Midianites, didn't understand the concept of a universal god. They saw their god as a tribal god belonging just to them. Moses was first introduced to the god of Abraham while still living in Midian (according to the biblical account of the burning bush). It makes sense that he would want to bring the Hebrews to the mountain where he had seen the burning bush. The Midianites believed that this mountain was where their god lived, and Moses would want the Hebrews to worship there. Crossing the Gulf of Reeds is the shortest and most direct route from Goshen to Midian.

2. Crossing at the Gulf of Reeds would have the Hebrews leaving Egyptian territory more quickly than following the caravan routes across Mafkat and then turning south to reach Midian.

3. Crossing at the Gulf of Reeds would allow the fleeing Hebrews one more chance to see their god's power over Pharaoh before leaving Egypt forever (the parting of the waters, and the destruction of Pharaoh's pursuing chariots when the waters closed). The Gulf of Reeds is the only body of water reasonably crossable that would lead the Hebrews out of Egypt.

It is for these reasons that I chose to have the Exodus follow the route shown in the map above.

CHAPTER 1

Amenhotep II, son of Thutmose III, the Pride of Amun, Great Son of Ra, Ruler of Iunu, Pharaoh of Upper and Lower Egypt, stood next to his broken chariot and watched helplessly as his chariot companies from Men-nefer vanished underneath the waters of the Southern Sea. A moment before, his chariots had been racing across dry land between the two walls of water that divided the sea across the southern mouth of the Gulf of Reeds. As the chariots bore down on the nearly two million Hebrew slaves escaping from Pharaoh's forces across the same dry land, the axles of the chariots all broke, as if by the hand of some unseen divine force. A heartbeat later, the two walls of water collapsed, covering his chariots and all traces of the Hebrews' escape to Midian across the sea.

Pharaoh watched the sea resume its normal shape, as if the waters had never been split by the might of the Hebrews' god. He stood motionless on the ridge above the seashore, waiting for some sign of his brave men. None appeared.

The enormity of what had just happened struck him deeply. He dropped to his knees next to the remnants of his own chariot and bowed toward the sea.

Five chariot companies! Twelve hundred brave men and horses, six hundred chariots, all gone. Destroyed by the god of slaves.

Pharaoh's hands clenched the sand, and he turned his face toward the sky and cried out in rage and grief.

Mighty Osiris, ruler of the underworld, accept these brave charioteers into your grace and grant them an afterlife, even though the funerary rites cannot be performed for them. Great Anubis, protector of the dead, gather the souls of those who were lost this day and convey them safely through the wasteland of demons so that they may find peace in the realm of the dead.

Pharaoh slowly rose to his feet and looked around. His chariot was broken beyond repair, its axle shattered on a rock as he led his forces after the Hebrews. His driver lay dead nearby – his head smashed against a rock when he had been thrown from the chariot. One of the horses was still harnessed to the chariot; the other had broken free and was nowhere to be seen. *The other horse is probably halfway to my army by now.*

Pharaoh carefully unhitched the remaining horse from the chariot's yoke and shortened what was left of the chariot's reins before reattaching them to the horse's bridle. He looked around for his khepresh, his blue war crown with the uraeus – the sacred cobra emblem – on the front, and saw it nearby where it had fallen from his head when the chariot had hit the rock. He grabbed the khepresh and mounted the horse. He placed the khepresh on his head, looked back at the sea one more time, and rode northwest toward his advancing army, which was following two or three days behind the chariot companies.

Anhur and Montu, last night I prayed to you to bring me victory against the Hebrews and against Moses. Now I pray to Amun, Sekhmet, and Sopdu to protect me until I can reach my army and have my soldiers escort me back to Men-nefer. Great gods of my fathers and of my kingdom, hear my prayers!

Pharaoh rode away from the Southern Sea with no food and no water. In the distance, he saw the hastily abandoned Hebrew camp. *Perhaps they left something behind that I can use.*

He reached the camp and saw that the Hebrews had indeed left much behind in their haste to escape from the advancing chariots. Pharaoh quickly found water, dried fruit, and unleavened bread. Too hungry and thirsty to care that he was eating the food of slaves, he quickly devoured the fruit and bread before searching for more to feed his horse and to take with him on the two-day ride to reach his advancing army.

After securing as much food and water as he could carry, he

2

set out again to the northwest. *Thank you, Sekhmet, for your gifts. When I return to Men-nefer, I will dedicate a new terrace for your temple at Waset... as soon as I can find someone to build the terrace, now that the Hebrews are gone.*

Pharaoh rode in silence, his mind replaying over and over again the calamities that began the day Moses returned to the palace at Men-nefer.

It was the ninth year of the reign of Amenhotep II, in the month of Peret Tybi, the first Month of Emergence – nearly seven months before the disaster at the Gulf of Reeds. The planting season had begun in earnest, and Pharaoh prepared for the two annual ceremonies to give thanks to the gods for the gifts of life.

The first ceremony was to Khnum and Hapi, the gods who controlled the flooding of the Ar River, to thank them for the floods that brought life to the farmlands along the river. The second ceremony was to Neper, Nepit, and Renenutet, the gods of grain and agriculture, to ask them to bless and protect the year's crops.

As the living god of Egypt, Pharaoh led most of the rituals that took place throughout the year, although all of the high priests from Karnak and Iunu were in Men-nefer to participate in and to oversee these rituals.

Pharaoh sat on the eastern terrace of his palace, enjoying the morning sun as he read dispatches from his emissaries in the kingdoms that surrounded the Middle Sea. He was interrupted by the arrival of Amenemipet, his Vizier, and Kenamun, the steward of Pharaoh's household and Amenhotep's childhood friend.

Pharaoh nodded to the two men, letting them know that they could approach.

"Great Pharaoh," they intoned, bowing.

"What brings *both* of you to see me?" Pharaoh put down the dispatches he had been reading.

Kenamun looked at Amenemipet, who answered, "The Priest of Midian desires an audience with you, Great Pharaoh."

"Midian?" Pharaoh asked. "Why would Midian be sending

an emissary? We haven't had any dealings with the Midianites in years."

"He didn't say, Great Pharaoh," Amenemipet replied. "Do you wish me to find out for you?"

Pharaoh stared absently at the tops of the city's many obelisks rising above the palace walls before answering. "No. Grant him an audience for this afternoon. And have all of the high priests present. This is a holy man and should be greeted by his fellow priests, even if the gods they worship are different."

"Yes, Great Pharaoh," Amenemipet and Kenamun responded before leaving Pharaoh's terrace.

A few hours later, Pharaoh sat on his throne. He carried the scepters of Egypt in his hands, and he wore the traditional red and white double crown of Upper and Lower Egypt and the wesekh collar of the Pharaoh. Along both sides of the throne room stood the high priests and their principal assistants.

Amenemipet announced that the Priest of Midian waited outside the throne room, and Pharaoh said, "Show him in."

A moment later, a tall man entered the throne room, accompanied by a shorter man. Pharaoh looked intently at the tall man and estimated that he must be about sixty years old. The shorter man looked older.

The tall man looked around the room and whispered to the shorter man, "It hasn't changed a bit. It's just the way I remember it."

When the two men reached the center of the room, they bowed to Pharaoh. "Welcome to Egypt, Priest of Midian," Pharaoh said. "I'm surprised that Midian would send us an emissary, given that we have had so few dealings with each other in my lifetime. And I couldn't help but overhear you a moment ago. Have you been here before?"

"Yes, Great Pharaoh," the tall man answered. "I grew up in Egypt. I spent most of my youth in the palace at Waset and in this palace."

"Really?" Pharaoh responded. "May I ask your name?"

"Certainly, Great Pharaoh. This is Aaron, my brother. My name is Moses."

Moses looked like he expected a reaction from Pharaoh at hearing his name. Getting none, he chuckled. "So like my brother to keep you in the dark about me."

"Your brother?" Pharaoh asked, confused. "Who is your brother?"

"My brother was your father, Thutmose III."

Pharaoh sat up as murmuring from the high priests broke the dead silence that followed Moses' proclamation. *My father had no brothers!*

Moses must have seen Pharaoh's confusion and disbelief. "Your father's mother, Hatshepsut, found me in a basket floating on the canal at Waset leading from the Ar River to her private apartments. She took me as her own son and declared me a Prince of Egypt."

Pharaoh smiled coldly. "And I suppose you can prove your claim?"

Moses shrugged. "Honestly, Great Pharaoh, I don't know if anyone still lives who was there when I was rescued and adopted by Hatshepsut. And since your father had my name stricken from every place in the kingdom, I doubt there are many who even remember when I left Egypt."

Pharaoh stared at Moses. *Is he mad, or is he telling the truth? It's easy to say that your name was stricken as a reason why your name appears nowhere in the kingdom. How can I find out if anything he says actually happened?*

Pharaoh was about to ask Moses another question when he saw Nebwawy, the aging High Priest of Osiris, step into the center of the room. "I remember, Great Pharaoh."

Moses spun around and looked at Nebwawy. He cocked his head and asked, "Nebwawy? Is that you?"

Nebwawy nodded, but he never took his eyes off Pharaoh.

Pharaoh motioned for Nebwawy to step forward. "What do you remember, Nebwawy?"

"Great Pharaoh, I remember Moses. I remember when he was found in the canal behind the palace at Waset, and I remember when your father cast Moses out of Egypt. This man, Moses, was indeed a Prince of Egypt and was raised as your father's brother.

5

But when it was learned that he was not a gift of the gods but rather the son of Hebrew slaves who were trying to save him from Hatshepsut's decree that the male children of the Hebrews be killed at birth, and when he chose to be acknowledged as a Hebrew after murdering your father's first Overseer of Works, your father banished him from Egypt and from the memory of Egypt."

Pharaoh nodded to Nebwawy and turned his attention back to Moses. "So you were once a Prince of Egypt, and now you're the Priest of Midian. You do get around, don't you?"

The high priests laughed.

Pharaoh held up his hand to silence his priests. "But if my father indeed banished you, why have you returned to Egypt?"

"I have returned for one reason, nephew, to collect something I left behind all those years ago."

There were several angry outbursts from the high priests when they heard Moses call Pharaoh "nephew."

"Don't ever call me 'nephew' again, Moses."

"Forgive me, Great Pharaoh." Moses bowed his head. "Being back in this place tends to bring out the arrogance of my youth."

Pharaoh nodded. "So what is it that you left behind and have come to collect?"

"My people, Great Pharaoh. I came back for them, and I want you to allow me to take them away. Let my people go, Pharaoh."

"What people?" Pharaoh demanded. "Midian is not part of my kingdom, and if you're referring to Egyptians, they're hardly 'your people' anymore, are they?"

"I'm not referring to Midian or Egypt, Great Pharaoh," Moses replied. "I'm referring to Goshen. I'm here for the Hebrews. I intend to lead them out of Egypt forever."

Pharaoh was impressed at the audacity of Moses to think that the two million Hebrew slaves in Goshen would just be turned over upon request. He shook his head. "I'm not prepared to discuss Goshen or the Hebrews at this time. Come back tomorrow, and we'll talk more about your claim to these people."

Kenamun motioned for two guards to escort Moses and Aaron out of the throne room. When only the Vizier, the high priests, and their assistants remained, Pharaoh turned to Nebwawy. "I want the whole story, Nebwawy. How did this man become a Prince of Egypt, and why was he cast out?"

6

Nebwawy nodded. "When your grandfather, Thutmose II, died, his only son, your father, was just two years old. Your grandfather's wife and half-sister Hatshepsut became regent. Since she was the daughter of a Pharaoh, she became Pharaoh herself and ruled until she died in your father's twenty-second year.

"Most of the building work being carried out by the Hebrew slaves was at Waset and Karnak at that time. We had Hebrews in the slave quarters at Waset and at Goshen. Hatshepsut became concerned that the Hebrews were breeding too many children, which she felt posed a risk to the kingdom. So she decreed that all male Hebrews be killed at birth as a way to reduce the population growth of the slaves. After all, Goshen lies at the eastern gates of the Ar River delta region, and nearly two million slaves in such a strategic location was a problem that required a drastic solution. She further decreed that the Hebrew slaves were only to be used for building works and agriculture. She didn't want them working in households in case of retaliation for her decree about the fate of the male children."

Pharaoh was surprised. He had never heard any of this, including anything about Hatshepsut being regent or being regarded as a Pharaoh in her own right.

Nebwawy continued his story. "One day, Hatshepsut was walking along the canal that led from the Ar River to her private chambers in the palace at Waset. She saw a basket floating in the canal, and she waded out and recovered it. Inside was the baby Moses. Hatshepsut had no children of her own, even though it was said that your aunt Neferure was her daughter. She wasn't. Hatshepsut didn't care that the child was a Hebrew boy who had been set adrift to avoid being killed by her own decree. She wanted a child of her own, so she named him Moses. A servant girl offered to find someone to nurse the child, and when the woman arrived, Hatshepsut knew instantly that it must be the child's mother."

"How?" Pharaoh asked.

"She had clearly given birth, and she wasn't sad that her baby had been killed by Hatshepsut's soldiers. If she had given birth to a girl, she would have been too busy to nurse Moses, and if she had given birth to a boy, she would have been grief-stricken. Instead, she looked excited to be nursing Moses."

Pharaoh nodded, gesturing for Nebwawy to tell him more.

"Hatshepsut ordered the woman to take Moses to the Children's Palace at Waset, where all of the children of the court were weaned. At the end of two years, Moses was to be presented to her, at which time she would either reject him or publicly acknowledge him as her son."

Pharaoh knew that this was normal for Egyptian nobility, having been raised in the Children's Palace in Men-nefer himself.

"Your father was almost five when Moses was presented to Hatshepsut. She publicly acknowledged Moses and credited his birth to the gods, not to the Hebrews. She named Moses a Prince of Egypt and second in line to the throne behind your father. As a Prince of Egypt, no law save Pharaoh's applied to him."

"How do you know all of this?" Pharaoh asked.

Nebwawy managed a weak smile. "I was Hatshepsut's chief spiritual advisor. She confided in me, making me the only other person who knew of Moses' true parentage. Hatshepsut made me swear to never reveal the truth. Since I am the High Priest of Osiris, my chief concern is the afterlife, and Hatshepsut made it clear that I would be denied an afterlife if I talked."

"And yet you're talking now," Pharaoh pointed out.

"That's because of what happened later, Great Pharaoh," Nebwawy replied. "As I was saying, Moses became a Prince of Egypt, and your father accepted him as an adopted brother. They grew up together in the palace at Waset, they both became great warriors, and they were the best of friends.

"When Hatshepsut died, your father was twenty-two and Moses was nineteen. Your father became Pharaoh, and Hatshepsut received the funerary rites of a Pharaoh for her accomplishments while regent. Moses carried out military campaigns in Kush, Punt, and Ethiopia to prevent an alliance with the Nubian Provinces to the south that could threaten the southern borders of the kingdom. Your father ordered that Moses' accomplishments be carved on a new terrace of the palace and in a new temple being finished at Karnak."

"Wait a moment," Pharaoh interrupted. "I've read every inscription in the palace at Waset and in every temple built in my father's lifetime. There's no mention that Moses led the campaigns in the south. The inscriptions say that my father and his generals led those campaigns."

"I know, Great Pharaoh," Nebwawy said. "I'm coming to that. In the thirtieth year of your father's reign, the building works at Waset and Karnak were finished. He ordered the Hebrews sent back to Goshen until the next building programs could be selected. Your father asked Moses to accompany the soldiers who were taking the slaves north. Thutmose also wanted Moses to inspect the northern defenses and survey Men-nefer for new building programs. Moses agreed.

"On the journey north, Moses got to know the Hebrews, and according to his own statements made later, his heart burned when he heard their prayers and songs. When he overheard them talking about Hatshepsut's decree to kill all newborn Hebrew males at the same time that he was rescued from the Ar River, he said that he started wondering if he might be Hebrew rather than Egyptian. He claimed that he was deeply affected by the way he saw the overseers treat the Hebrews. When the Hebrews reached Goshen, he saw your father's Overseer of Works beat a slave to death and then start beating another slave the same way. In a fit of rage, he killed the Overseer of Works."

"But as a Prince of Egypt, he had no fear of punishment, right?"

"Correct, Great Pharaoh. Moses was above the law, but the Overseer of Works was a high government official, and his murder was reported to your father. Moses made his inspection of the northern defenses, but when he arrived in Men-nefer, your father was waiting for him. Moses was escorted into this very room. Priests, officials, and military officers were all here, and guards stood at every entrance and exit.

"When your father demanded to know why Moses killed the Overseer of Works, Moses admitted that he suspected he might be Hebrew and not Egyptian. I was ordered to reveal what I have just told you as confirmation of Moses' suspicions. Your father then insisted that Moses decide whether he was a Prince of Egypt or the son of slaves. Moses declared that he was the son of slaves, much to everyone's shock.

"Your father was devastated. As a Prince of Egypt, Moses was above the law, but as a son of slaves who was condemned at birth, he should have been dead. Killing the Overseer of Works was done while Moses was still a Prince of Egypt by decree of

9

Hatshepsut, and as a Pharaoh in her own right, her word was law. But Moses could not remain a Prince of Egypt if he acknowledged that he was Hebrew, and he could not be sent to Goshen in case he led a revolt against Pharaoh and Egypt to free the Hebrew slaves. The only choices your father had were for Moses to be killed or to be banished.

"Your father was reluctant to kill the man he had called brother for most of his life. Moses declared that he would never lead the slaves in revolt against Pharaoh or Egypt, so your father decided to banish Moses. He warned Moses never to return. He then ordered Moses to be denied an afterlife by striking his name off every wall, pillar, obelisk, terrace, and entryway in every palace, official building, tomb under construction, and temple in the kingdom. All of Moses' accomplishments were attributed to your father or other men loyal to him. Your father also decreed that, because Hatshepsut had allowed a Hebrew to become a Prince of Egypt and inflict such anguish on your father by raising a Hebrew as his brother, Hatshepsut's name was to be stricken as well. He couldn't deny her an afterlife since she was already entombed, but he wanted to prevent anyone from remembering her in the future."

"So that's why my father asked me to continue his efforts to have Hatshepsut's name stricken from the kingdom," Pharaoh said. "I never understood, so I didn't have the workers make it a priority."

Nebwawy nodded. "In the thirty-first year of your father's reign, thirty-two years ago, Moses was taken out past the northeastern border forts along the edge of the great desert. He was given food and water for a week and ordered to start walking east. Your father's charioteers watched until he disappeared into the distance. Then they returned to Men-nefer."

For the entire time that Nebwawy answered Pharaoh's questions about Moses, the high priests and their assistants stood silently around the throne room, spellbound by the tale.

Pharaoh leaned back in his chair. "I was born five years after Moses was exiled. I imagine that his name had been stricken by then, which is why I had never heard of him."

Amenemipet stepped forward. "What are you going to tell Moses when he returns tomorrow, Great Pharaoh?"

Pharaoh stood. "I don't care if Moses was a Prince of Egypt or the King of Babylon. No one walks into my kingdom and demands the release of my slaves. They're mine, and mine they'll remain."

Late in the afternoon on the day of the disaster at the Gulf of Reeds, Amenhotep stopped for the night in the wilderness of Mafkat. He fed and watered his horse before eating some of the dried fruit and bread that he had acquired from the abandoned Hebrew camp. He sat down next to a tree, removed his khepresh, and stretched out.

As the last light of the sun disappeared in the west, he closed his eyes. *Great god Ra, father of kings and bringer of light, travel safely through the realm of demons, and rise again tomorrow. Light my way home.*

The sun did indeed rise the next morning, and after eating a quick breakfast and watering his horse, he set out again to the northwest. He tried to focus on his surroundings, but his mind continued replaying the events of the previous seven months.

Moses arrived at the palace on the morning after his first audience with Pharaoh, accompanied by Aaron, Moses' Hebrew brother. They were escorted to the throne room, where Pharaoh waited for them along with the high priests and military officers.

"Nebwawy has given me the details of your time in Egypt, Moses," Pharaoh stated as Moses stood before him.

"It's not a very happy story, is it, Great Pharaoh? Still, all things happen for a reason."

"You were warned by my father not to return to Egypt. Why did you disobey him?"

"I was sent by the god of my fathers to free his people," Moses answered.

"So now they're *his* people and not yours?" Pharaoh mocked

Moses. "Well, I don't know this god, and I don't know you. But I do know the people of Goshen, and I see no reason why I should set them free on your say-so."

"Then let me take the people of Goshen into the wilderness to worship our god," Moses suggested. "The people of Goshen need to return to the proper worship of our god."

"How far into the wilderness?" Pharaoh asked.

"Three days east of Goshen."

"Just the men of Goshen?"

Moses shook his head. "No, Great Pharaoh. Women and children, too. And we'll need to take our flocks with us."

"Why your flocks?" Pharaoh demanded.

"They must be sacrificed to our god," Moses replied.

"And what guarantee do you give me that your people will return to Goshen when they're finished sacrificing and worshiping?"

Moses just smiled. "What guarantee would you accept from a defrocked Prince of Egypt and a Hebrew?"

Pharaoh shook his head. "I'm not so easily fooled, Moses. Three days east is a three-day head start on my soldiers as you lead the people of Goshen to escape from Egypt. The answer is no."

"I warn you, Great Pharaoh," Moses said sternly. "My god will not be pleased with you if you refuse me. Let my people go."

"Go into the wilderness to sacrifice and worship, or go free from Egypt altogether?"

"Both," Moses answered.

"No. That's my final word."

Moses shook his head and turned to leave the throne room. "Remember, I am not responsible for what happens next."

What happened next was that Moses unleashed the demons of the underworld on the people of Egypt.

Moses came to see Pharaoh again and again to make the same demand that the Hebrews be let go. Pharaoh offered compromises to allow some of the Hebrews to sacrifice and worship three days into the wilderness, but not all. He even offered to allow all of the Hebrews to sacrifice and worship as long as they only ventured one day into the wilderness. But Moses rejected each of Pharaoh's compromises and unleashed another calamity on the people of Egypt.

For three months, Moses remained in Men-nefer and punished the people of Egypt in the name of his god. After enduring the loss of the season's crops, the death of the flocks and herds of Egypt, piles of dead frogs everywhere, boils, infestations of flying insects, burning hail, and utter darkness that blocked the sun and even kept torches from giving off any light, Pharaoh finally ordered Moses to leave Men-nefer and never show himself to Pharaoh again.

"If I ever see you again, Moses, I will have you killed," Pharaoh shouted at Moses as the guards escorted Moses and Aaron out of the throne room.

Moses left Men-nefer and journeyed to Goshen. When he arrived, he unleashed the tenth and most terrible calamity ever to hit Egypt. The firstborn males, females, and beasts were all killed in a single night, including Pharaoh's firstborn son, Prince Thutmose.

CHAPTER 2

As Pharaoh rode through the wilderness of Mafkat on the day after the disaster at the Gulf of Reeds, the pain of that terrible night still burned inside of him.

Moses killed my son. But it was my grief and my anger that brought the eleventh calamity on my people.

On the night that Moses unleashed the tenth calamity on Egypt, Pharaoh woke to the sound of wailing. It was as if the entire city of Men-nefer were in anguish.

What's going on? Has Moses unleashed yet another catastrophe on my kingdom? Weren't nine enough?

Pharaoh strode into the hallway outside the royal apartment and nearly fell as his foot caught on something lying on the floor. Looking down, he saw one of his guards – eyes open with a surprised expression frozen on his lifeless face.

Is the city under attack? Has someone breached the palace?

Pharaoh checked the guard for any wounds. Finding none, he returned to his chamber and retrieved his sword. Clutching it in his hand, he returned to the hallway and stepped over his fallen guard.

Around the corner, Pharaoh saw two more guards and a serving girl lying on the floor – dead – all of whom had the same blank stare and astonished look on their faces.

What has happened?

He heard wailing coming from the harem, where the women of the royal family and of the court lived in the palace. He headed in that direction and saw Tiaa, his royal wife and the mother of his firstborn, running towards him.

"What is it, Tiaa?" Pharaoh demanded as she approached. "What is happening?"

"It's Thutmose, our son," she sobbed. "Come quickly!"

Pharaoh followed her to the corridor housing the apartments occupied by his eleven sons, which ran parallel to the harem's main corridor. Tiaa led him into the apartment of his firstborn and heir, the older of his two sons named Thutmose.

Prince Thutmose lay on his bed, surrounded by priests and several of his brothers.

Pharaoh's daughter, Iaret, turned away from the bed – tears streaming down her cheeks. "Father…"

Pharaoh reached the bed and stared at the face of his son. The face had the same look as the dead guards and serving girl that he had encountered.

"There is no life in his body," the priests intoned. "Thutmose, Prince of Egypt has crossed the barrier into the netherworld."

The priests began chanting to Osiris to protect and welcome the soul of Pharaoh's son. Pharaoh moved past them and knelt next to his son's bed. He reached out and felt Thutmose's face. It was stone cold.

"What is happening?" Pharaoh choked on the words. "Who has killed my son?"

There was a loud clatter outside Thutmose's apartment. A moment later, Ahmose, his chief general, strode into the room.

"Forgive me, Great Pharaoh," he said from the doorway.

"What is it, General?" Pharaoh whispered hoarsely.

"The city is filled with the dead, Great Pharaoh. There's not a house in the city that isn't mourning a loss."

Pharaoh turned away from his son to face his general. "What is happening to my people, General?"

"I don't know, Great Pharaoh. But it appears that the dead are all firstborn sons or daughters."

"Thank the gods you weren't firstborn, Father," Iaret noted.

Pharaoh's face was grim as he stood. "That's true. I'm my

father's second son. My older brother and mother were killed in an accident when I was a child."

"I, too, am a second son, Great Pharaoh," General Ahmose said. The expression on his face was one of pain. "But my firstborn is a daughter, and she was found... dead... a short while ago."

"I'm sorry about your daughter, General. I remember her. She was a lovely girl." Pharaoh bent down and kissed the forehead of his lifeless son, and then he strode out of the apartment, signaling for General Ahmose to follow him.

"Send messengers to every corner of the kingdom and find out if this calamity is targeting all firstborn of Egypt or just the firstborn of this city." Pharaoh ordered.

"It will be done, Great Pharaoh!"

Over the next several hours, reports came in from all quarters of the capital city. The death toll was already in the hundreds by the time the first rays of the morning sun reached Pharaoh's terrace. There were fifty dead soldiers and servants in the palace alone, all of whom had already been removed. Only Prince Thutmose's body remained where it had been found. The priests had prayers to complete before the funerary rites could begin for the Prince of Egypt. It would take seventy days to complete the mummification process before the prince's body could be entombed.

"Bodies are piling up in all quarters, Great Pharaoh," Amenemipet said as he stood next to Pharaoh on the terrace. "What shall we do with them? As the sun rises higher in the sky, the stench of the dead will choke the air."

Pharaoh looked up at his Vizier. "Have the soldiers haul the dead to the Giza plateau and bury the bodies in a mass grave. Have the other cities bury their dead in the desert, too. And send priests to perform whatever funerary rites can be given quickly to ensure an afterlife for each of the dead."

"Yes, Great Pharaoh."

Tiaa approached her husband and knelt before him. "The priests have taken our son to be prepared for burial. Is it still your wish that he be interred in your tomb in the Valley of the Kings?"

Pharaoh nodded. Amenhotep's tomb, which was still under construction in the valley west of Waset, had several chambers where the children and wives who predeceased him would be entombed. "Make certain that the engineers seal the chamber well so no one will disturb our son's eternal rest."

Tiaa nodded. "I will see to it."

Pharaoh saw the tears on Tiaa's face as she rose. *She grieves. But is she grieving for the loss of her son or for the loss of her position as my royal wife and queen should I name the son of one of my other wives to succeed me?*

Several days after the death of Prince Thutmose, Pharaoh met with his advisors in the palace.

"Moses is in Goshen," General Ahmose announced. "An officer from your navy confirmed it. And it appears that Goshen is the only part of Egypt that was spared from this and the other calamities that have plagued your kingdom since Moses returned."

Pharaoh slammed his fist onto the table. "Moses! A ghost from the past who walks in here like the messenger of Set. Is he responsible for these deaths? Did my firstborn die because I refused to let the Hebrews follow Moses out of Egypt?"

"I don't know," General Ahmose said. "But no mortal hand was behind all of these deaths. It was either our gods or his god."

Pharaoh looked around the room. "And how do I fight against a god who can do this to us? What weapons do we possess that will kill a god?"

"None," General Ahmose admitted.

Amenemipet cleared his throat. "Great Pharaoh, what do we do about the Hebrews? If their god can kill our firstborn in a single night, what else can he do if we keep the Hebrews in Goshen?"

Amenmose, the Mayor of Men-nefer, interrupted. "There's a more important problem that we have to solve immediately. How are we going to feed the people of Egypt? There is no food."

Sennefer, the Mayor of Waset and the Overseer of the Granaries and Fields, Gardens, and Cattle of Amun, stood. "Amenmose is correct, Great Pharaoh. The crops and most of the cattle were destroyed by the calamities unleashed on us by Moses. I know we must mourn our dead, but the living are in terrible danger if we don't do something quickly."

"And if we find food, what's to keep Moses from destroying that as well?" Amenemipet demanded. "He's already proven that he can reach out and destroy any part of Egypt he wants. If we keep the Hebrews in Egypt, what will the next calamity be? Will any of us survive it?"

Pharaoh regarded his Vizier with a mixture of anger and grief. *Moses and his damnable Hebrew slaves. For over four hundred years, they have served us as we built the most glorious kingdom in the world. Am I to lose it all now because Moses returned from Midian? He killed my son. He killed the firstborn of Egypt. He destroyed our crops and killed our livestock. Clearly, there is nothing he won't do to achieve his purpose. What will be next for us? Will he unleash the crocodiles of the Ar River to eat us all? Will he allow our enemies to walk in and strip our very bones of whatever flesh remains? I am Pharaoh. My priests call me the "living god" of my people. But if I can't fight Moses' god, what do I do? My people look to me to protect them, but how can I protect them against a god who can do what Moses' god has done to us? Yes, two million slaves will be hard to replace, but won't it be harder to replace every Egyptian in the kingdom should Moses' god decide to do something worse? It's time to end these catastrophes against Egypt, and I see only one way to do it. He killed my son. He will kill no more sons and daughters of Egypt.*

As Amenemipet took his seat, Pharaoh nodded. "It's all the same problem. If we keep the Hebrews in Egypt, we risk an even worse calamity than the last one. If we're going to feed our people and rebuild what Moses has already destroyed, the Hebrews cannot remain here."

"You'd just let them go?" General Ahmose asked incredulously.

Pharaoh shook his head. "No, not let them go. Drive them out."

Pharaoh rose to his feet – his resolve turning to rage against the Hebrews and against Moses. "General, send soldiers to Goshen. Drive the Hebrews out of their homes and out of Egypt. Send them east following the same route that Moses took out of

Egypt when my father drove *him* out. They can take whatever they can carry, and they can take their flocks and herds, but nothing else. I want them gone. I don't care if they die in the wilderness as long as they're out of Egypt as quickly as possible. And any who refuse to leave or leave too slowly… kill them!"

"Yes, Great Pharaoh!"

"And then I want your men to sack Goshen. It's the most fertile land in Egypt. If they haven't finished harvesting their crops, or if they can't carry out all that they've already harvested, there may be food there that can be distributed across the kingdom. Send word to Admiral Thuti that I want him to use the navy to help with the food problems. Have him send ships to transport farmers north and bring the food they find south; have him send ships up the Ar River to Nubia and the southern provinces to see if their crops, flocks, and herds are as damaged as ours are; and have him send ships to our neighbors and see what food and livestock we can purchase to replenish our losses and to keep our people alive until the next planting season."

"It will be done," General Ahmose said. "But if we buy grain, fruit, and livestock from our neighbors, won't they learn of our plight? What if they try to exploit the situation?"

"General, I can assure you that our neighbors and enemies already know about our plight," Pharaoh responded. "Their emissaries undoubtedly sent messages to their masters as soon as Moses began punishing us for refusing his demands. Yes, they may decide to exploit the situation. But they might not. I don't know, but I do know that our people will starve if we don't get food. I can only deal with what I know. It'll be up to the army to defend Egypt should our enemies, or even our allies, decide to attack us while we're so vulnerable."

"Yes, Great Pharaoh."

Pharaoh turned to his Vizier to say something, and then he looked back at General Ahmose. "And send a squad of chariots to follow the Hebrews. I want to make certain that they leave Egypt and don't try to double back and attack us."

"Yes, Great Pharaoh."

Even though Pharaoh ordered the nearly two million slaves in Goshen to be freed and driven out of the kingdom, the people of Egypt were busy mourning the loss of their firstborn, their cattle, their crops, and the homes destroyed by the burning hail that Moses had unleashed. Slaves were the last thing on their minds.

Pharaoh's soldiers arrived in Goshen in Shemu Epiphi, the third Month of Harvest. They ordered every Hebrew to leave Egypt or be killed. The people of Goshen raised their voices in songs of praise to their god and gathered on the eastern bank of the Ar River. Moses gave the signal, and the Hebrews left Goshen and made their way east toward Canaan.

The squad of chariots, sent to watch the Hebrews leave, followed the tracks in the sand left by the former slaves. The chariots kept far enough back so the Hebrews wouldn't notice them.

At the beginning of Shemu Mesore, the fourth Month of Harvest and the end of the Egyptian year, Pharaoh met with his advisors again.

"The Hebrews have left Egypt, Great Pharaoh," General Ahmose reported. "Couriers from Goshen arrived this morning. The Hebrews have crossed into the eastern wilderness."

Pharaoh chuckled. "Can you image how the Canaanites will react when they see two million Hebrews marching across their lands?"

Pharaoh's advisors laughed.

"They aren't heading toward Canaan, Great Pharaoh," General Ahmose said.

"Where are they heading?" Pharaoh demanded.

"According to the squad of chariots that were following them, they turned south when they passed the northern tip of the Gulf of Mafkat. They're heading into Mafkat toward Succoth."

Pharaoh leapt to his feet. "Mafkat? That's hardly the most direct route out of Egypt. That makes no sense. Mafkat is a peninsula, bordered by the Gulf of Mafkat to the west, the Gulf of

Reeds to the east, and the Southern Sea to the south. If Moses is leading the Hebrews to Midian, he should have gone around the Gulf of Reeds before turning south. If he were heading for Canaan, he wouldn't have turned south at all. If they're in Mafkat, they could threaten our turquois mines. They could turn back and threaten our eastern border! What's Moses playing at?"

"I don't know, but they've definitely turned south," General Ahmose reported.

"Could Moses be so stupid as to trap his people between three bodies of water?" Amenemipet asked.

"He didn't seem stupid when he unleased calamity after calamity on my kingdom," Pharaoh said to his Vizier. "And don't forget, he was once a Prince of Egypt. According to Nebwawy, he was a very successful one. Moses doesn't impress me as someone who is stupid – only cunning and ruthless."

"Then what's he doing in Mafkat?" Mayor Amenmose asked.

A plan formed in Pharaoh's mind, fueled by anger and grief – the memory of seeing his young son dead was still raw in his heart. "I cannot allow the Hebrews to threaten our eastern border, potentially wreaking more havoc against us than they've already caused. Maybe this is an opportunity for us to extract revenge for the calamities caused by Moses and his god."

"Pharaoh?" General Ahmose inquired.

"If they continue south, they'll be trapped by two gulfs and the Southern Sea. If we attack, we can reduce their numbers far better than Hatshepsut ever did."

"And the survivors?" Amenemipet asked.

"Returned to Egypt."

The room erupted in protest over Pharaoh's plan to return the Hebrews to Egypt. "Great Pharaoh," Amenemipet said over the din, "Is it wise to bring them back after what has already happened? What will Moses do to us then?"

"Nothing. Killing Moses will be the first thing we do. The Hebrews who survive will be dragged back here, but things will be different."

"How so?" Mayor Amenmose asked.

"First of all, we will prevent them from breeding unchecked. The men will all be castrated, and the women will be bred with Egyptians and slaves from other lands. Their race will no longer be pure, and no slave will be allowed to breed without permission. Second, we won't let them return to Goshen. They'll be spread out across Egypt so they can be controlled more easily. We won't make the same mistakes as our ancestors."

There were nods around the table.

"How many soldiers do you want to take?" General Ahmose asked.

"One division," Pharaoh answered. "That will leave one division from here to protect the northern borders, and the two divisions from Waset to protect the southern borders and provinces. I think five thousand soldiers should make quick work of the Hebrews. I also want five chariot companies to lead the expedition. If the chariots can herd the Hebrews into a position where they're trapped against the water, then the soldiers can arrive and finish them off."

"Six hundred chariots against two million Hebrews?" General Ahmose asked.

"Twelve hundred of the finest charioteers from the most powerful army in the world against two million exhausted, unarmed slaves," Pharaoh corrected him. "They'll probably start killing each other to escape from us."

General Ahmose nodded. "When do you want to set out?"

"As soon as the preparations can be completed, General."

As the final preparations were being made for the six hundred chariots to leave Men-nefer, Tiaa approached Pharaoh.

"Good hunting, my Husband."

Pharaoh put a hand on her shoulder. "I will avenge the death of our son."

"Nothing can bring our son back," Tiaa reminded him. "Do what's right for your people."

"I'm doing this to protect my people from an enemy much larger than any we've faced before."

Tiaa nodded. "Come back safely, my Husband."

Pharaoh thumped his chest with his fist. "I'll be home soon with Moses' head on my lance."

22

Tiaa's eyes opened wide. "That will look perfect on the eastern wall of the city."

Pharaoh turned and left to join the charioteers waiting for him at the city gates.

Tiaa watched him leave the palace with a wicked smile. *Take all the time you need, my Husband. I have plans of my own to set in motion while you're gone.*

The sun was setting twelve days later when Pharaoh's chariot companies reached the ridge above the Hebrews, who were camped on the southeastern tip of the Mafkat peninsula. Pharaoh's army division was still at least three days behind.

"Look at them down there," Pharaoh said to his company commanders as they observed the former slaves spread out against the seashore below them.

"Do we attack now or wait until dawn?" one of his commanders asked.

Before Pharaoh could answer, he heard a shout from the Hebrews below and knew that he and his charioteers had been spotted. The shout was picked up by other Hebrews, and soon the screams of the frightened former slaves filled the evening air.

In the distance, Pharaoh saw Moses standing on a great rock next to the water. Moses lifted his arms, and a pillar of fire and smoke fell from the sky, creating a barrier between Pharaoh's forces and the Hebrews.

"What is that?" his company commanders exclaimed.

Pharaoh shook his head. "It appears that Moses and his god are up to their old tricks." Looking back at his charioteers, he added, "Clearly we can't attack until morning. Order the men to make camp, and post guards to watch what the Hebrews are doing down there."

"Yes, Great Pharaoh."

Before dawn the next morning, Pharaoh woke to the sound of shouts from the guards watching the Hebrews. The sky was growing lighter as he reached the top of the ridge and saw... no one.

The Hebrew camp below the ridge was deserted.

"Where are they?" he demanded.

The guards pointed to the east. Pharaoh looked where they were pointing and gasped.

Where before there had been the southern mouth of the Gulf of Reeds, now there were two walls of water with a wide strip of dry land in between. Pharaoh saw that the tracks from the Hebrew camp led straight to the opening in the sea.

Their god parted the Southern Sea and gave them dry land to escape from us? Who is this god of theirs?

"Why wasn't I informed about this?"

"Great Pharaoh," the captain of the guards responded, "We couldn't see what they were doing. The smoke obscured the entire camp. It wasn't until the sky lightened that we saw..."

Pharaoh nodded curtly. *In one night, their god parted the sea, and two million Hebrews escaped without being seen or heard! How long have they been gone?*

Pharaoh saw that the pillars of smoke and fire were dissipating. He turned and ordered his charioteers to prepare to follow the Hebrews. *They're not going to escape me so easily. I will see Moses dead before this day is over.*

Pharaoh put on his armor and his khepresh, and then he mounted his chariot. Drawing one of his lances, he shouted to his men, "The Hebrews think they can escape us, but they're wrong. Don't fear what their god has done for them. Use it against them. Follow me!"

Pharaoh's chariot driver flicked the reins, and the horses reared before racing down the ridge after the Hebrews. Six hundred chariots followed in close formation.

They rode through the abandoned Hebrew camp, following the tracks in the sand that marked the passage of two million former slaves. As they crested the ridge overlooking the seashore, Pharaoh's chariot hit a rock and stopped suddenly. Pharaoh's chariot driver flew over the front of the chariot and lay motionless. Pharaoh stayed in the chariot, but it had tilted to one side and could not move.

"Follow them!" Pharaoh shouted to his men. "But bring Moses to me alive. No one kills him but me!"

The chariot companies raced past Pharaoh down the ridge and onto the strip of land between the two great walls of water. Pharaoh leaped from his chariot and stood on the edge of the ridge, watching his chariots follow the Hebrews east through the sea.

Mid-afternoon on the day after the disaster at the Gulf of Reeds, Amenhotep turned north and continued riding toward his advancing army.

Pride and grief killed my charioteers. I mourned for my son, and I wanted revenge against Moses. Twelve hundred charioteers are dead. I suppose I should be grateful that I didn't lose the army division as well. Now I have to return to Men-nefer and explain that the god of the Hebrews is greater than the gods of Egypt. Oh great Ra and mighty Sekhmet, give me the strength I need to face my people after this defeat.

Pharaoh stopped for the night. The food and water were nearly depleted, but he saw to his horse before finishing the last of the rations.

The ghosts of the firstborn of Egypt and of his dead charioteers haunted his dreams that night, and when he awoke in the pre-dawn stillness, he was grateful that the night was over. He mounted his horse and rode north.

An hour after dawn, he reached high ground and looked out at the most welcome sight he had seen in days. Spread out on the plains below him was his army division.

Pharaoh patted the horse's neck. "We made it. Thank the gods, we made it."

Pharaoh nudged the sides of the horse and rode toward his waiting soldiers, knowing that they would wonder why he was returning alone. He dreaded having to explain to them what had happened at the Gulf of Reeds.

CHAPTER 3

Pharaoh rode into the army encampment unchallenged. He knew that the khepresh would identify him as Pharaoh – no one else would dare wear Pharaoh's war crown – but he still saw looks of surprise and confusion on the faces of his soldiers.

They're wondering why I'm alone and riding on a horse instead of my chariot. How do I tell them that the entire chariot force was lost?

Pharaoh saw General Ahmose approaching. He dismounted and handed the reins of the horse to one of the soldiers.

"Thank the gods you're all right, Great Pharaoh!" General Ahmose exclaimed when he reached Amenhotep. "Yesterday, we caught a riderless and half-starved horse with the markings of your personal chariot. We feared the worst."

Gesturing toward the south, General Ahmose asked, "Where are the charioteers that were with you? Where is your escort?"

Pharaoh saw that a large group of soldiers had gathered and were listening. "It was a trap," he said. "We never had a chance."

"A trap set by Hebrew slaves?" There was a tone of disdain in the General's voice at the idea.

Pharaoh shook his head. "No, a trap set by their god."

General Ahmose escorted Pharaoh to his tent. Once they were out of the soldiers' earshot, Pharaoh told the general what had happened at the Gulf of Reeds.

"The Hebrew god opened up the sea, so Moses could lead the slaves to safety, and then closed the sea to kill your charioteers?"

The shock was evident in General Ahmose's face. "How could this happen?"

Pharaoh shook his head. "Does it really matter, General? It happened. My quest for vengeance has failed. Tomorrow morning we return to Men-nefer and start repairing the damage that Moses and his god brought upon us."

"Yes, Great Pharaoh."

The army set out at first light, heading north the way they had come. It would take fourteen days to reach Men-nefer, and the soldiers made certain that they didn't let Pharaoh hear them voice their disappointment about the campaign against the Hebrews.

Most of the soldiers didn't know the details about what had happened at the Gulf of Reeds, but they knew that twelve hundred charioteers and horses were lost. Open speculation about the loss of the chariot companies was discouraged by the officers of the division.

Three days before the army reached Men-nefer, as the evening shadows lengthened across the wilderness, Pharaoh sat down with General Ahmose in Ahmose's tent.

"We'll be back in Men-nefer soon." General Ahmose handed Pharaoh a cup of beer and a platter of dried fruit and meat.

Pharaoh accepted the food and drink, and he leaned back in his chair. "Quite different from the last time we returned home from a campaign, eh?"

General Ahmose nodded. "The Mitanni fought well."

"They did," Pharaoh agreed. "Do you remember when their forces from the city of Qatna attacked us while crossing the Orontes River? We decimated them. We captured more than two thousand prisoners on that campaign, not to mention the seven princes we took at Kadesh. We brought home gold, silver, slaves… even a complete Mitanni chariot."

"They thought that you were still grieving the loss of your father." General Ahmose smiled. "You showed them that grief can be turned into strength. They learned a hard lesson about underestimating you."

Pharaoh ate some of the fruit on his platter. "They were arrogant even in defeat, weren't they? Those seven princes were defiant even as I killed each of them one by one. I hung their bodies upside down on the prow of my ship so their people could see what happened to those who defy me. Then I mounted six of the bodies on the walls of Waset and sent the remaining one to Nubia to remind them of the consequences of rising up against me."

Pharaoh stared at his platter. "Now look at us. Six hundred chariots lost, including the charioteers and horses, no prisoners, no slaves, no tribute or plunder... nothing to show for spending a month in the desert chasing after slaves. We never fired a single arrow at them. There was no fighting, no military engagement at all. And yet we still lost all of our chariots. If your men had been there, I have no doubt that we would have lost them, too."

General Ahmose leaned forward. "Great Pharaoh, you cannot blame yourself for what happened. You went up against a god. How can you defeat a god?"

"Aren't *I* supposed to be a god?" Pharaoh slammed his platter onto the table. "Isn't that what the priests tell everyone? I'm the 'living god of Egypt,' and yet with that, with all the might of my military, I'm no match for the god of slaves! And now, instead of returning to Men-nefer in triumph, I'm returning in humiliation. All because, in my grief and anger, I charged after the Hebrews on a campaign of vengeance, even after their god had already shown himself to be more powerful than I am... and my priests. The blood of those charioteers is on my hands, General. Mine."

The two men sat in silence for a while. Then General Ahmose asked, "Is there any reason to return to Men-nefer openly?"

"What do you mean?"

"Instead of you leading the division into the city for all to see that the chariots are all missing and that the campaign did not go as you wanted, send the division back to Men-nefer a company at a time. They'll blend in with the other soldiers that are coming and going to help with food distribution, and no one will know that the campaign is over. The soldiers will go straight to the city barracks. I can send messengers to Amenemipet and Mayor Amenmose, letting them know that you're arriving at the city in secret with a small escort, and you'll be waiting at the barracks until Amenemipet can arrange for you to return to the palace. That'll give you time to decide how you want the people to find out what happened."

Pharaoh nodded. "I like that idea. It will give me time to plan for what's coming next."

"Next?"

"Oh, come on, General." Pharaoh picked up the platter again. "You know that by now the Ethiopians, as well as the Canaanites, Mitanni, Assyrians, Babylonians, Hittites, and the rest of the states in the eastern region of the Middle Sea, will have heard what Moses and his god did to us. They'll know that I freed the Hebrews, and they'll eventually find out that the Hebrews escaped from our clutches when my chariots were destroyed by their god. How long do you think it will take them to decide to exploit our weakness? How long do you think it will take the southern provinces to decide that they no longer have to accept our rule? How will the kingdom survive if the tribute stops flowing from other nations or if the Nubians stop providing us with gold? War is coming, General, and we're not going to have much time to prepare for it."

General Ahmose nodded. "I've been wrestling with the same thoughts. I just didn't know when to broach the subject with you."

Pharaoh smiled. "I'm grateful that you see it, too. Tell me, if you were in my position and knew that war was coming, what would you do?"

"In our current state? I'd do everything I could to prevent the war."

"How?" Pharaoh demanded. "By suing for peace from our enemies? By showing the world that we're weak and helpless?"

"No. By attacking first before they're ready."

"We're in no condition to conquer our enemies."

General Ahmose shook his head. "We don't have to conquer them, Great Pharaoh. We need only make a show of force. Think of it as an expedition to acquire slaves. We just lost two million slaves, and we'll need more before the planting and harvest seasons. If we can start a campaign in the eastern states along the Middle Sea and capture more slaves than have ever been captured before, not only will it show our enemies, and our allies, that we're still a great military power, it will show your people what you're willing to do to help them overcome what we've lost. Your enemies will be caught off guard, and they'll be thinking long and hard about whether they're strong enough to go up against your armies if you're in a position to launch a military campaign so soon after what has just happened."

As Pharaoh stared at General Ahmose, a smile slowly crept across his face. "Brilliant, General. Brilliant. But can we pull this off, and how long do we have to prepare?"

"The armies of Egypt are more than up to the task, Great Pharaoh. And after what has just happened, they'll be itching to prove themselves in battle. As for when, I'd guess that we have less than five months to plan and begin the campaign. We need slaves ready to work the fields as soon as the floods from the Ar River recede."

"That doesn't give us much time."

"No," General Ahmose agreed. "But we have no choice, so we'll make it work."

"We'll need the senior commanders from the divisions at Waset to come to Men-nefer as soon as possible. We have to determine how many soldiers to take on the campaign and how many to leave behind to defend the kingdom should the southern provinces take advantage of the situation."

"If we take all of the Nubian archers with us, the southern provinces won't have much left to mount a rebellion with against the soldiers we leave behind."

Pharaoh nodded. "Good plan."

General Ahmose called for his scribe. "I'll have messengers sent to Men-nefer and Waset immediately to set things in motion."

The scribe entered the tent and prostrated before Pharaoh. General Ahmose dictated the messages he wanted sent to Men-nefer and Waset, and then the scribe left the tent to carry out the general's orders.

The two men ate in silence for a while.

"What do you suppose I'll find when I get back to my palace?" Pharaoh asked finally.

"Chaos and intrigue, Great Pharaoh. Chaos and intrigue."

"Explain."

General Ahmose hesitated. "It's not my place, Great

30

Pharaoh."

"I insist, General."

General Ahmose put down his platter and walked over to the entrance of his tent. He looked around before returning to his seat and moving it closer to Pharaoh. After he sat down, he leaned forward and whispered, "Very well. Your firstborn son is dead, leaving you with ten sons and one daughter that you've acknowledged. Your royal wife only has one more son to advance as your heir, Prince Amenhotep, your fourth-born son. If Queen Tiaa wants to remain your royal wife, she has to convince you that Prince Amenhotep should succeed you.

Pharaoh nodded but said nothing.

"Merytamon, your third wife, is mother to your second-born son, Prince Webensenu. As the second-born, he is the easy choice for heir, making her your new royal wife. I believe that Queen Tiaa will do everything she can to keep that from happening. Sitamun, your second wife, is mother to your third-born son, the younger Prince Thutmose. You have one other wife, Meratum, and four concubines – two of whom bore you sons. If the queen will stop at nothing to have Prince Amenhotep succeed you, then Princes Webensenu and Thutmose are in danger, as are their mothers. And so is anyone who would encourage you to select someone other than Prince Amenhotep to be your heir. I imagine that the harem and the children's apartments in the palace are buzzing with intrigue by now."

Pharaoh chuckled. "You see my problems very clearly, General. Your spies must be at least as good as Amenemipet's. But you forgot one point."

"What point?"

"The queen has a lover. She doesn't know that I know, but I do. I just don't know who he is yet. If she moves against me, she can easily have anyone killed who stands between her son and the throne, making her regent until Prince Amenhotep comes of age. She'd probably have all of my other children, wives, and concubines killed, just to be safe. I have no doubt that you and Amenemipet would be next on her list to eliminate so that there'd be no one left who might do to her what she'll do to me."

"That's treason!"

"That's Tiaa. She is perhaps the shrewdest woman I've ever

31

known. She's also the most corrupt. I don't remember her being like that when I first met her, but she certainly is now. If she's allowed to rule Egypt, even as regent, she'll tear the kingdom apart with her ambition and greed. She might even kill her own son just to remain regent. She could never be Pharaoh because she doesn't descend from a line of kings, but as regent, she'd wield the same power."

General Ahmose shook his head. "What are you going to do?"

"Watch and wait. If I'm right, she's not working alone. I want to know who her allies are so they can all be dealt with at the same time. Otherwise, I'll never be safe, and neither will my sons. I know I'll have to choose a successor eventually, but I want to see which of my sons is the most worthy. I don't want to choose one simply because of his age."

"And what about the people, Great Pharaoh?"

"The people?"

"As you said before, the people regard you as the 'living god of Egypt.' Are you worried about how they'll react to news of your loss against the Hebrews?"

Pharaoh thought about this for a moment. "That will likely depend on the food situation when we return. There are few things worse to deal with than hungry Egyptians. If we've located enough food to get us through the next planting season, the people will be more forgiving. Busy people rarely have time to think about how angry they are, and this year's planting and harvest should keep most of my people busy working in the fields."

Pharaoh drained his cup. "I was remiss in my duties by not finishing my father's work of removing Hatshepsut's and Moses' name and memory from Egypt. It should be easy enough to convince the people that Hatshepsut and Moses are to blame for what has happened and that the Hebrews were the real calamity upon Egypt. If I keep the people focusing their anger on Hatshepsut and Moses instead of on me, that should give me time to restore Egypt's rightful glory. And if the military campaign that you suggested yields a large number of slaves, then my people should forget about the Hebrew god's triumph and be satisfied."

"Very clever," General Ahmose noted.

"Thank you. That just leaves the priests."

32

"The priests?"

Pharaoh nodded. "Moses and his god humiliated them. And don't forget that their living god – me – failed to protect them by defeating Moses and his god. Their power comes from making the people believe that our gods are omnipotent, including me. I failed them when Moses unleashed his calamities on Egypt. That could easily shake the people's faith in our gods. If the people turn from the worship of the gods and stop paying tribute or stop working the lands controlled by the temples, the priests' wealth will dwindle, and their influence over the people will be lost. They may well decide that Egypt needs a new living god, since I've proven myself less than worthy to bear that title."

"But you're not the first Pharaoh who has been defeated in battle," General Ahmose pointed out. "Even your father lost battles. Defeat in battle is not the same as no longer being a living god."

"But I wasn't defeated in battle. There *was* no battle! I was defeated by a god, and that could shake the faith of the people to their core. If you were a priest, would you find it easier to restore the people's faith in me and the gods, or would you find it easier to find a new living god that could be used to rebuild the people's faith and obedience to the priests?"

"If I were a priest, and you had been defeated in battle, I would tell you that the gods were angry with you and to build a new temple as a way to get back in their good graces," the General replied cynically. "And if you had been victorious in battle, I would tell you to build a new temple as a gift to the gods for the victory. But I see what you mean. Again, what are you going to do?"

"Watch and wait. What else can I do? I can't defend myself against a weapon I can't see. I have to wait until one of the priests tips his hand. Then I'll know where and how to respond."

General Ahmose rose from his chair and knelt before Pharaoh. "I am sworn to protect you and the kingdom, Great Pharaoh. It appears that you will have enemies all around you. Whatever I can do to keep you safe, you have only to ask. I and my sword are yours."

Pharaoh put his hand on his general's shoulder. "And what of your soldiers, General? Will they continue to support me even after this defeat and humiliation?"

"I'll deal swiftly and harshly with any who don't, Great Pharaoh. And I believe that our next campaign will more than prove to them that you are worthy of their unwavering loyalty."

Pharaoh rose from his seat and motioned for General Ahmose to stand. "Thank you, General. Thank you."

"It is an honor to serve Pharaoh," General Ahmose stated, grasping Pharaoh's outstretched arm.

As the army marched closer to Men-nefer, General Ahmose sent companies of soldiers ahead so that the entire division wouldn't arrive at the capital at the same time.

As Pharaoh approached the Ar River, he looked across at his capital city. Its white walls stood out against the stone and brick buildings inside. His palace, which was visible from far away, dominated the city. The two great pylon towers flanking the main entrance of the palace rose higher than the city's principal temple, which stood on a hill near the palace. Banners lined the top of the towers. From across the river, Pharaoh saw the carvings on the towers, boasting of Egypt's strength and glory. Obelisks, memorials to the military achievements of past pharaohs, rose above the city walls. *There will be no obelisks raised to my campaign in Mafkat or the calamities caused by the Hebrews and their god.*

Pharaoh glanced beyond the walls of Men-nefer and saw the pyramids, tombs, and funerary temples of Sakkara – where members of royal and noble families were entombed – to the west and northwest of the city. *I suppose things could be worse. I could have died with my charioteers in the Gulf of Reeds, denying me an afterlife, or General Ahmose could be escorting my body home to be buried.* Pharaoh gazed at the pyramids for a while longer and then pressed his heels into the side of his horse. The horse immediately picked up its pace as Pharaoh continued riding toward the quarters of Men-nefer's army garrison.

Pharaoh arrived at the barracks at Men-nefer with General Ahmose and a hundred soldiers shortly after sunset in mid-Akhet

Thoth, the first Month of Flood. He had been gone an entire month, and he was impatient to hear news about how his kingdom was recovering from Moses' calamities. Amenemipet and Mayor Amenmose were both waiting at the barracks for Pharaoh to arrive.

"Welcome back, Great Pharaoh," the two officials intoned as Pharaoh dismounted. Pharaoh nodded and motioned for the two to follow him.

General Ahmose led Pharaoh and the two officials into his quarters at the far end of the barracks. Once inside, he ordered a servant to fetch refreshments, and then he offered the men seats. Pharaoh removed his khepresh and sat down first.

"What happened out there?" Amenemipet asked once they were alone.

Pharaoh gave a quick account of the campaign against the Hebrews. When he described what happened at the Gulf of Reeds, the two officials gasped but said nothing.

Pharaoh then recounted his conversation with General Ahmose and outlined his plans for the military campaign and the efforts to finish removing Hatshepsut's and Moses' name from across Egypt. He then summarized his concerns about what his wives and the priests might be planning.

"We have seen evidence of that already, Great Pharaoh," Amenemipet stated. "But I can talk to you about that as we return to the palace."

Pharaoh nodded. Then he asked about the condition of his kingdom and the people.

"The repairs to the city are nearly complete," Amenemipet began. "Most of the fire damage has been repaired, the dead have been removed, and the last of the remnants of the calamities have been cleared. Life is returning to normal."

"What about the food?" Pharaoh demanded.

"Fortunately, Lower Egypt was hit the hardest by the calamities. The southern provinces fared better, and their surplus food has been coming north, thanks to the navy, for many days. Even flocks and herds from the south have been coming north. Your Vizier in Nubia has been coordinating to have all excess herbs, fruit, and livestock sent down the Ar River as fast as your ships can carry them. The fish have also returned to the river. Evidently, there is more food for them now that the frogs have

35

gone. Our fishermen are harvesting fish in numbers I've never seen before, so our people will not starve."

"What about Goshen?"

"Their crops were untouched by the calamities, as you suspected, and little had been harvested when our men arrived. The crops have all been harvested and distributed across the kingdom. We seized everything else the Hebrews left behind, and we're still going through it all."

"What about trading for food from our neighbors?"

Amenemipet smiled. "It's amazing what gold can buy in the world. Flocks, beasts, fruit, and herbs have been arriving daily and are also being distributed across the kingdom."

Pharaoh felt relieved. "I guess the food crisis is over then."

"Not entirely, Great Pharaoh," Amenemipet responded. "We still don't have enough grain to feed all of the people. There is enough to keep the people from starving, but the people will be very weak if we don't find more grain before the next harvest season."

"How can I launch a campaign to keep our enemies from rising against us if our people – especially our soldiers – are weak?" Pharaoh demanded. "Is there no grain that can be bought from our neighbors?"

Amenemipet shook his head. "We've bought all that they could spare, but it's not enough, even when you add that to what we salvaged from Goshen and the southern provinces."

Pharaoh shook his head. Grain was a staple in the Egyptian diet, and without it, his people would not fare well. *How can I bring back slaves if my soldiers are too weak to fight? How can I defend my kingdom? There has to be grain somewhere.*

Pharaoh's mind searched for a solution to the problem. Then he remembered something. "The palace has its own granaries, doesn't it?"

"Yes," Amenemipet replied. "So do most of the cities and the houses of the nobility of Egypt. It's part of the defense against sieges and drought."

"And the temples have granaries as well?"

Amenemipet nodded. "Vast granaries, Great Pharaoh."

"Between all of those granaries, is there enough grain to keep the kingdom well-fed until the next harvest?"

Amenemipet thought about it for a moment. "Barely, Great Pharaoh. But the nobles and the priests will be furious."

Pharaoh snorted. "I'd rather them be furious and reasonably full than smug and overstuffed with bread, wouldn't you?"

Amenemipet nodded.

"Good. I want all granaries in Egypt seized and the grain distributed evenly across the kingdom... starting with the palace and city granaries here and at Waset. We'll make certain to plant enough next season to replace what is taken, but this is a matter of survival."

Pharaoh turned to General Ahmose. "General, see to it. All grain stores anywhere in the kingdom are to be seized and distributed to the people."

"It will be done, Great Pharaoh," the general responded.

After the meeting was over, Amenemipet led Pharaoh to the palace. General Ahmose sent a squad of twenty soldiers to protect Pharaoh and his Vizier as they walked through the city.

"What did you mean earlier about my wives and the priests?" Pharaoh asked as they made their way toward the palace.

"Tiaa has started putting her plots into motion," Amenemipet whispered so the soldiers wouldn't overhear. "She wants to secure her position quickly. My spies are trying to keep an eye on what's going on, but she's not using her usual agents this time."

"Who is she using?"

"Priests. Amenemhat, the young High Priest of Amun from Karnak, has practically taken over the palace with his priests in your absence. Tiaa is using his priests to do her dirty work, and I don't have enough spies to watch them all."

"Why are priests from Karnak and not Iunu in Men-nefer? And what about the Medjay, my guards?" Pharaoh asked. The Medjay were an elite force of Nubian soldiers who protected the palaces, the royal tombs, and the treasury, along with performing other special services on behalf of the Pharaoh.

"I don't know why Tiaa is using priests from Karnak, Great Pharaoh, other than perhaps the High Priest of Amun at Iunu is old, and his priests seldom trouble themselves with what happens here in your capital. Tiaa has most of your Medjay guards positioned outside the palace and is using the priests from Karnak to guard the palace interior."

Pharaoh turned to one of the soldiers. "Go back to General Ahmose and tell him I need two more squads at the palace immediately. They are to take position within the palace and serve as guards around my apartments and the princes' apartments."

"Yes, Great Pharaoh." The soldier turned and ran back to the barracks.

"A very wise precaution, Great Pharaoh."

When Pharaoh and Amenemipet arrived at the palace, Kenamun, Pharaoh's Chief Steward, was waiting to greet them. He stood between the two obelisks in front of the avenue of sphinxes that lined the way to the palace entrance at the base of the two pylon towers.

"More soldiers will be arriving shortly," Pharaoh told his boyhood friend as they entered the palace grounds. "The soldiers are responsible for the protection of me and my sons. Any priest, or anyone else who tries to interfere with their duties, is to be immediately arrested. Understood?"

"It will be done."

Two of the soldiers accompanied Pharaoh, Kenamun, and Amenemipet to Pharaoh's apartment. The rest marched toward the corridor where the princes' apartments were located. A few moments later, Pharaoh heard what he assumed to be the surprised grunting of priests who were being relieved of their guard duties for the princes.

When Pharaoh reached the corridor outside of his apartment, he turned to Kenamun and Amenemipet. "Thank you both. Let's all meet first thing in the morning. The presence of so many priests makes me think that we need a strategy for dealing with the intrigue undoubtedly targeting me and my sons."

"Yes, Great Pharaoh," both men responded before leaving Pharaoh with the two soldiers serving as his escort.

After allowing the soldiers to search the apartment, Pharaoh entered. As he crossed the sitting area, he removed his khepresh and placed it on a nearby table along with his armor and wrist cuffs. Then he entered the bedchamber and tumbled face first onto the bed – the first bed he had slept in for a month. He was asleep before he could kick off his sandals.

CHAPTER 4

Amenemhat, the High Priest of Amun from Karnak, woke as the first rays of the morning sun rose over the palace walls at Mennefer. After offering a prayer of gratitude to Ra for safely passing through the realm of demons, he turned to the woman lying next to him.

"Wake up, my beloved," he whispered into her ear as he nuzzled her bare shoulder.

The woman stretched and looked sleepily into her lover's eyes. "Good morning, my darling," she purred. "Is it time to get up, or it is time to continue what we started last night?"

Amenemhat smiled and kissed her passionately. He pulled back the covers, exposing her naked body, but before he could mount her again, he heard soldiers outside in the hallway.

"What is it?" she asked, seeing the look of concern on his face.

"Soldiers in the palace," he hissed. He leaped from the bed, grabbed his robes, and began dressing.

"How do you know?" she asked.

"Because my priests wear soft sandals that barely make a sound when they walk, and I hear the stomping of heavy sandals and the sound of spears striking the stone floors."

The woman got out of bed and began to dress. "Do you think my husband is back from hunting down the Hebrews?"

Amenemhat blanched at the thought. "Don't you think there would have been fanfare throughout the city if Pharaoh had returned?"

Tiaa, Pharaoh's royal wife, shrugged as she put on her jewelry. "You tell me. I was in Waset when he returned to Men-nefer after his first military campaign."

"Whether he's back or not, we'd better find out why there are soldiers in the palace and why my priests didn't warn us." Amenemhat gazed at Tiaa as she finished dressing and combing her long black hair. The pale linen sheath dress complimented her figure and the color of her skin, and her jewelry shimmered in the low light. He was aroused and wanted to take her again, but she slipped on her sandals and walked toward the entrance of her bedchamber.

Tiaa moved aside the curtains that separated the bedchamber from the sitting area of her apartment. She crossed the sitting area to the antechamber with its washing pool, peered down the corridor, and then retreated back to the sitting area. She glanced through the curtains lining her terrace and returned to her bedchamber.

"There are soldiers at the entrance to the harem and outside my terrace," she whispered. "You'll have to go out through the courtyard at the far end of the corridor and go around to the other side of the palace if you want to avoid them."

Amenemhat held her tightly. "Anything you say, my love."

Tiaa kissed him quickly. "Just go!"

Amenemhat hastened across the sitting area to the antechamber, looked around for the soldiers, and then raced down the corridor away from the entrance to the harem and the soldiers standing guard.

Kenamun entered Pharaoh's apartment in the palace at Men-nefer with Amenemipet, a servant, and two soldiers. The morning sun shone on Pharaoh's eastern terrace, but his bedchamber was still dark.

"Pharaoh?" Kenamun stood just inside Amenhotep's bedchamber.

"Who's there?" Pharaoh responded groggily.

"It's Kenamun, Great Pharaoh. I'm here with Amenemipet as you requested."

"Is it morning already?" Pharaoh stirred. "I feel like I just lay down."

Kenamun stepped back into the sitting area and motioned for the servant to help Pharaoh clean himself and change into a fresh linen kilt. Kenamun heard the servant pour water into a basin, followed by sloshing.

Pharaoh appeared a few moments later with his shaved head and face still wet. He sat down next to the curtains, which billowed in the morning breeze along the terrace. The servant dried Pharaoh's head and placed the wesekh collar around his neck. Amenhotep's wesekh – one of the symbols of Pharaoh's rank – was in the form of Horus the falcon, with the body of the bird in the center and the wings spread outward around Pharaoh's neck. The wesekh was made of gold and silver tubes, but throughout the design were beads made of turquoise, lapis, feldspar, jasper, and carnelian. The servant fastened the collar's gold clasps in the back, and then he placed the nemes – the traditional striped headdress with its gold uraeus – on Pharaoh's head. The servant handed Pharaoh his gold cuffs and withdrew from the apartment to fetch food.

Once Pharaoh had placed the cuffs on his wrist, he gestured for Kenamun and Amenemipet to sit.

"What's the latest here in the palace?"

Amenemipet answered. "The priests were rounded up as soon as the additional soldiers arrived from the barracks. They protested being relieved of their guard duties and were all arrested. General Ahmose is housing them in the chariot stables."

"And my family?" Pharaoh asked.

"There are soldiers on duty outside each of your sons' apartments, guarding the entrance into the harem, along the terraces, and outside your apartments. You and your sons will have soldier escorts until you order otherwise."

Pharaoh nodded and looked at Kenamun. "What about my wives and concubines? What mischief have they begun?"

"Nothing that I can prove yet," Kenamun replied. "Tiaa moved faster than the others when she invited Amenemhat and his priests to take over the security of the palace. With most of the priests in custody, her spy network is damaged, but she has other spies among the servants. I know she talked to your sisters and some of the concubines, but I haven't seen her talking to your other wives."

"Anything else?"

Kenamun stared at the floor.

"Out with it," Pharaoh demanded.

"Again, I can't prove it, but it appears that she wasn't alone this morning. The soldiers interfered with my spies seeing who it was, but there was definitely a man seen running down the harem corridor away from her apartment."

"And you have no idea who it was?"

"No, Great Pharaoh."

Pharaoh nodded. "And apart from the soldiers, does anyone know that I'm back in Men-nefer?"

"Not as far as we know, Great Pharaoh," Kenamun and Amenemipet responded.

Pharaoh stood. "Then it's time to inform my family."

Tiaa exited her apartment and walked down the corridor to the harem's entrance. The two soldiers snapped to attention when she passed. As Tiaa walked through the palace, she saw soldiers everywhere.

What are they all doing here, and where are Amenemhat's priests? Who would dare let soldiers into the palace? It must have been Kenamun. I don't care if he IS Pharaoh's childhood friend, I'll have him flogged for this.

She rounded the corner that led to Pharaoh's apartments and recognized Kenamun and Amenemipet walking away toward the throne room. "Kenamun!"

Kenamun stopped and turned toward Tiaa. "Yes, my Queen? Did you need something?"

"What are all of these soldiers doing in the palace?" she demanded as she reached the two men. "And what happened to the priests I assigned as guards?"

"The soldiers have replaced the priests to supplement the

Medjay guarding the palace, my Queen," Kenamun replied calmly. "The priests were removed during the night."

"Why?"

"I had my orders, my Queen."

"Orders? And just whose orders can supersede my own?" Enraged, Tiaa shouted at the top of her voice.

"Mine."

Tiaa froze when she recognized the voice. She slowly turned her head and saw Pharaoh standing there, staring at her with a dark look on his face.

Pharaoh gestured for Kenamun and Amenemipet to walk away as he watched his wife bow to cover the look of shock on her face.

"My Husband, I had no idea you had returned to Men-nefer. No messages were sent announcing your arrival. Was the campaign a success?"

"The campaign went badly, and I don't wish to discuss it with you. By what right do you replace my loyal Medjay guards with priests? And since when is the palace become a temple to Amun?"

Tiaa straightened up trying to appear calm. Only her eyes betrayed any fear. She hesitated answering.

Pharaoh heard approaching footsteps and stepped back into the shadows.

"Where are all of my priests?" a voice shouted. "I've searched the entire palace, and I can't find any of them…"

"High Priest," Tiaa interrupted, turning toward the voice. "You honor us with your presence."

"My presence?" Amenemhat sounded confused as he approached her. "What…"

Amenemhat stopped short when he reached the corridor that led to Pharaoh's apartments and saw Pharaoh standing there.

He shot a glance at Tiaa and then immediately dropped to his knees. "Great Pharaoh! I had no idea you had returned. Welcome back!"

Pharaoh looked down at the High Priest of Amun and began

to understand whom his wife had been with that morning. *So Amenemhat is Tiaa's lover. No wonder she turned to him to seize control of the palace when I left. I'll have to watch them both very closely. A queen is terrible to cross, but a High Priest is even more so. I'll have to be careful.*

"Why aren't you at the temple in Karnak?" Pharaoh asked coldly. "I know of no festivals or rituals to Amun that require you to be in Men-nefer at this time."

Amenemhat regarded Pharaoh. "I'm here to look after the spiritual well-being of your family, Great Pharaoh," he responded with the manners of a cobra eyeing its prey. "My thoughts were only to help fill the void left in their souls when their living god set out on the campaign against the Hebrews, which I trust was a success."

"It was not." Pharaoh snapped more harshly that he intended. *I know what void you were filling last night, priest.*

Before Amenemhat could ask another question, Pharaoh held up his hand. "The living god has returned. The void is filled. You are no longer required here. Return to your temple with your priests.

"Yes, Great Pharaoh." Amenemhat hastened from Pharaoh's presence.

Tiaa pouted once Amenemhat had left. "That was rude."

Pharaoh waved his hand dismissively and walked past his royal wife in the same direction that Kenamun and Amenemipet had taken.

"Don't walk away from me, Husband," Tiaa said sternly. "I want to talk about what happened with the Hebrews."

"Not now, Tiaa." Pharaoh continued walking away.

"And what about my son, *Great Pharaoh*?" Tiaa's voice was shrill. "If the campaign went badly, how are you going to get justice for my son?"

Pharaoh whirled around and glared at Tiaa, who shrank somewhat from the rage in his eyes. "*Our* son, Tiaa," he growled. "He was *my* son, too. And it's not for *you* to question *me* on how I get justice for what was done to Egypt *or* to our family. You're not Pharaoh. *I* am. Remember your place."

"Yes, Great Pharaoh." Tiaa's voice was contrite, but there was still an edge to it.

Pharaoh turned his back on her and walked away. When he reached the throne room, Kenamun and Amenemipet were waiting for him.

"How did it go?" Kenamun asked.

Pharaoh snorted. "It would appear that Amenemhat was with her last night."

"The High Priest of Amun from Karnak? Amenemipet looked surprised. "That explains a lot, but it's not good. He has spies everywhere. He knows more about what's going on inside the kingdom than I do."

"That must change," Pharaoh stated. "I don't care if you have to recruit more spies or if you choose to start killing his, but I don't want anyone knowing more about what's going on than you. Understood?"

"Yes, Great Pharaoh."

"We'll continue this discussion a little later. I need to arrange for Amenemhat's arrested priests to be returned to Karnak, and I have to meet with the captain of my Medjay guards and give him new orders. Meet me back here in an hour."

When Amenemipet and Kenamun met Pharaoh in the throne room an hour later, Kenamun said, "There's another matter I must bring to your attention, Great Pharaoh."

Pharaoh motioned for him to continue.

"It pertains to your safety. Specifically, poisons."

"Poisons?" Pharaoh was surprised. "Why poisons?"

"Because one of the food tasters who samples your food each meal fell ill this morning. I don't know if it's from poison or some other malady, but I can't take any chances where your health is concerned."

"How is the taster?"

"He's still quite ill," Kenamun replied. "He's being tended to by the physicians, and I'll let you know when his condition changes."

Pharaoh shook his head. "I have always known that you had my food tasted, but I thought it was more for show than to actually save me from poisoning."

"No, the threat is quite real," Kenamun explained. "This is just the first time anything has happened that might suggest an attempt to poison you."

Kenamun continued. "For ages, poisons have been one of the favored tools of assassination by the nobility. Even Hatshepsut was fascinated with them. One of her serving girls swore that Hatshepsut actually died while mixing a poison made of seeds from Ethiopia."

"What do we do about that?" Pharaoh asked.

Kenamun looked concerned. "There's little we can do about slow-acting poisons, but we can defend against the faster-acting ones by increasing the number of food tasters."

"Will that help?"

"Possibly. My worry is that someone might bribe your current food tasters. If the taster administers the poison, he could sample your food safely because he'd already know where the poison is. We need to bring in new tasters and switch them often so no one will know which taster is going to check your food. We should also have one taster check the food before it's brought out, and another taster check it before you begin eating. That will make it harder to bribe the tasters and give any potential poison more time to show itself. I'd recommend doing the same for the princes. Now that the succession is unclear, they're all in danger."

"And there's nothing we can do about slow poisons?" Pharaoh asked.

Kenamun shook his head. "No, Great Pharaoh. It's said that the poison Hatshepsut was mixing could take days before the first signs appeared, and then several more days before killing its victim."

Amenemipet spoke up. "Let's ban these seeds from Ethiopia immediately. There may be other slow-acting poisons, but at least we can defend against this one."

Pharaoh nodded. "Do it."

Turning to Kenamun, Pharaoh added. "I want to have a banquet for my family and for the senior officials tonight. Have the new tasters in place by then. I want my food and the food of the princes tasted by new people in front of my entire family. And watch for who reacts to this. That will help us identify anyone already thinking about using poisons in the food."

"A brilliant plan, Great Pharaoh!" Kenamun smiled. "I'll see to it."

That evening, Pharaoh held the banquet in the palace. Apart from Amenemipet, his Vizier, Mayor Amenmose, and General Ahmose, only Pharaoh's wives, concubines, children, siblings, nieces, and nephews attended.

Pharaoh had not held a banquet for his entire family since before Moses arrived, and Pharaoh felt it was long overdue. He wanted to reconnect with his family after the defeat at the Gulf of Reeds, and he wanted to let his family in on what would be happening over the next several months.

A forest of columns in the shape of palm trees and papyrus reed bundles lined the banquet hall. The brightly painted columns stood in pairs on either side of the hall, carved with hieroglyphs that gave the history of Egypt and the great deeds of the gods and pharaohs. The ceiling above the hall, supported by wooden lintels and headers resting on the columns, was adorned with images representing the sky. The light from the braziers around the hall danced as the evening breeze blew in through the windows along the upper part of the hall between the columns and the ceiling.

Kenamun had the kitchen prepare a meal of herbed fish and fruit, but Pharaoh insisted that there be no breads or other dishes made with grain.

The new tasters sampled the food before any of the men ate. Tiaa and the other women noticed the change but made no comments. Tiaa looked particularly annoyed.

"Why are we all together tonight, Father?" Prince Webensenu asked once the meal was over and the dancers had left the hall.

Pharaoh smiled at his second-born son. "It's been too long since we were all together – well before we lost your oldest brother. And there are things that have happened and are about to happen that I want to tell you all."

"Did you crush the Hebrews?" Prince Amenhotep asked.

48

Pharaoh shook his head. "No, they escaped my grasp."

"How, Father?" the young prince asked.

Pharaoh told his family what had happened at the Gulf of Reeds. He left nothing out.

Prince Amenhotep had a look of wonder on his face. "So they escaped through a canyon of water? I wish I could have seen that."

"I wish I could forget it," Pharaoh said. Then he added, "It's clear to me that Egypt will no longer be punished now that the Hebrews are gone. I say 'good riddance.' *They* were the real calamity on Egypt, and now that they're gone, we can rebuild and once again be the envy of the world!"

"How?" Tiaa asked. "Our cities and temples are what made us the envy of the world, and without anyone to build them for us, we will slowly decay and fade into a distant memory."

Pharaoh shook his head. "We will have slaves to build for us again."

"Where will these slaves come from?" Tiaa demanded.

Pharaoh outlined the initial plans for his next military campaign.

"May I go with you, Father?" Prince Webensenu asked.

Pharaoh smiled. "Not yet, my son. Soon you'll be old enough to accompany me, but not now."

"Is Webensenu now your heir, Father?" Princess Iaret asked.

Pharaoh's wives tried to shush the princess, but Pharaoh answered her question. "I haven't chosen my new successor, Iaret. I want to pick the son who is the most worthy; the one who shows the most promise and skill at being Pharaoh. I'll make my decision when I think the time is right."

Pharaoh watched the reactions of his wives and concubines. Most simply nodded, but Tiaa had a contemptuous look on her face and fidgeted with her jewelry nervously, as if it were suddenly too heavy or was irritating her skin. Her gaze darted to each of Pharaoh's other wives and concubines like each one of them was her mortal enemy.

"Is there anything else going on that you want to tell us?" Prince Webensenu asked.

"Yes there is," Pharaoh said. "You probably noticed that there was no bread with our supper tonight. Egypt is still very low on grain, and we have to be careful how much we eat if we're going to make what we have last until the next harvest."

"But we have dozens of granaries here at the palace," Tiaa said. "We should have plenty of grain to last us."

"We did, but not anymore." Pharaoh stated. "I've had the grain stores here at the palace and at the palace in Waset emptied and distributed to our people…"

"You gave away our grain?" Tiaa cried.

"Not just *our* grain. The granaries of the nobles, the cities and towns, and the temple granaries are also being emptied and distributed to the people."

"You can't take the grain from the temples!" Tiaa sounded incredulous. "That's for the gods!"

"It's not the gods who get fat on the temple grains, it's the priests." Pharaoh's voice turned cold. "And you forget yourself once again, Tiaa. As Pharaoh, my word is law, and none can overrule me. If I decide to distribute all of Egypt's grain stores so that my people will have bread to eat, then that's what will happen. Don't ever tell me what I can and cannot do again. Remember, you're only my royal wife for as long as *I* say you are."

Tiaa fell silent but glared at Pharaoh with a look of near-hatred.

Tiaa stormed back to her apartment in the harem after the banquet. Her rage was difficult to mask. Soldiers saluted as she passed, but she ignored them all.

Only his royal wife for as long as he says I am? Who does he think he is? He should remember that he's only Pharaoh for life, and there have been many Pharaohs whose reigns were cut short.

She entered the antechamber of her apartment. As she crossed the sitting area, she felt two arms wrap themselves around her shoulders.

"My darling," a man's voice whispered.

Tiaa turned around. "Amenemhat!" She kissed him. "What are you doing here?"

"I had to see you, my love," the High Priest whispered.

"Pharaoh's soldiers can't keep me from you."

Tiaa kissed him again and again.

"In a moment, my love." Amenemhat pulled away. "I have something for you."

Amenemhat untied a bag from his jeweled belt and handed it to her. "My agents in Ethiopia sent me this to give to you. It's just the first of several bags being sent."

Tia opened the bag excitedly. "My seeds!"

Amenemhat looked at the light brown seeds with dark brown spots that filled the bag. "What are they for?"

"They're the seeds of the castor plant. They can be used to cure skin conditions, if you're careful, and they can be used to ease headaches and eye conditions."

"You don't have any of those, my darling."

Tiaa smiled. "I know. If you break the seeds open, the meat inside can be distilled into a poison that will kill in the most terrible way."

"How terrible?"

"Stomach pain, vomiting, uncontrollable liquid bowel movements, burning in the chest, parching of the mouth and skin, and then death. It can take several days to die, and the first symptoms don't even show up for a day or two."

"And what do you plan to do with such a poison?"

"I have a few things in mind." Tiaa closed the bag and placed it in a chest on a nearby table. "I also have something to tell you. Pharaoh has ordered all granaries emptied and the grain distributed to his people throughout Egypt. This includes the granaries here in the palace, in the nobles' houses, in all of the towns, and in the temples."

"No! He can't do that!"

"He already has. He sent soldiers to make it happen, and anyone who resists will be arrested. When I protested, he reminded me that he can replace me as royal wife any time he wants."

Amenemhat shook his head. "The other priests and the nobles will band against him. There may even be an uprising."

"Not from the people. They'll love him for being willing to distribute his own grain so that they can eat bread. It could even help them stop blaming him for the loss of their firstborn."

"Is that why he did it?" Amenemhat asked. "To secure the

love of the people? Doesn't he realize that power is more important than the love of his people?"

Tiaa took Amenemhat's hand in her own. "Who knows? But if the nobles are angry enough to move against Pharaoh, wouldn't you rather they be working with us rather than working on their own? We don't want their wrath to accidently turn on us, do we?"

"Are you suggesting that we convince the nobles to join together with us to help usher in a new Egypt? One with you as regent perhaps?"

"Perhaps," Tiaa purred.

Amenemhat kissed her. "Oh, how I love you, my Queen!"

"I know."

CHAPTER 5

Pharaoh's assertion that other nations had heard of the departure of the Hebrews proved to be true. Less than a month after his return to Men-nefer, Pharaoh received an emissary from Ethiopia.

A chamberlain escorted the emissary into the throne room, where Pharaoh and many of his military officers and civil advisors were gathered. This was the time of year that Ethiopia paid its annual tribute to Egypt, and Pharaoh and his officials were anxious to see what their southern neighbor had sent

"The Emissary from Ethiopia," the chamberlain bellowed.

A tall man in flowing robes, a leopard skin sash, and an elaborate Ethiopian headdress with plumes and gold accents walked to the center of the room and faced Pharaoh.

"Greetings *great* Pharaoh of Egypt." The emissary's tone sounded like he was mocking Amenhotep.

Pharaoh stared expressionless at the Ethiopian, ignoring the man's subtle disrespect. "What news from your master?"

The emissary drew himself to his full height. "My master instructs me to say that he will be unable to pay the annual tribute this year. Possibly for the next several years as well, Pharaoh."

"And why is that?" Pharaoh's expression turned dark. "Why is your master abandoning his obligations to Egypt?"

"Great Pharaoh," the emissary began, "my master no longer believes that Egypt has the strength to enforce those obligations. We received news that your army was lost chasing after escaping slaves, who were led by the former Prince of Egypt who first conquered and subjugated our lands. And, after all, if you cannot win a military campaign against mere slaves and one of your own former princes, how can you expect to retain control of your subjugated kingdoms?"

Angry murmurs arose from around the throne room, but Pharaoh held up his hand, and the room grew eerily quiet. "So your master believes that my armies were destroyed and that the loss of the Hebrews is sufficient justification for an act of defiance against Egypt?"

The emissary nodded confidently.

Pharaoh roared with laughter. The sound echoed around the throne room, startling the emissary and the assembled Egyptian officials. "Your master is a fool, then. What happened with the Hebrews was not a contest of armies. My forces never even engaged the Hebrews. It was a contest between their god and my gods, and on that day, their god won. It was no military victory for the Hebrews. I lost only six companies of charioteers against the Hebrew god; the rest of my armies are intact and ready to enforce my will."

"They weren't d-d-destroyed?" Sweat beaded on the emissary's brow.

Pharaoh shook his head and leaned forward in his chair. "Your master would do well to remember Egypt's military victories against his kingdom. We've already seen that his armies – and his gods for that matter – are no match for mine."

Pharaoh gestured north, toward the empty city of Goshen. "The slave city of Goshen now lies empty, waiting to be filled with new slaves. I'd rather fill it with captives from campaigns to the east and the north, but I'm certain that my people wouldn't mind if I filled it with captives from the south. Tell your master that if the tribute doesn't keep flowing as before, I'll lead my armies against him, destroy him and his armies, and drag his people back to Goshen in chains to replace the lost Hebrews. Now, go!"

The emissary bowed low and quickly backed out of the throne room.

"And you tell your master that I am still *HIS* MASTER," Pharaoh shouted after the retreating Ethiopian. "You remind him of that!"

"Yes...yes, Great Pharaoh!"

Pharaoh met with General Ahmose, Admiral Thuti, and the other assembled military officers shortly after the emissary from Ethiopia left the palace.

"I anticipated that Ethiopia would be the first to openly defy us after the loss of the Hebrews," Pharaoh said. "Now that it has happened, we need to finalize our plans for the campaign and launch it as quickly as we can. It won't take long for the kingdoms in the north and the east to follow Ethiopia's lead."

Pharaoh pointed to the map on the table in his council chamber. "If we treat this campaign as an expedition for prisoners and to keep our enemies from moving against us, I recommend that we do not attack the Assyrians, Mitanni, or Hittites directly. If we land our forces north of Joffa but south of the Assyrian and Hittite borders, we can sweep south, driving prisoners and other tribute toward Egypt."

Admiral Thuti looked closely at the map. "There are a number of places where we can land the ships, Great Pharaoh, but it will take every ship in the fleet to get your soldiers to northern Canaan. If you plan to take your chariots on this expedition, we'll have to make multiple trips to transport the horses and other equipment."

"What if we land the foot soldiers and archers first?" General Ahmose suggested. "They could establish a beachhead while the navy goes back to pick up the chariots. The charioteers would have no difficulty catching up to the lead companies of the army once they arrive in Canaan."

"That's a sound strategy, General." Pharaoh looked around the table and saw heads nodding in agreement.

"When do you want to begin the campaign?" Admiral Thuti asked.

"Peret Mechir, the second month of Emergence," Pharaoh replied. "We have just enough people to begin the planting, but we'll need new slaves in place to tend to and harvest the crops. We'll have to land our forces at the beginning of the month and sweep through the region as fast as we can to prevent disaster."

"How many forces do you want to take on the expedition?" General Ahmose asked.

"Three divisions of foot soldiers, all of the Nubian archers, and most of the remaining chariots, leaving behind as many chariots as are necessary to serve as couriers. The fourth division of foot soldiers will be spread across the kingdom to defend against attack and to escort the arriving prisoners to Goshen."

"How many prisoners are you hoping to capture?" Admiral Thuti asked.

"As many as we can, Admiral. Certainly more than have ever been captured before."

"Once the chariots have been offloaded, I can have the navy move south slowly so some of the prisoners can be sailed back to Egypt as they are captured. It might make it easier for the army if they don't have to herd all of the prisoners back to Egypt by land."

Pharaoh nodded. "Good plan, Admiral. Deliver the prisoners to Goshen, turn around, and return to load the next group of prisoners. The army will follow the land route back to Egypt, driving the remaining prisoners toward Goshen."

Pharaoh ordered his scribe to write down everything that had been decided. Then he looked around the room. "Can we be ready to start the expedition in four months at the beginning of Peret Mechir?"

"Yes, Great Pharaoh!"

The Vizier, Amenemipet, waited for Pharaoh outside the council chamber.

"May I have a word with you, Great Pharaoh?"

"Certainly. Walk with me."

The two men walked toward Pharaoh's apartment. They passed a number of cats curled up in the pools of sunlight across the floor while other cats played and chased any mice, rats, and jerboas that tried to invade the palace.

When they were out of earshot, Amenemipet whispered, "The High Priest of Amun is still in Men-nefer, despite your instructions to return to Karnak."

"Is Amenemhat entertaining Tiaa while he disobeys my instructions?"

"Yes, Great Pharaoh."

Pharaoh snorted.

"And it appears that he has agents in Ethiopia purchasing seeds."

"*Banned* seeds?" Pharaoh asked.

"Yes. He's already delivered the first bag of seeds to her. One of my agents found it in her apartment this morning."

"Does she know what to do with the seeds?"

"I'm not certain, but the seeds haven't been touched yet, so if she knows, she's taking her time creating the poison."

Pharaoh shook his head in disgust. "What else is she up to?"

"She's making changes to the kitchen staff, which is infuriating Kenamun to no end. And it looks like many of the changes are to exchange Kenamun's people for Amenemhat's priests in disguise."

"She can poison anyone in the palace if she has control of the kitchen!"

"I know, Great Pharaoh. But we have to move cautiously. If we can find a way to discredit the people she has placed into the kitchen, we could replace them without her protesting. Otherwise, we risk her discovering that we suspect her."

Pharaoh paced angrily at Tiaa's treachery. "Anything else?"

"Yes, your daughter Iaret asked to see you in private."

Iaret came to see Pharaoh shortly before supper, and she was escorted to Pharaoh's private terrace. Extra guards had been posted to make certain that they were not overheard.

At fourteen years old, Iaret was already a striking beauty. She was Pharaoh's only daughter and the oldest child of his second wife, Sitamun. She was his oldest surviving child, having been born a month after the late Prince Thutmose, Pharaoh's first-born son by Tiaa. Her next oldest sibling by Sitamun was Pharaoh's third-born and favorite surviving son, Prince Thutmose.

She gave Pharaoh a kiss, sat down in the seat next to his, and accepted a plate of fruit from her father. She gazed intently at her father, noting the sad expression in his eyes that had been there ever since he returned from Mafkat.

"Why are you so sad lately, Father? Is it because of that bad man who came and took the Hebrews away from you?"

Pharaoh smiled at his daughter. "Partly, yes."

"I don't want to make you sad."

"How could you do anything that would make me sad?" Pharaoh asked.

"If I tell you what I came here to tell you, it'll make you sad.

Pharaoh put a hand on his daughter's hand. "Just tell me what you came to tell me, Iaret, and let me worry about whether or not it makes me sad."

Iaret stared at the fruit on her plate. "Did you know that there are hidden corridors all through the harem?"

"I've heard rumors over the years, but I've never gone looking for them. Have you?"

Iaret nodded. "I found them years ago. I use them to spy on the other women. It's good to know what other people are up to, don't you think?"

Now more than ever. Pharaoh patted Iaret's hand.

Iaret continued. "There's a hidden corridor that leads from my apartment to Tiaa's apartment."

Pharaoh tried to appear calm. "Have you been spying on her?"

Iaret smoothed a wrinkle on her gown. "She doesn't sleep alone, you know. There's a priest who spends almost every night with her. It's been going on for a while."

"Which priest?"

"I don't know, Father. They whisper a lot, but the only word I can hear clearly is 'regent.' I've never seen his face. Oh, and he brings her strange gifts."

"Like what?" Pharaoh asked.

"Like a bag of seeds that can be made into poison. She wants to use it on Webensenu and my brother Thutmose so her son Amenhotep will be next in line for your throne."

"You heard her planning to kill Webensenu and Thutmose?"

"Yes. I warned Thutmose to stay away from her, but I can't get close to Webensenu. She has him watched day and night."

"What else is she up to?" Pharaoh made a mental note to have Amenemipet and Kenamun watch Webensenu more closely.

"She's planning something in the kitchen. She has been taking the priests that used to guard the palace while you were in Mafkat, and she has been assigning them to the kitchen as food servers. She wants them to tamper with your food and the princes' food."

"How does that make you feel?"

"Angry. Whatever she's planning, I don't want her to succeed. She's not trying to be a good wife to you; she's doing whatever will make Prince Amenhotep the next Pharaoh."

"Has she approached you to participate in her schemes?" Pharaoh asked.

Iaret nodded. "Yes, Father. She has approached all of the women in the harem – all of your wives, concubines, sisters, and cousins who live in the palace. I don't think the rest of them see what her real plans are, because she lies very well. But I know the truth; I hear what she says when she doesn't think anyone is listening."

Pharaoh regarded his daughter carefully. "And you have no interest in helping her succeed?"

"No, Father!"

"Do you want to help me?"

"Yes, Father."

"Even if it means pretending to help her?"

Iaret smiled a wicked smile. "That sounds like fun!"

"It's also dangerous, Iaret. I don't want you getting hurt."

"Trust me, I can handle Tiaa and her priest."

Pharaoh called for a servant to fetch Amenemipet and Kenamun.

When Amenemipet and Kenamun arrived, Pharaoh quickly told them what Iaret had learned about Tiaa.

"We need to keep Tiaa off balance, so she has to spend time dealing with what we're doing, rather than taking the initiative to advance her own plans," Pharaoh said.

"We need to get those priests out of the kitchens and out of the palace," Kenamun said angrily.

"And we need to keep the other women in the harem from supporting her," Amenemipet pointed out.

"How do we do that?" Pharaoh asked.

Iaret giggled.

"You have something to contribute, Iaret?"

Iaret smiled. "Yes, Father. Host another banquet for the royal family, and have someone tamper with your food. Make certain that one of Tiaa's men brings you your food and tastes it, but don't let him know that it's been tampered with. When he falls over dead, look at Tiaa like you're accusing her of the deed. Everyone in the hall will see that you think she's behind it. Then your guards can take you from the hall. Amenemipet will arrest all of Tiaa's agents in the kitchen and the rest of the palace, and Kenamun can replace them with people loyal to you. Tiaa will lose allies in the harem, and it will set her plans back while she deals with what happened."

"Brilliant!" Amenemipet exclaimed.

Iaret blushed. "We used to do it all the time in the children's palace. If you want to get someone in trouble, hurt yourself and blame someone else. It always works."

Pharaoh laughed. "And if someone we trust approaches Tiaa afterwards and offers to help, we can stay a step or two ahead of my *dear* wife."

"I can do that," Iaret offered.

"What do you think?" Pharaoh asked Amenemipet and Kenamun after Iaret left his terrace and returned to her apartment in the harem.

"I think she may be one of the sneakiest and cleverest young women I've ever met," Amenemipet said with admiration. "She's wise beyond her years, and she has a clearer mind for strategy than someone twice her age. If she weren't your daughter, I'd make her one of my spies."

"If her plan works and we can get rid of Tiaa's agents in the palace, she'll make things much easier to handle around here," Kenamun added.

Pharaoh nodded. "Let's plan the banquet for tomorrow night. I'd like to get Tiaa's agents out of the palace and Iaret secured in

Tiaa's inner circle as quickly as possible."

The banquet was a beautiful affair. A gentle breeze blew through the palace, causing the curtains to sway and billow. The musicians had chosen a lively tune, and the dancing girls did their best to keep up with the tempo in the warm evening air. When the tune was done, everyone applauded. The dancing girls began a slower and more titillating dance as servers brought in the food.

The tasters stepped forward to sample each of the dishes before they were served. Pharaoh ignored his taster and watched the dancers as their whirling became more frenzied. Just as Pharaoh reached out his hand to accept the platter of food from the taster, the taster's eyes rolled back in his head, and he fell. The serving platter clattered loudly against the stone floor, causing the dancing girls to stop and stare at what was happening.

Pharaoh stood and looked down at his taster, who was convulsing on the floor. A moment later, the convulsing stopped. The taster's eyes were open, but he wasn't breathing.

Pharaoh immediately glared at Tiaa as guards rushed in to escort Pharaoh and the princes out of the hall. All eyes were on Tiaa, and Pharaoh saw her expression change from confusion to fear. She stared at Pharaoh's face, and he could tell that she knew he was accusing her of the murder.

The guards ushered Pharaoh and the princes back to their apartments, leaving Tiaa surrounded by the concerned and enraged members of Pharaoh's family.

Iaret visited her father later that night.

"It worked perfectly, Father," Iaret giggled. "After you left, everyone just glared at Tiaa. She claimed that she had nothing to do with it, but no one believed her. She finally fled the hall and went back to her apartment."

"When are you going to approach her?" Pharaoh asked.

"I'll give her a couple of days to regain her composure," Iaret replied. "Then I'll step in as the ally she's been looking for."

"Just be careful, Iaret," Pharaoh warned. "She's not one to underestimate."

"Neither am I, Father."

By the next morning, Amenemipet's men had arrested all of Tiaa's agents inside the kitchens and the rest of the palace, including the few of Amenemhat's priests who had not already been captured. Her agents were replaced with people loyal to Pharaoh. No one ever spoke about what happened to her agents, but Amenemipet knew where the bodies had been buried.

Tiaa was still in a rage the next night when Amenemhat snuck into her apartment in the harem.

"Tell me you didn't do this!" she hissed when she saw him.

"Of course I didn't, my love."

"And none of your priests tried something on his own?"

"I can assure you that none of my priests did this. If one of the other High Priests tried to move against Pharaoh, I'd know nothing about it."

Tiaa fumed. "I have to find out who was behind this. Everyone in the palace thinks I did it!"

"What about my priests that you placed here in the palace?" Amenemhat asked.

"Amenemipet arrested them all! And Kenamun has brought in a phalanx of tasters that are loyal only to him and to Pharaoh. Kenamun's planning to use two tasters instead of one, and he's rotating them so that not even the tasters will know whose food they'll be sampling until the last moment. How am I supposed to tamper with people's food now?"

"You'll just have to find a different way to administer your poisons, my love."

Tiaa glared at her lover, but her gaze softened. "You're right. It's time to start working with those seeds you brought me."

Amenemhat held up his hands in a gesture of caution. "But use them sparingly. It's now forbidden to bring seeds from Ethiopia into Egypt, so it'll be difficult to get you more anytime soon."

Tiaa threw a silver goblet across the room. She stared at its dented shape in the low light.

"What else can go wrong?"

Amenemhat reached his arms around her and slid her gown from her shoulders. "Let me make something right for you, my darling."

Neither Amenemhat nor Tiaa noticed a faint snickering sound as Iaret left her hiding place inside the walls and returned to her own apartment.

CHAPTER 6

At the end of Akhet Phaophi, the second Month of Flood, Prince Thutmose's sarcophagus was laid to rest in one of the chambers in Pharaoh's tomb in the Valley of the Kings near Waset before being sealed behind a wall of stone. Pharaoh ordered guards placed around the tomb to prevent the prince's body and treasures from being desecrated by robbers.

Pharaoh's barge pulled into the royal docks of the port city of Peru-nefer. Pharaoh always loved coming here, but he had never seen the port so busy before. It was an amazing sight.

Peru-nefer, originally called Avaris when it was the capital city of the Hyksos invaders more than a century earlier, lay along the easternmost branch of the Ar River just south of the Middle Sea coast and northwest of Goshen. Not only was the city where most commercial shipments arrived to be taxed before heading up the Ar River to Men-nefer and Waset, it was also the home port and shipyards for Pharaoh's royal navy.

The rowers raised their oars, and Pharaoh's barge glided to a stop in front of the spacious home that served as Amenhotep's northern palace. Little more than a compound surrounded by lush gardens, it was Pharaoh's favorite place to get away and rest from the toils of ruling the most powerful kingdom in the known world.

Pharaoh's Medjay guards exited the barge and secured the dock area before Pharaoh disembarked. Pharaoh looked around the port, amazed at how fast it had grown since he first visited with his father twenty years earlier. Merchant ships representing dozens of kingdoms were tied to every open space along the docks. On the north end of the harbor, near the shipyards, Pharaoh's navy was preparing to leave on the military expedition to northern Canaan.

Pharaoh's three oldest sons – Princes Webensenu, Thutmose, and Amenhotep – had accompanied him on the trip north. He had never brought them to Peru-nefer before, and he knew that the port would provide endless distractions for them. He wanted to bring his daughter Iaret with him as well, but she was deeply imbedded in Tiaa's plots in the palace at Men-nefer, and Pharaoh needed her to remain close to his royal wife.

Pharaoh came to Peru-nefer to inspect the preparations for the expedition, which was leaving Egypt in less than a month. He also wanted to get away from the constant intrigue and gamesmanship going on in his palace at Men-nefer.

It's not that I mind my wives and concubines being affectionate, but they're being unusually and overly affectionate, and I know that they're only doing it to curry favor for their sons or to secure their own positions should the selection of my next heir lead to a change in who my royal wife is.

Pharaoh stared absently across the harbor at the ships. *I'm grateful that Tiaa has a lover and has made no attempt to show renewed affection. I'm not certain I'd ever trust her in my bed again. Besides, I'm aware that she has other plans for how to secure her surviving son, Amenhotep, as my heir. Merytamon, my third wife, has visited my bed several times over the past weeks to secure Webensenu as my heir. I've always enjoyed our times together, but there's no warmth in her dalliances; no sense of true intimacy. Even Meratum, my fourth wife whose son has little chance of being named my heir, has visited my bed a number of times. Her sexual frolicking borders on the acrobatic, but she, too, lacks any warmth in our coupling.*

The three princes joined Pharaoh on the dock, and Pharaoh motioned for the captain of his Medjay guards to send men to the palace to secure the compound. *And then there's Sitamun, my second wife. Unlike Tiaa, who has always wanted to help me rule,*

Sitamun has only wanted to please me and give me a home filled with affection and honesty. Yes, she has visited my bed more than usual lately, but she never once made me feel like she was doing it to secure favor for her sons. She makes me feel like she's doing it because she genuinely cares for me and supports me while I do what I have to do to secure my kingdom. She has also raised our daughter, Iaret, who has proven to be my truest ally. Of all of my wives and concubines, I trust Sitamun the most. I just hope that trust is not misplaced.

Pharaoh watched the Egyptian and foreign merchant ships with great interest, but then he noticed that priests were boarding each of the ships as they docked. *What are they doing?*

Admiral Thuti approached Pharaoh, along with two scribes carrying dispatches. "Welcome to Peru-nefer, Great Pharaoh. And welcome, Princes of Egypt." The admiral bowed to Pharaoh and his sons.

"How go the preparations?" Pharaoh asked, keeping his eyes on the priests working along the wharf.

"We're right on schedule," Admiral Thuti replied. "The Nubian archers have already arrived, and companies of soldiers and charioteers arrive daily. They're staging west of the town so they won't be seen by the foreign merchant ships."

Pharaoh pointed toward the merchant ships. "Speaking of merchant ships, why are priests boarding the ships coming and going from the harbor?"

"They're collecting import and export taxes, Great Pharaoh."

Pharaoh was troubled by this. "And how long have the priests been handling import and export taxes here?"

"For nearly ten years, Great Pharaoh," the admiral replied. "It began during your co-regency with your father."

"Did my father decree that the priests should handle taxation?"

"Not to my knowledge, Great Pharaoh."

"And does anyone know what happens to the taxes they collect?" Pharaoh was growing angrier. He was tired of the priests moving in on every aspect of governing his kingdom.

"Is it not delivered to your treasury?" The admiral sounded confused.

"No, it's not. That means it's being taken to the temples. Do you know whose priests those are?"

Admiral Thuti looked toward the merchant ships and the priests. "The temples of Ra, Osiris, Amun, and Isis all have priests working here. I believe they alternate days so that all of the priests working the port on any given day are from the same temple."

Pharaoh tried to contain his rage. *It's bad enough that I have to provide tribute to all of the temples in my kingdom. It's bad enough that I have to constantly build new temples to the gods for the priests to live in luxury. But now I find that the priests are stealing from my treasury by intercepting taxes that they should never have been allowed to collect in the first place?*

"This ends now, Admiral," Pharaoh spat. "I want the garrison here at the port handling all taxation along with the Vizier's men. Send messengers to the garrison commander and to Amenemipet in Men-nefer to see to it immediately. And any priests who refuse to leave Peru-nefer and return to their temples where they belong are to be arrested. I don't want to see any priests near the wharf unless they're here to bless the ships... from a distance."

"Yes, Great Pharaoh."

"And have Amenemipet use the Medjay to transport the collected taxes to the treasury."

"Yes, Great Pharaoh."

Pharaoh watched the priests for a few more moments. *The priests will have to answer for what they've been doing here, but I'll deal with them when I return from Canaan.*

Pharaoh's Medjay guards escorted Pharaoh, his sons, and the admiral's two scribes to the palace. The princes were fascinated by the gardens, which were quite different from those at Men-nefer.

Prince Webensenu immediately set out to explore the gardens and the palace, but he returned a short while later with a confused expression. "Where are all the cats, Father?"

Webensenu loved cats, and the palace at Men-nefer had many cats inside the palace and across the grounds of the royal compound. Webensenu's apartment was where many of the cats spent their time because he always had food on hand for them.

"They usually spend the day along the wharf, but they come back at night," Pharaoh explained. "I think you'll find that the cats here are larger than the ones we have a Men-nefer. There's more for them to eat here."

The princes scampered off to explore the compound. Pharaoh sat down in the shade and motioned for the scribes to hand him the dispatches. He then waved them off and began reading.

The first dispatch was from Ashur-nadin-ahhe I, the Emperor of Assyria. Pharaoh had alliances with the Assyrians to defend the eastern region of the Middle Sea from the expanding Mitanni Empire. Amenhotep read the dispatch and then put it down. *The Assyrians are abandoning our alliance and refusing to pay tribute. That was to be expected.*

Pharaoh picked the second dispatch, which was from Artatama I, the Emperor of the Mitanni. *No more tribute from the Mitanni.*

The third dispatch was from Muwatalli I, Emperor of the Hittite Empire. *No more tribute from the Hittites either.*

The final dispatch was from Agum III, the King of Babylon. *The Babylonians claim that they have no tribute to send. That's original.*

Pharaoh gestured for the two scribes to approach. "When did these dispatches arrive?" he demanded.

"Over the past three days, Great Pharaoh," one of the scribes responded.

"Admiral Thuti knew that you'd be here today, which is why he didn't send the dispatches on to Men-nefer, Great Pharaoh," the second scribe said.

"Are the emissaries still in the city, or have they left Egypt already?"

"They left as soon as they delivered their dispatches, Great Pharaoh," the first scribe replied.

Pharaoh nodded and handed the dispatches to the first scribe. "Take these to the Vizier in Men-nefer immediately."

"Yes, Great Pharaoh," the two scribes intoned. They bowed and left the palace.

All of the northern kingdoms have stopped sending tribute. They must be preparing for war. It's a good thing the expedition to Canaan will be leaving before the end of the month. If we can move faster than they do, it could force them to reconsider our perceived weakness, which should prevent an invasion of my kingdom.

That evening, Pharaoh and his sons dined on the terrace. As predicted, the cats had returned to the palace for the night, and Webensenu was delighted to see how much bigger they were than the cats at Men-nefer.

After the servants had cleared the platters away, Pharaoh regarded his sons. *I said that I wanted to test my sons to see who would make the best heir to my throne. This is a good time to start. They know that I'm invading Canaan, but I've never told them why it's important that I do so. I wonder if any of them can work it out.*

"You saw the preparations being made for my expedition into Canaan today," Pharaoh began. When the princes nodded, he continued. "Who can tell me *why* I'm invading Canaan?"

Prince Webensenu spoke up first. "To replace the slaves that you lost when the Hebrews left Egypt."

"And why is that important?"

"Because we need slaves to tend to our crops and to build our cities and temples," Prince Amenhotep answered.

"That's true. Are there any other reasons to invade Canaan?"

"To bring back plunder," Prince Amenhotep blurted out. "You told us that the northern kingdoms have stopped paying tribute, and the treasury needs plunder from Canaan to replace what was lost from the north."

"But don't we have gold mines in Nubia? Can't they supply my treasury?"

"Not enough, Father," Prince Webensenu replied. "It takes much gold to maintain your kingdom, and that gold has to come from somewhere."

"Good answers." Pharaoh turned toward Prince Thutmose, who had said nothing up to this point. "Thutmose, don't you have anything to add?"

Thutmose met his father's gaze. "Yes, Father. Slaves and plunder are important, and you need them. But I think there's a more important reason why you need to attack Canaan."

"What is that reason?" Pharaoh asked.

Prince Thutmose spoke slowly, as if still working through the idea in his mind. "You mentioned that the northern kingdoms are refusing to pay tribute because they think that we're weak after the loss of the Hebrews. They know that we're a rich country, and you told me once that rich weak countries invite invasion. If you attack all of the northern kingdoms directly, you'd never be able to defeat their combined forces. If you attack them one at a time, you'd leave yourself open to attack from one of the others. But if you attack northern Canaan, just south of the borders of the northern kingdoms, and overwhelmed the tribes who live there, plundering and taking their people as prisoner so soon after losing the Hebrews, you'll demonstrate that you're still strong – strong enough to defend against invasion and strong enough to teach them all a lesson in loyalty and obedience."

Prince Thutmose fell silent but never looked away from Pharaoh.

Pharaoh smiled. *That was a very well thought-out answer from one so young. He saw the real problem, and he identified a solution. His brothers saw only the obvious benefits of invading Canaan, not the strategic benefit.*

"You are correct. The most important reason that I'm invading Canaan is to prevent the northern kingdoms from moving against us. Slaves and plunder are just the spoils of war that we'll be bringing home with us."

Princes Webensenu and Amenhotep nodded in understanding. Thutmose beamed at his father.

Pharaoh and his sons remained in Peru-nefer for three more days, watching the preparations for war. On the fourth day, Pharaoh sent his sons back to Men-nefer on the royal barge. He remained in Peru-nefer to oversee the final preparations and to plan for the invasion of Canaan, which he believed was better done away from Tiaa and her plots.

A servant quietly entered Tiaa's apartments in the palace at Men-nefer and crossed the antechamber. She stood waiting at the entrance to the sitting area until Tiaa acknowledged her.

"What do you want?" Tiaa demanded.

"My Queen, Princess Iaret desires an audience."

Tiaa smiled. "Send her in, and then pass the word that we're not to be disturbed."

"Yes, my Queen."

The servant escorted Iaret into the sitting area and then withdrew.

"Good morning, Iaret," Tiaa said, gesturing toward a nearby chair.

"Good morning, my Queen," Iaret responded. "How are you today?"

"Fine. Just fine. And I told you to call me Tiaa when we're alone. We're family, after all."

"Yes, Tiaa." Iaret smiled.

"That's better. What have you done about the favor I requested?" Tiaa had asked for help getting more of her spies into the palace.

Iaret smiled. "It's done. All of the people are in place just where you wanted them. Kenamun doesn't suspect a thing."

"And have you given any more thought to what we discussed the other night?" Tiaa had insinuated that she might be looking for ways to tip Pharaoh's choice of heir to her surviving son, Prince Amenhotep.

Iaret nodded.

"And you understand that it may involve your brother, Thutmose?"

Iaret pouted slightly. "I'm Pharaoh's oldest surviving child, but I'm not being considered as a potential heir. I'll support any heir who will guarantee my position as the royal princess and give me a role in his government."

Tiaa grinned. "I'll see to that, my dear."

"Then I'm with you, Tiaa."

Tiaa nodded and reached for a chest on the table next to her. She opened it and withdrew a leather bag. She opened the bag and poured a few of the seeds into her hand. "Good. Do you know what these are?"

Iaret leaned forward and looked at the seeds. They were light brown with dark brown spots. She shook her head. "No. What are they?"

"They're called castor seeds," Tiaa replied, pouring the seeds back into the bag and returning the bag to the chest. "It's said that

Hatshepsut had developed a poison from them. I've even heard a rumor that it was the poison that killed her."

"I've never heard of them before," Iaret lied. "What are you going to do with them?"

"I haven't decided yet," Tiaa replied. "But I want to try to recreate Hatshepsut's poison. Do you think you can find me some cats?"

"Cats?" Iaret sounded confused. "Is that part of how you make the poison?"

Tiaa shook her head. "No. I just need cats. About a dozen. Take them from Prince Webensenu's apartment. They seem to congregate there."

"That's because he feeds them," Iaret said.

"Well, if they're well fed, then they'll be easier to catch."

Iaret nodded. "Anything else?"

"Not now, Tiaa replied. "Just bring me the cats."

"When do you need them?"

"By next week."

Iaret stood, bowed to Tiaa, and left the sitting area.

Iaret knew exactly what the seeds were. *I need to report this to Amenemipet. She IS planning to use the seeds to make poison. But why does she need the cats, and why do they need to come from Webensenu's apartment?*

Iaret hastened to find her father's Vizier.

She has no idea that I told Kenamun and Amenemipet about the spies that she asked me to sneak into the palace, nor does she know that Amenemipet's spies are watching all of her new spies. As long as she doesn't find out, she'll believe that I'm loyal to her.

She found Amenemipet in the throne room surrounded by several chests and pallets filled with gold, silver, and rich fabrics. Amenemipet chuckled to himself as he examined each item carefully. A scribe stood nearby, writing down everything that Amenemipet said.

"What's all this?" Iaret asked, looking intently at the fabrics.

"The tribute from Ethiopia," Amenemipet replied, holding up

a dispatch from Egypt's southern neighbor. "It finally arrived, and the King of Ethiopia included a very apologetic message begging for your father to forgive the misunderstanding about why it arrived so late. He claims that his emissary delivered the wrong message, and he proclaims his undying loyalty to your father and to Egypt."

Iaret snorted. "If he knew that my father's army was heading for Canaan, do you think that the tribute would have arrived so soon?"

"I doubt it."

Amenemipet saw a strange expression on Iaret's face. "Is there something you need to see me about?"

Iaret nodded, and Amenemipet dismissed the scribe. Once he and Iaret were alone, he asked, "What's wrong? Has Tiaa found out that we know who her new spies are?"

Iaret shook her head. "No, but I did just meet with her. She showed me the castor seeds and asked me to bring her a dozen cats from Webensenu's apartment."

"Why cats? And why from there?"

"I don't know, but I thought you should be made aware of what she wants from me."

Amenemipet rubbed his face with his hands. "Go ahead and get her the cats. We'll just have to watch her more closely to find out what she's up to."

A week later, just a few days before Pharaoh's expedition was to sail from Peru-nefer, Kenamun made his rounds through the palace at Men-nefer. Twice a day he inspected the placement of the guards and servants, and he also made certain that no priests were lurking inside the palace or anywhere inside the compound.

The priests are becoming more of a problem now that Pharaoh has forbidden them to collect taxes, which took away one of their primary sources of income. Between that and taking all of their grain stores, the priests are almost ready to rise up against Pharaoh.

He turned the corner and saw a dark shape lying in the

middle of the floor. Moving closer, he saw that it was just a cat. As he walked past it, he noticed that its eyes and mouth were open. He reached down and touched it. It was stone cold.

A dead cat inside the palace? I'll have a servant take care of it.

Kenamun continued his rounds. By the time he returned to the kitchens, he had discovered four more dead cats inside the palace.

This isn't normal. I don't believe that five cats all died of old age on the same day. Something killed them. I'd better alert Amenemipet. Perhaps he knows what's going on.

Pharaoh, General Ahmose, and Admiral Thuti stood on a platform facing the foot soldiers, archers, charioteers, and sailors who were about to depart Peru-nefer for northern Canaan. In all, there were over twenty thousand of Pharaoh's men standing in the staging area. Even though it was well before midday, the sun's heat was already sweltering. Only the breeze blowing from the Middle Sea made the day feel tolerable.

After Pharaoh made an offering to Ra and Amun, he made an additional offering to Anhur and Montu, the Egyptian gods of war. Pharaoh may have been angry with the priests, but he knew better than to fail in his duty to the gods of Egypt.

Once Pharaoh had concluded making the necessary offerings and prayers, he faced his men. The company commanders stood in front of their men to repeat what Pharaoh said, since the men standing away from the platform wouldn't be able to hear Pharaoh's voice. "Our expedition into Canaan is about to begin. This expedition will be unlike any we've undertaken. We must convince our enemies that we're still the strongest kingdom in the world and that taking sides against us is folly. We must replace as many of the Hebrew slaves as we can before the harvest season begins. And we need plunder to replace the tribute that our enemies, in their foolishness, have stopped sending to us."

Pharaoh gestured toward his fighting men. "I know that many of you had your faith in Egypt shaken when the chariots sent against the Hebrews were lost. But now is your chance to prove to the world that our might has not abated one bit. I need you to fight harder than you've ever fought before. And in return, when we reach Egypt at the end of the campaign, you will receive a bounty for every prisoner taken who is physically able to work in the fields, build our cities, and build our temples. And you will all share in the plunder we take from the tribes of Canaan!"

Cheers rose from the ranks of soldiers and sailors facing Pharaoh.

"Fight like lions, and you'll be rewarded. Take every bit of plunder, and you'll share in the riches. Capture prisoners, and you'll receive a bounty for every one who can become a viable slave. Fight by my side, and we'll make the world shake in fear of our might! Who is with me?"

The soldiers and sailors cheered.

"Who is with me?"

The soldiers and sailors cheered louder.

"WHO IS WITH ME?"

The soldiers and sailors began chanting Pharaoh's name while pounding the butts of their spears on the ground and stomping their feet. Pharaoh let this continue for a moment, allowing their energy to fill him with pride and confidence.

Pharaoh raised his arms, and the soldiers and sailors grew quiet to hear what he said next. "Admiral Thuti, is the fleet ready?"

"It is, Great Pharaoh!" Admiral Thuti shouted.

"General Ahmose, are our forces ready?"

"They are, Great Pharaoh!"

Pharaoh opened his arms wide, as if he were trying to encircle the men standing below him. "Then load the ships!"

The sailors ran for the ships as the soldiers gathered their gear and marched in columns toward the harbor and the waiting navy. Only the charioteers returned to their tents to wait for the navy to return for them in a few days.

Pharaoh looked at his general and admiral. "Let's join the men."

"Yes, Great Pharaoh!"

CHAPTER 7

Iaret entered Tiaa's chamber and was alarmed to find several dead cats strewn across the sitting area.

"My Queen? It's Iaret."

"In here." The voice came from behind a heavy curtain on the opposite side of the sitting room from Tiaa's bedchamber.

Iaret followed the voice and pulled aside the curtain. Tiaa sat in front of a large table covered with several jars, bowls, and tools needed to extract the poison from the castor seeds that Amenemhat had provided to her. As Iaret entered the room, she saw Tiaa applying a paste to the claws of a fidgeting cat.

"Hold this cat still for me," Tiaa instructed.

Iaret obeyed and reached one arm around the cat's belly while stroking the cat's head to calm it down. Tiaa finished applying the paste and put the brush back into a stone bowl on the table. She then took the cat from Iaret and set it down on the floor.

"What were you doing?" Iaret asked.

"Remember the poison I told you about? The one made from castor seeds?"

Iaret nodded.

"I finished making a small amount, and I want to see if it can be delivered using a cat's claws."

"Why?"

"Because if it can't be administered in food or drink, it can be delivered under the skin. The palace cats like to scratch people who play with them, and if the cat has the poison on its claws, the poison will get into the person it scratches."

"And by 'person,' you mean Prince Webensenu?" Iaret knew of Prince Webensenu's love for cats.

Tiaa flashed a wicked smile.

Iaret was impressed and terrified. Then a thought occurred to her. "Is that why there are so many dead cats around the palace lately?

Tiaa nodded, washing her hands in a stone bowl filled with clean water. "The cats keep licking the poison off their claws and dying before they can scratch anyone. If one more cat dies, I'm going to abandon the idea of using their claws to administer the poison and come up with a different method."

Iaret watched the cat that Tiaa had just put on the floor. It shook the paw that had the poison on it and then proceeded to lick the paw. Within a few moments, the cat began to spasm uncontrollably. Then it stopped moving altogether. Its eyes were wide open and fixed, and its mouth was agape.

"Damn!" Tiaa slammed her fist on the table.

"I thought this was a slow-acting poison," Iaret commented. "The cat died in only a few moments from licking the poison."

"It's only slow-acting when administered through the skin. If it's swallowed, it acts very quickly."

Iaret shuddered at the thought. "Do you want me to call a servant to remove the dead cats?" Iaret was concerned that the cats would begin to stink.

"Yes, thank you."

Iaret summoned a servant, who appeared and began gathering the dead cats in Tiaa's apartment. When the last cat was removed, Tiaa covered the bowl containing the poison and motioned for Iaret to follow her into the sitting area.

"What are you going to do now?" Iaret sat next to Tiaa facing the terrace.

Tiaa reached into a small chest on the nearby table and extracted a leather bag. She opened it and drew out the contents. It was a copper ring in the shape of a cobra about to strike. It looked like an ordinary ring, except for the copper spike sticking out of the underside.

"I call this my 'cobra ring.' I can dip the spike in the poison and press it into the skin of the person I want to kill."

Iaret looked at the ring. The sacred cobra design was typical of the jewelry worn by the royal family. "It's beautiful, but aren't you concerned that you might accidently stick yourself with the spike?"

Tiaa waved dismissively. "I'm not stupid, Iaret. Poisoning has a certain risk to the poisoner, but I've always been careful."

"I didn't mean to imply that you're stupid." Iaret tried to sound as contrite as possible. "I was just concerned that the spike could accidently stick you instead of your intended victim."

Changing the subject, Iaret added, "It definitely kills cats, but have you tried it on a person yet?"

"Not yet." Tiaa eyed Iaret closely. "Any suggestions?"

"It would have to be someone who wouldn't be noticed or missed," Iaret suggested. "Amenemipet and Kenamun watch the palace too closely for one of the servants or guards to be an effective victim."

Tiaa agreed. Then she asked, "What is your opinion of Amenemipet and Kenamun?"

"As it relates to what?" Iaret wasn't certain what Tiaa was asking.

"As it relates to manipulating the succession or potentially setting up a regency should Pharaoh pass into the next world sooner than expected."

Iaret smiled. "Kenamun is easy. He's Pharaoh's boyhood friend, and his loyalty to Pharaoh personally is unquestioned. He will oppose anything that he perceives to be a threat to Pharaoh's person or well-being. Amenemipet is harder. I've heard him say several times that, as Vizier, his loyalty is to Egypt, not to any one particular Pharaoh or regent. He will defend Egypt to his last breath, even if it means going against the reigning Pharaoh."

"You mean Amenemipet might actually go against your father if he believes it's in Egypt's best interest?"

Iaret nodded.

Tiaa sat back with a stunned look on her face. "How close are you to Amenemipet?"

"Close enough."

Tiaa leaned closer to Iaret. "Can you approach him and see where he stands with Egypt's current situation? Does he blame Pharaoh for our plight? Does he agree with Pharaoh's decision to seize the granaries of the nobles and the temples? Does he have an opinion about who from among your father's sons should be the next Pharaoh?"

"I can try to find out," Iaret offered.

"Good. He could be a great ally if he can be convinced that Pharaoh is not capable of ruling Egypt much longer."

"I think a lot will depend on how the campaign into Canaan goes," Iaret pointed out. "If the campaign goes well, support for Pharaoh will increase across Egypt, and your plans could easily fail. If it doesn't go well, you'll have potential allies from all quarters of the kingdom, including the military."

Tiaa stared at Iaret.

Iaret shifted uncomfortably in her chair. "Have you considered sending a private message to the Hittites or the Assyrians that Pharaoh has brought his army so close to their borders? If Pharaoh should be killed in battle, it would be easier for you to move against Princes Webensenu and Thutmose to secure Prince Amenhotep's position as the next Pharaoh and your position as regent."

Tiaa snorted. "Leave strategy to the experts, child. If the Assyrians or Hittites attack Pharaoh and defeat him, no child of Pharaoh will sit on the throne of Egypt. They will either put one of their own princes on the throne or annex Egypt to become part of their Empire. No, alerting our enemies won't improve my position and that of Prince Amenhotep one bit. Pharaoh must come home and die here in Egypt for my plans to work."

Tiaa gestured toward the entrance to her apartment, signaling that the meeting was over.

After Iaret left, Tiaa reached inside the leather bag and pulled out another ring. This one was also made of copper, but it was not a ring like one a noble or great lady would wear. This one was simple, like what a servant or slave would wear. It, too, had a spike protruding from the underside.

Tiaa held the two rings in her hands. *If I'm not the one who administers the poison, I don't have to worry about sticking myself in the hand, do I?*

She put both rings back in the bag and closed it up before putting the bag back in the chest.

"You did well, my Princess." Amenemipet sounded pleased. "Let her continue to underestimate you. Then, when her plans crash around her, she'll never suspect that you are the instrument of her demise."

"Thank you, Amenemipet. She was positively disgusted with me when I suggested alerting the Assyrians or Hittites. However, when I told her that your first loyalty was to the kingdom, I've never seen her look so surprised."

"Let's keep her thinking that I might be persuaded to support her. It'll keep me alive longer, and I just might be able to infiltrate her spies before she has the chance to move against me."

Iaret nodded. "What about the poison?"

"That still concerns me," Amenemipet admitted. "I'm grateful to finally know why so many cats have died lately, but if she administers the poison through the skin, she could strike a person days before the first symptoms showed. It would be impossible to prove that she was the poisoner. It's good to know about the cobra ring. I'll make certain my people watch her when she's wearing it, in case she tries to poison someone."

"Should we try to substitute the poison with something that's not harmful?" Iaret asked.

Amenemipet shook his head in frustration. "I don't know. We may have to, but I don't like the idea of having to try to create something that looks and smells the same without killing. And I don't want you handling the poison under any circumstances. You're taking a huge risk as it is."

"We already have enough on Tiaa to charge her with treason. Why are we waiting?"

"Because we need the names of the people helping her. We know that the High Priest of Amun from Karnak is her lover, but we're not sure if he's plotting against Pharaoh with her. We also don't know what nobles or other priests have joined her plot. Until we know all of that, we need her alive."

"I'd be happier if she were dead," Iaret stated.

"So would I, but the plot against Pharaoh must die with her. If it doesn't, we may lose our link to the other conspirators, and we can't protect your father if that happens."

Iaret shook her head. "And if she manages to convince any of Pharaoh's siblings to join her?"

Amenemipet looked anxious. "Then we're in real trouble."

Iaret nodded, but her expression was clearly unhappy.

The saltwater spray coming off the Middle Sea stung Pharaoh's face as his ship led the Egyptian fleet toward the northern Canaan coastline. He stood near the prow, willing the fleet's destination to appear.

It feels good to be on campaign again. My father launched a major military campaign every few years. It has been nearly nine years since I've been on campaign.

Pharaoh looked back at the soldiers sitting in rows along both sides of the ship.

These are no conscripts or inexperienced soldiers. They are professionals all – the finest fighting force in the world! I know I came close to losing the loyalty of my men after the loss of the chariots at the Gulf of Reeds, but Amenemipet was right. By offering the men a bounty for every slave AND a share of the plunder, I've ensured that they'll fight harder than ever before. They'll return home in triumph and enjoy the wealth that goes with their success. I must remember to give the soldiers in the division that remained behind the same bounty and share of the plunder as well. I don't want them feeling left out. Having them remain in Egypt is vital to the defense of the kingdom, and they must be rewarded for their service.

Pharaoh faced forward again. *Amenemipet was also right that I use some of the plunder to compensate the nobles for their lost grain. It's only fair, but I'm not going to use the promise of payment to keep the nobles from joining forces against me. Only loyal nobles will share in this plunder. The priests will get their* usual tribute for the gods, but I have no intention of compensating THEM for their lost grain. The temples had eighty percent of all grain stores in the kingdom, and there is no reason for them to have so much for so few. Besides, they've been stealing port taxes from my treasury for years. I consider them already fully paid for whatever I took to save my kingdom.

Pharaoh sat next to his soldiers as the swells of the eastern Middle Sea grew stronger.

Soon we'll arrive in Canaan, and I'll be facing enemies that I can see again. No more gods, no more wives and priests plotting in shadows. Just my army against whatever forces that the Canaanite tribes can muster against us. That's a fight we know how to win.

A servant ushered Amenemhat and his acolyte Kaaper into the courtyard of a house owned by Khaemtir, one of the chief nobles in Men-nefer. The late afternoon breeze caused the treetops to sway, casting ever-changing patterns of light on the stone floor.

"Greetings, Khaemtir," Amenemhat intoned as his host bowed in respect for the high priest's office.

"Greetings, High Priest of Amun." Khaemtir gestured toward the nearby benches. "To what do I owe this visit? You're a long way from Karnak."

"I am here to ensure the spiritual well-being of the nobles of the kingdom." Amenemhat sat and accepted the tankard of beer offered by the servant.

Khaemtir nodded. "Most kind of you."

"I understand you recently suffered a grievous loss," Amenemhat said smoothly as his eyes looked like a cobra regarding a potential prey.

"To what are you referring?" Khaemtir asked blandly.

"Your firstborn, Khaemtir. Surely that was a grievous loss. And I understand that your granaries were also seized by Pharaoh's men."

"I appreciate your concern for my son, but the granaries are hardly something that should attract the notice of the High Priest of Amun," Khaemtir said.

"And yet here I am." Amenemhat pretended to be supportive. "Your well-being is important to me."

Khaemtir stared at the priest and his acolyte. "My family and I are coping with the loss of my son, High Priest. As far as my grain goes, though, I see no reason why this matter should involve someone of your position. Weren't your granaries also seized and distributed to the people? Surely you lost more than I did. And, after all, if our grain was needed to ensure the survival of the kingdom, it was a small tax to pay to Pharaoh for his protection over all of us, wasn't it?"

"Of course, Khaemtir. Of course. And I'm grateful that you see it that way. We certainly wouldn't want lingering hostilities toward our Great Pharaoh to cloud our judgement during these difficult times. Would we?"

"No, High Priest, we certainly wouldn't."

Amenemhat stood. "It would seem that your well-being requires none of my assistance. Should that ever change, please reach out to me immediately."

"I don't wish to be a burden upon you, High Priest."

"It is no burden, Khaemtir. I am here to support you at any time."

"Most kind, High Priest."

The servant escorted Amenemhat and Kaaper out. Once they were out of earshot of Khaemtir's compound, Amenemhat turned on Kaaper.

"What was that? This is the second noble that I've visited on *your* recommendation who didn't seem to have any issues with our beloved Pharaoh. I've had my priests sowing discontent among the nobles for weeks now, and Khaemtir was one of twelve that you assured me would be receptive to joining the Queen's plans for the future of the monarchy. I saw no evidence that he's interested in joining anything at all! I'm warning you, Kaaper. If there's a third noble on your list who doesn't seem receptive to the Queen's desires, it will go very bad for you. Do you want to revise your list?"

Kaaper stood silently for a moment. Then he shook his head. "No, High Priest. I stand by my list. I met with Khaemtir and five other nobles in his courtyard to discuss the current state of Egypt. He was furious with Pharaoh and was ready to storm the palace that night. They all were."

"Then what happened between then and now?" Amenemhat demanded.

Kaaper shrugged. "Perhaps he was concerned that you were testing him on Pharaoh's behalf. If he thought you were Pharaoh's man, he wouldn't confess his anger to you, would he?"

Amenemhat scratched the back of his head and stared at his acolyte. Finally, he said, "That's possible. So how do I get them to talk to me the way they talked to you?"

Kaaper presented an idea. Amenemhat thought about it and then nodded. "We'll try that. But if it doesn't work, the realm of demons waiting for you will be the least of your worries!"

Kaaper, Khaemtir, and the five other nobles sat around the courtyard of a compound near the southern wall of Men-nefer after nightfall the next day.

"Pharaoh still has to answer for the loss of our firstborn," Khaemtir stated. "And he owes us for the indignity of stealing our grain. That grain came from *my* fields. *My* workers planted it, tended to it, harvested it, threshed it, and placed it in my granaries. I gave tribute to Pharaoh and the priests from the harvest. I should have been allowed to keep the remainder!"

There were murmurs of agreement from the other nobles.

"And yet Pharaoh lost a son, and he gave up his own grain stores first," Kaaper pointed out.

"He had no choice but to give up his own grain stores," Pensekhmet snapped. "My family descends from pharaohs of old. I should be exempt from any such *taxes*. Pharaoh had no right to take my grain."

"And what is he going to do about the loss of my slaves?" Sharek demanded. "I had over a hundred Hebrews working my fields. Pharaoh just let them leave Egypt and didn't do anything to stop it."

"But they weren't *your* slaves, Sharek," Khaemtir said. "The Hebrews belonged to Pharaoh. He only assigned them to your fields."

"And didn't you petition Pharaoh to let the Hebrews go after you lost your firstborn?" Wadjmose asked.

"Of course I did," Sharek snapped. "We all did. And it doesn't matter who *owned* the Hebrews. They were working in *my* fields, and Pharaoh just let them go. It was his decision, and it was done without any compensation to those of us who lost slaves in the deal."

"So what are we going to do about it?" Khaemtir asked. "Sitting here being angry will accomplish nothing. Either we bring our grievances to Pharaoh when he returns from Canaan, or we take more direct action to redress our grievances."

"Like what?" Pensekhmet demanded.

"I don't know," Khaemtir confessed. "Perhaps we find someone else who could help us redress our grievances."

"Like who?" Wadjmose asked.

Amenemhat stepped out of the shadows and walked into the center of the courtyard. "Like me."

Senebsen, one of Pharaoh's younger concubines, entered Tiaa's antechamber. She had no children with Pharaoh, but she was one of Pharaoh's favorites. Senebsen waited until a servant appeared and escorted her to Tiaa's sitting area.

Tiaa gestured for Senebsen to sit next to her as the servant poured both of them a drink before retiring from Tiaa's apartment to the central hallway of the harem.

"I wanted to talk to you, Senebsen," Tiaa said warmly. "I want to know where you stand on the issue of the Pharaoh's next heir."

"Isn't Prince Webensenu the next in line as the oldest surviving son?" Senebsen asked cautiously.

"Ordinarily, yes, but Pharaoh said that he plans to select the son who is most worthy, not just the one who is the next oldest."

Senebsen nodded. "I've spent very little time with the princes, my Queen. Pharaoh prefers that I serve him... in other ways."

Tiaa smiled. "And I've heard that you serve him well in those ways. But he'll seek the advice of all of his wives and concubines before he chooses his heir, and he'll want your honest answer."

"How can I give him an honest answer if I don't really know the sons he'll be choosing from?"

Tiaa patted Senebsen's arm. The copper cobra ring flashed in the light. "If you're not certain, then would you accept the advice of your queen?"

"You want me to tell Pharaoh to select Prince Amenhotep, don't you?" Senebsen accused.

Tiaa nodded. "He's the best choice."

"Because he's your son, and you'd be regent if anything happened to Pharaoh?"

"No, because he's been trained along with my late son, Prince Thutmose, to be Pharaoh."

Senebsen shook her head. "Pharaoh would see through that suggestion in a heartbeat. Prince Webensenu should be the next heir. I won't give Pharaoh any other suggestion than that."

Tiaa stood, hiding her anger. "Then we have nothing more to discuss."

Senebsen stood, and Tiaa grabbed her arm tightly. "You'd do better to give Pharaoh no answer, my dear. You don't want me as your enemy."

Senebsen fled from Tiaa's apartment.

Tiaa smiled and removed the cobra ring. *Now we wait to see if the poison works.*

Senebsen took ill three days later. Tiaa visited her daily to watch the effects of the poison. It took two days for Senebsen to die once the symptoms appeared, and they were terrible to watch.

Tiaa ordered that no messenger be sent to Pharaoh about Senebsen's death. Tiaa didn't want Pharaoh to find out until he returned.

"Was it Tiaa?" Amenemipet demanded.

Iaret nodded. "She was wearing the cobra ring when Senebsen came to see her, Tiaa threatened her, and then I saw Tiaa grab her arm with the same hand that had the ring on it. Tiaa visited her daily, and I'm sure it was to watch the progress of the poison."

Kenamun, who was with Iaret and Amenemipet, clasped his hands on his head. "For her to move against one of Pharaoh's concubines – his favorite – shows that she's not afraid of the consequences. Her plans must be well-developed indeed."

"Or she doesn't think that the deed can be tied back to her," Iaret suggested. "After all, the only benefit she gets from killing Senebsen is to cause Pharaoh pain and plant fear in the other wives and concubines. That's hardly proof of her involvement."

"But you saw her with the ring on, and she grabbed Senebsen's arm, right?" Kenamun asked.

"Yes. I had a clear view from my hiding place in the wall of Tiaa's apartment."

"She's moving too quickly," Amenemipet said. "With Pharaoh on campaign, we can't have her accused of treason."

"Then I need to stay even closer to her," Iaret stated.

Amenemipet shook his head. "No, it's too dangerous."

"We don't have a choice," Iaret insisted. "I'm the only one of us that she trusts."

"She's right," Kenamun agreed. "There is no choice."

Amenemipet hung his head. "Please be careful, my Princess. Pharaoh will have me skinned alive if something happens to you."

CHAPTER 8

Pharaoh stood on the hill overlooking the beach in northern Canaan. Most of his navy had unloaded the soldiers and returned to Peru-nefer to pick up the charioteers, chariots, and horses. The soldiers had secured a large area around the beach so the army wouldn't be vulnerable while waiting for the chariot companies to arrive.

General Ahmose approached and stood next to Pharaoh. "The encampment is set up, Great Pharaoh. I've sent out scouts to see if any tribes are nearby. What are your orders?"

Pharaoh turned away from the beach where the last of his soldiers were disembarking. He looked toward the army's camp and was pleased with the progress. *My men work quickly. It seems a shame to have them doing nothing until the chariots get here.*

"I'd like my navy to return to Egypt with the first consignment of prisoners and plunder after they deliver the chariots. We should be able to conduct several raids before the chariots arrive, don't you think?"

General Ahmose smiled. "I do, indeed, Great Pharaoh."

Pharaoh gestured for the general to follow him to the camp. "We should raid in all directions. The Assyrians and Hittites will know we're here by now, but they don't know our intentions yet. Let's keep them off guard for a while longer. Then, when we move south with our full force, it will confuse them even more. I don't need them attacking from our rear while we're plundering the settlements and emptying Canaan of every able-bodied person we can capture."

"A wise plan, Great Pharaoh. I'll pass the word to the company commanders to move out as soon as the scouts return."

"Thank you, General."

The scouts returned the next afternoon. After they reported to General Ahmose, the general and the company commanders met with Pharaoh to review the options. Pharaoh selected the villages and settlements that seemed to be the most promising, and the company commanders left to inform their men.

The next morning, two thirds of Pharaoh's men, including half of the Nubian archers, left camp to raid the villages and settlements that Pharaoh had selected. Pharaoh, General Ahmose, and the rest of the soldiers remained behind to secure the camp and the beach where the navy would land the chariots.

Pharaoh watched the soldiers march out of camp with a sense of longing. *I wish I were going with them on these raids. But all I can do now is wait for them to return. I hope I haven't sent them into any Hittite or Assyrian traps.*

Iaret entered Tiaa's apartment in the harem and sat down next to her in the sitting area. Iaret glanced at Tiaa's hands and didn't see the cobra ring. She relaxed.

"I want to talk to you about Prince Webensenu," Tiaa began as she offered Iaret refreshments.

"What about him?" Iaret accepted a fig from Tiaa.

"The thirteenth anniversary of his birth is this week, and it's time to be looking for a suitable wife for him. But I'm concerned that he might not know anything about the art of coupling yet."

Iaret was confused. "You're concerned about his coupling skills and finding him a wife? I thought…"

Tiaa held up her hand. "Yes, I have plans for the young prince that don't include him ascending the throne of Egypt, let alone getting married. But as the royal wife, it's my duty to find him a wife and make certain that he knows what to do with her to produce an heir. If I don't carry out this duty, it will arouse suspicion. Besides who would suspect me of trying to hurt a prince when I'm busy finding him a wife and having him properly taught in the other *manly* arts?"

Iaret was impressed with Tiaa's logic. "How can I help?"

Tiaa leaned forward. "Finding the young prince a wife will take time. We have to weigh the advantages and disadvantages of selecting an Egyptian noble's daughter or the daughter of a foreign ruler or dignitary. Much will depend on your father's success in Canaan. But in the meantime, we must see to his education in the ways of men and women. Talk to him. Find out if he has been with a woman yet, and if so, who it was. Also find out if any of the slave girls here in the harem have caught his eye. I think it's better that he learn from someone he's already attracted to, don't you?"

Iaret nodded.

"And on the subject of marriage, we need to find you a husband."

Iaret blushed. While she had some experience in the arts of coupling – thanks to Hannu, one of her personal guards whom she had grown fond of – she was not ready to be relegated to the role of wife to some foreign prince or spoiled noble's son. "I think that can wait until all of our plans have borne fruit. It's a distraction we don't need just yet."

Tiaa's shoulders slumped somewhat. "I guess you're right. But I do love matchmaking, so don't be surprised if I send the occasional man your way, okay?"

Iaret nodded. She stood to leave.

"Talk to Prince Webensenu today, if possible," Tiaa said as Iaret reached the antechamber.

"I will, my Queen."

Iaret stepped into the corridor and left the harem, tossing the fig uneaten into the courtyard. *She must be crazy to think that I'd ever accept food or drink from her.*

90

Iaret wasn't able to see Prince Webensenu until later that day. At his suggestion, they had supper together in his apartment.

One of the cats that always seemed to be in Webensenu's apartment jumped into Iaret's lap, and she absently scratched it behind its ears. The cat purred, watching the food on the table closely.

Looking around, Iaret commented, "There aren't as many cats in here as usual."

"I noticed that, too," Webensenu admitted. "But I have seen a number of dead cats around the palace. I'd like to know what's killing them."

Iaret nodded, holding onto the cat so it wouldn't interfere with the servants who were serving the meal.

"I'm surprised that you wanted to see me," Webensenu said once the servants had withdrawn from the room.

"I don't get to see you that much," Iaret explained, letting the cat jump down onto the floor. "And besides, there's something we have to talk about."

"It's not about Tiaa and her plots, is it?" Webensenu picked up a fig and ate it. "My mother has told me all about them. Evidently Tiaa approached my mother to enlist her help in making certain that I don't get chosen as father's heir."

Iaret knew about Tiaa's conversation with Merytamon, Webensenu's mother, but she pretended to be surprised. "It's not about Tiaa's plots concerning the next heir, but she is involved."

Webensenu looked at Iaret suspiciously as he reached for his flagon of beer. "What is it about, then?"

"The anniversary of your birth is this week. As the royal wife, it's Tiaa's duty to find you a suitable wife."

Webensenu spit out the sip of beer he had just taken. "A wife?!"

Iaret giggled at his discomfort. "You're a prince of Egypt, brother. And you're the same age as Father was when he was betrothed to Tiaa."

"But a wife..."

Iaret cocked her head to one side. "Have you never been with a woman?"

Webensenu blushed furiously.

"Don't worry about it. Part of the process of finding you a

wife also includes making certain that you know what to do with her once you take her to your bed. Come on. Surely at least one of the women in the harem has caught your eye. I could arrange for her to teach you what you need to know. It was done for Father, you know."

"It was? I never heard that."

Iaret nodded. "The woman lives in a house in Waset and has slaves of her own. Father was very grateful for what she taught him, and from what I've gathered from Tiaa and my mother, she taught him well. I can arrange the same for you, if you'd like."

Webensenu took a bite of the fish dish and stared past the terrace curtains that billowed gently in the evening breeze. Iaret saw a faint smile appear.

"There *is* someone in the harem, isn't there?"

Webensenu looked at his half-sister and nodded. "One of the girls who arrived just before the Hebrew calamities. Her name is Shayari, and she has the most amazing eyes I've ever seen."

"Just her eyes?" Iaret asked coyly.

Webensenu laughed. "No, not just her eyes. She's beautiful. If I had to pick one, it would be her."

"Leave it to me, brother. Leave everything to me."

"Tiaa's actually looking to have Prince Webensenu trained in the art of coupling while she finds him a wife? What's she playing at?"

It was late that night, and Iaret sat with Amenemipet and Kenamun in the room that Amenemipet had set aside for private conversations. Iaret had just finished telling the two men what Tiaa and she had discussed earlier that day, and Amenemipet shook his head with a look of amazement on his face.

"Have you talked to this Shayari yet?" Kenamun asked.

"I told her that Tiaa and I wish to speak with her in the morning. Shayari's to find me, and then I'll take her to see Tiaa."

"Do you think that Tiaa plans to use Shayari in her plots?" Amenemipet asked.

Iaret shrugged. "Possibly. Or it could be that Tiaa's just keeping up appearances by performing the duties of the royal wife.

You have to admit that it's a brilliant way to deflect suspicion from her should anything happen to Webensenu. Why would she be finding him a wife and having him educated in coupling if she plans to kill him?"

"You'll need to stay close to Tiaa and Webensenu," Kenamun noted. "If this is all part of her larger plan, then she could be recruiting agents who don't even know they're her agent."

"Shayari will have to be watched, too," Amenemipet pointed out. "There's no telling what Tiaa might trick her into doing."

"I can't be everywhere," Iaret reminded them.

"No, I know." Amenemipet glanced at Kenamun. "We'll have to assign guards and some of the new servants to help you."

Changing the subject, Iaret asked, "Is there any word from my father in Canaan?"

"The fleet made it safely to the landing area in northern Canaan," Amenemipet replied. "He established a beachhead and was waiting for the navy to return with the chariots. My reports from Peru-nefer say that the navy sailed for Canaan with the chariots this afternoon. We haven't heard anything else, but we should when the navy returns to Peru-nefer. I'll keep you informed."

"Thank you. Does he know about the death of his concubine Senebsen?"

Amenemipet shook his head. "Not yet. Tiaa doesn't want him distracted while on campaign, and I happen to agree with her on this one point."

Shayari entered Iaret's antechamber the next morning and waited to be escorted into the presence of Pharaoh's daughter.

When the servant brought Shayari into Iaret's sitting area, Iaret immediately understood why Webensenu was fascinated with her. She was a lovely girl with long, curly dark hair and a slender figure like a dancer's. Her almond-shaped eyes seemed to catch the light and glow.

"How did you come to be here in the palace, Shayari?" Iaret

asked, gesturing for the girl to sit.

"I was a gift from the King of Babylon, my Princess," Shayari answered softly. Her voice had a soothing quality to it.

"And how are you in the arts of coupling?"

Shayari's face flushed and she looked at her hands when she answered. "There have been no complaints, my Princess."

"How many men have you been with?" Iaret needed to know if Shayari could teach or if she'd be learning along with Webensenu.

"Four in Egypt, my Princess. Three before I left Babylon."

"Were any of them inexperienced?"

Shayari glanced at Iaret with a curious look on her face. "Yes, my Princess. Two had never been with a woman before."

"And you taught them how to be with a woman?"

Shayari nodded.

"Good. Are you acquainted with Prince Webensenu?"

Shayari blushed again. Iaret saw a hint of a smile on her lips.

"Ah, I see that you are. Good. The queen has begun looking for a suitable wife for the prince, but he needs to be trained in the arts of coupling before he marries. He has expressed an interest in you."

Shayari's head snapped up and she looked intently at Iaret.

"He could become the next Pharaoh of Egypt, Shayari. He must be well trained in *all* of the manly arts. Pharaoh's master-at-arms will handle his military training, Pharaoh and his Vizier will train him to rule wisely, but you will train him to be with women and, ultimately, produce an heir."

Shayari nodded.

Iaret stood. "Come with me. The queen wants to see you, and I'm certain that she'll have additional instructions for you."

Pharaoh was sitting with General Ahmose when the first scout returned to the camp.

"What news?" the general demanded.

The scout caught his breath. "I bring wonderful news from the companies sent north, great Pharaoh! We attacked four settlements and captured all of their people with no losses. Two of the settlements were merchant colonies. The plunder is rich indeed and was being loaded onto more than fifty pack animals as I left to bring you the news."

"How many prisoners altogether?" Pharaoh asked.

"Nearly a thousand, including women and children, great Pharaoh!"

General Ahmose dismissed the scout. Turning to Pharaoh, he said, "Fifty pack animals of plunder and a thousand prisoners? That's wonderful news indeed!"

Pharaoh smiled. "Those merchant colonies were on the border of Assyrian territory. Not only have we made the Assyrians wonder what we're up to, but we've hurt their southern trade. It's a good start."

More scouts arrived throughout the day, and each had similar reports to make.

"If this keeps up, the fleet will be full when it sails back to Egypt," General Ahmose noted.

Pharaoh nodded. "Good. My people need to see quick success in Canaan if we're to stop the spread of discontent being sown by my priests and unhappy nobles."

Well after sunset, Shayari approached the corridor that led to the apartments of Pharaoh's sons. The Medjay guards searched her quickly; her translucent linen sheath dress provided no hiding places for any weapons or items that could harm Prince Webensenu.

One of the guards escorted her to Prince Webensenu's apartment and stood at the entrance when she went inside.

She stood in the antechamber and looked around. Then she cleared her throat. "My Prince?" she called softly.

"Come in," she heard a voice say nervously.

She smiled and entered Webensenu's sitting area. The prince sat in a chair near the terrace, watching her walk toward him.

When she reached the center of the room, she gently lowered herself to her knees. Looking down at the floor, she asked, "What is your desire, my Prince?"

Webensenu didn't answer. She glanced up and saw that he looked nervous. She flashed him a warm and understanding smile. He returned the smile and motioned for her to stand.

She stood and walked slowly toward him in a way designed to stir his desires. When she reached his chair, she stopped and stared into his face.

"What do I do?" he whispered.

"I'll show you, my Prince." Shayari reached up and slipped her dress off her shoulders. It slid silently to the floor. She held out her hand, and Webensenu took it. He stood, and she led him to the bedchamber. She drew the curtain closed as they entered.

"Relax, my Prince. Tonight is all for you."

Shayari left Webensenu's apartment shortly before sunrise the next morning. The guard hid a smile as she walked past him and headed back to the harem.

After she returned to her quarters, she cleaned herself, changed clothes, and left to find Princess Iaret.

"How did it go last night?" Iaret asked as Shayari entered her sitting area.

"I think he enjoyed himself, my Princess," Shayari said softly.

"I imagine he'll need lots of instruction before he weds."

"All men do, my Princess. But he's a quick learner."

Iaret giggled as she glanced at one of her guards standing across the room. The guard's face remained neutral, but Iaret saw him look at her and wink. "The student can only be as good as the teacher," she commented.

Shayari looked down. "Yes, my Princess."

"Will you see him again tonight?"

"Yes, my Princess."

Iaret picked up a bag of coins from the table next to her and handed the bag to Shayari. "From the queen."

Shayari looked surprised. "I am a slave, my Princess. She owes me no payment."

"You're doing a service for the royal family – possibly for the next Pharaoh. That deserves a reward."

Shayari reached for the bag of coins hesitatingly. Iaret thrust the bag into her hands.

"Accept the gift, Shayari. And if Prince Webensenu has good things to say about coupling with you, you can expect more in the future."

"Yes, my Princess."

Shayari visited Prince Webensenu's apartment again that night.

Iaret didn't see her half-brother again until the next afternoon.

"You seem to be in high spirits, brother," she said as she saw him approaching across the courtyard from the stables.

Webensenu blushed and grinned at her. "Shayari is amazing!"

Iaret smiled. "I had hoped so. I take it you're an attentive student?"

Webensenu nodded, blushing harder.

Iaret put her hand on his shoulder. "Then enjoy the learning, brother. She truly is a lovely girl, and she enjoys the teaching as much as you appear to enjoy the learning."

Webensenu's eyes opened wide. "You've spoken to her?"

"Of course," Iaret acknowledged. "I have to be certain that you have the right teacher."

Webensenu answered quickly. "She *is* the right teacher,"

Iaret nodded. "Then enjoy your time with her."

Shayari visited Prince Webensenu's apartment every night for the next two weeks.

Iaret met with Shayari every morning and gave her another bag of coins from Tiaa.

On the first morning of the third week, Iaret said, "The queen wishes to speak with you before you return to your quarters. She wants to know how things are going with Prince Webensenu."

"Yes, my Princess." Shayari stood, but Iaret remained seated. "Will you be there?"

Iaret shook her head. "No, I have to go meet with the Nubian delegation in the throne room. Don't worry, though. The Queen is happy with you; she just wants to hear from you how the prince is doing."

Shayari left Iaret's apartment and walked down the corridor to Tiaa's apartment. When she was escorted into the Tiaa's sitting area, an older man stood just behind the queen.

"My Queen," Shayari intoned as she lowered herself to her knees.

"Come here, child." Tiaa gestured to a chair.

When Shayari was seated, Tiaa said, "I need your help, Shayari."

"Anything, my Queen."

Tiaa gestured to the man standing behind her. "This is the royal physician. He's just been telling me that Prince Webensenu is not well."

Shayari blanched. She knew that it was common for slaves to be blamed for the smallest of things in the palace. "My Queen, I haven't done anything…"

Tiaa held up her hand, and Shayari fell silent. "It's nothing that you've done. Prince Webensenu has a condition that's getting worse because he refuses to let the physicians treat him for it. If he takes the treatment, he'll be fine in no time. If he doesn't, he'll get worse. He says that he won't take anything until his father returns to Canaan, but the physicians have told me that he might not make it that long. That's why I need your help."

"What can I do, my Queen?"

Tiaa gestured for the physician to speak. He held up a bowl with a cover on it. Lifting the cover, Shayari saw a white powder inside. "This is the medicine that will cure him," the physician said. "It needs to be administered under his skin, and time is running out."

Tiaa regarded Shayari closely. "You seem fond of Prince Webensenu, Shayari."

Shayari smiled. "I am, my Queen."

"And you don't want to see anything bad happen to him, right?"

"No, my Queen!"

Tiaa reached into a leather pouch and extracted a copper ring similar to the one that all of the slave girls in the harem wore. Tiaa held up the ring so Shayari could see the spike at the bottom. "I need you to wear this ring when you go to him tonight. The medicine will be on the spike. Be careful not to touch it! It will cure him, but it will make you sick, since you don't have the condition it's intended to cure. While you're coupling with the prince, prick him with the spike in the back of his calf muscle. I'm told that's the best place to administer the medicine."

The physician nodded in agreement.

"And then what?" Shayari asked.

"Nothing," Tiaa said. "Enjoy the rest of your night with him, bring the ring back to me in the morning, and continue doing what you're already doing like nothing happened."

Tiaa leaned forward. "Will you help me to help Prince Webensenu? Can I count on you?"

Shayari nodded. "Of course, my Queen. Anything to help you and the prince."

Tiaa smiled and leaned back. "Thank you. Stop by on your way to see him tonight, and I'll give you the ring. It'll have the medicine on it already. Remember, don't touch the spike!"

As soon as Shayari left her apartment, Tiaa turned to the man. "You played your part well, priest."

"Thank you, my Queen. I'll tell High Priest Amenemhat that all is arranged for Prince Webensenu's... future. But what about the girl?"

Tiaa chuckled and held up her cobra ring. "The prince won't be the only one who feels the spike. She'll meet the same fate with twice the dose when she brings me back her ring in the morning."

"Why twice the dose?"

"So she'll die before the prince starts getting sick." Tiaa placed both rings back in the pouch. "Alive, she can tell people what I asked her to do. Dead, there's no one to point the finger at me."

CHAPTER 9

Pharaoh's charioteers disembarked. Rows of chariots brought from the ships soon lined the beach below the army encampment. Once the horses were unloaded and harnessed, charioteers drove up the hill to join the waiting soldiers.

Pharaoh's new driver brought Pharaoh's war chariot up the hill and stopped in front of Amenhotep and General Ahmose, who watched from the ridge above the beach. This chariot, replacing the one lost at the Gulf of Reeds six months earlier, had extra quivers built in for arrows and spears. It was slightly larger than Pharaoh's previous war chariot, and when Amenhotep mounted the deck next to the driver, he immediately appreciated the extra space.

The driver drove Pharaoh to the army encampment. Pharaoh watched the activity around the encampment with great interest. Most of the soldiers had returned from their raids and were taking their plunder and prisoners down to the beach.

Within a few hours after the chariots were unloaded, the ships were filled with plunder and thousands of prisoners to take back to Egypt. Admiral Thuti made arrangements with General Ahmose for the next rendezvous, and then the fleet sailed for home.

Pharaoh and General Ahmose convened a war council that evening with the company commanders to review the battle plans.

Because a great river separated western and eastern Canaan, Pharaoh decided to keep his forces in western Canaan, between the river and the Middle Sea. The army would move south through western Canaan, deployed in a crescent shape with the lower tip of the crescent to the east near the river. This would force any settlers, villagers, and townspeople that the army encountered to flee toward the coast where Pharaoh's navy would be waiting for them. The chariots would take positions at the southernmost tip of the crescent so they could move around to the south and prevent any potential prisoners from escaping.

If Pharaoh's strategy worked, western Canaan would be almost entirely cleared of people and plunder by the time the campaign ended and the army returned to Egypt.

"Inform your men to get as much rest as they can," Pharaoh said at the end of the war council meeting. "We move out at first light."

Shayari stopped by Tiaa's apartment on her way to see Prince Webensenu.

"Here is the ring." Tiaa held up the copper ring. "Take off your ring and give it to me."

Shayari obeyed. Tiaa gave her the spike ring, and Shayari placed it on the middle finger of her left hand. She looked at the spike and found it hard not to touch it.

"Do you remember my instructions?" Tiaa asked.

Shayari nodded. "Yes, my Queen. In his calf muscle."

"And you're to return here and bring me that ring as soon as you leave him in the morning."

"Yes, my Queen."

Tiaa gave Shayari her warmest smile. "Thank you again for helping me, Shayari. What you do tonight will save the young Prince's life. I'll make certain that you are royally rewarded."

"That's not necessary, my Queen."

"Nonsense." Tiaa escorted Shayari across the sitting area to the antechamber. "You're helping the monarchy. That service must be rewarded. Now, you go and enjoy yourself with Prince Webensenu, Shayari."

"Yes, my Queen."

Shayari smiled to the guards as she passed through the entrance to the corridor where the princes' apartments were located. At Prince Webensenu's request, the guards no longer searched Shayari when she arrived for their nightly coupling.

She entered the prince's apartment and immediately crossed the sitting area to the bedchamber, where he waited for her. She slipped off her translucent dress before entering, making certain not to snag the material on the ring's spike. Then she entered the bedchamber and drew the curtain closed behind her.

Prince Webensenu waited for her in bed. She knelt on the edge of the bed, rubbing her right hand along his legs and thighs. As she leaned down to teach him something new, she clutched his left leg with her right hand and moved her left hand around the back of his right leg.

She waited until he was in the throes of ecstasy before pressing her left hand against his calf muscle. He must not have felt the prick of the spike because he didn't react to anything other than the pleasure she was giving him.

Shayari rose before dawn the next morning while Prince Webensenu was still asleep. They had coupled several times during the night, and Shayari took a moment to stretch before putting on her dress and leaving Webensenu's apartment.

She walked quickly to Tiaa's apartment in the harem. Tiaa was already awake – waiting for her.

"How did it go last night?" Tiaa asked as Shayari slipped the spiked ring off her finger.

"He never felt a thing, my Queen," Shayari replied as she handed the spiked ring to Tiaa and took back on her own ring.

Tiaa placed the spiked ring in a leather pouch, and for the first time Shayari noticed that Tiaa wore a beautiful copper ring on her finger with a cobra worked into the design.

"You have done me and the royal family a great service,

Shayari." Tiaa handed Shayari a bag of coins that felt heavier than any bag she had received so far.

Shayari accepted the bag and clutched it in her left hand since she had no folds in her translucent dress that could conceal anything. "Thank you, my Queen. Is there anything else you need from me?"

Tiaa patted her on her shoulder. "Not a thing, my dear. You may return to your quarters. I believe Princess Iaret will want to hear about last night's coupling, but there's no reason to mention what you did for me or anything about the medicine that you gave Prince Webensenu."

Shayari felt a slight sting on the back of her shoulder as Tiaa led her to the antechamber, but she assumed that it was just the bite of a flying insect. She pushed it from her mind and returned to her quarters to wash and change before meeting with Princess Iaret.

"Shayari's ill," Iaret said to Amenemipet and Kenamun two days later in Amenemipet's private meeting room. "She's showing the same symptoms as Senebsen did, but it's taking hold of Shayari much faster."

"Tiaa must have used a stronger dose of poison on her," Amenemipet speculated.

"But why poison her at all?" Iaret looked distressed. "She wasn't part of Tiaa's plans. She was just a slave girl who was coupling with Webensenu."

"Are you certain that she wasn't part of Tiaa's plans?" Kenamun asked. "After all, it was Tiaa's idea to find a slave girl for Webensenu. Perhaps she's already done what Tiaa wanted her to do, and it's time for her to be eliminated."

Iaret shuddered. "If she's already done what Tiaa wanted, does that mean that Shayari poisoned Webensenu?"

"He's not showing any symptoms," Amenemipet stated. "But that doesn't mean he hasn't already been poisoned."

"If she poisoned Webensenu, how could it have happened?" Kenamun asked. "I thought we were watching Shayari closely."

"We were," Iaret confirmed.

"Did she ever meet with Tiaa alone?" Amenemipet asked.

Iaret blanched. "Yes. Three days ago. Tiaa wanted to see Shayari, but I couldn't be there because I had to meet with the Nubian delegation."

Amenemipet shook his head. "That's probably when she either poisoned Shayari, or when she gave Shayari the poison to give to Webensenu. Or both."

"Then we're too late, and I failed." Iaret felt angry with herself.

"We all failed, my Princess," Amenemipet said gently. "We were all supposed to be watching what was happening, and we didn't prevent this tragedy."

"Is it possible that Tiaa killed Shayari because she *didn't* poison Prince Webensenu?" Kenamun asked.

Amenemipet shrugged. "It's possible, but I can't see Tiaa killing an agent until the job was done."

"If Prince Webensenu *was* poisoned," Iaret speculated, "then Tiaa's one step closer to having Amenhotep named as my father's heir. Only my brother, Thutmose, stands in her way. We have to protect him, but it can't look like I'm doing it, or Tiaa will come after me next."

"You need to embed yourself deeper into her plots, my Princess," Amenhotep stated. "We have to know what she's planning if we're going to stop her before it's too late."

Iaret nodded. *I'll keep close to Tiaa so I can be there when she's finally brought down. I'll see her dead and buried before I let her hurt my brother or tear apart my father's kingdom.*

Death took Shayari quickly and painfully.

Prince Webensenu was devastated when he learned that she had died. He spent hours in the royal chapel next to the palace – where the royal family members made their daily supplications to the gods – praying for her to be granted an afterlife, something that most slaves would automatically be denied.

Iaret found him in the chapel and quietly knelt next to him. She wanted to comfort him, but she also didn't want to interrupt his prayers.

After nearly an hour, Webensenu looked at her. His grief was clearly evident on his face. "Why did the gods take her from me?" he lamented. "She was beautiful. She was gentle. She was precious to me."

Iaret put her hand on his shoulder. "I don't know. Only the gods know why they do what they do." *Of course, I don't believe for one moment that this is the work of the gods. This is Tiaa's doing. Has she arranged for you to meet the same fate?*

Webensenu stood, and Iaret did the same. Silently, he turned and walked out of the chapel back to the palace. Iaret walked next to him, not wanting to intrude on his thoughts.

When they reached the central courtyard of the palace, Webensenu turned to face his half-sister. His face, head, and chest were covered in sweat. "I don't feel well..."

Webensenu collapsed at Iaret's feet.

"Guards!" Iaret shouted as she knelt beside Webensenu. His skin was wet and clammy, but his forehead was burning up. He twitched and shuddered, just as Senebsen and Shayari had when the poison began to tear them apart from the inside.

Five Medjay guards arrived and saw Webensenu sprawled on the stone tiles of the courtyard. They looked from him to Iaret with confusion on their faces.

"Take him to his quarters," Iaret ordered.

"Yes, my Princess," the guards intoned. Four of the guards bent down and picked up the prince. The fifth guard held their spears. As the four guards carried Webensenu across the courtyard toward his apartment, Iaret stopped the fifth guard.

"Go find the Vizier. Tell him what happened, and tell him to meet me in Prince Webensenu's apartment as soon as he can get there."

"Yes, my Princess."

Iaret followed the four guards to Webensenu's apartment. They laid him down on his bed, and Iaret covered him with the pelt of a tiger to keep him warm.

"One of you go and fetch the physician," Iaret instructed. "The rest of you take positions around the apartment. No one enters or leaves without *my* permission. Understood?"

"Yes, my Princess."

One guard left to find the royal physician while the other three took up posts outside the bedchamber, next to the terrace, and just inside the sitting area next to the antechamber. Iaret stayed with Webensenu, watching helplessly as he writhed in pain.

Amenemipet arrived a short while later with the fifth guard and was stopped by the guard posted at the entrance to the sitting area.

"My Princess, it's Amenemipet," he called.

"Let him in," Iaret commanded.

The guard stepped aside, and Amenemipet hastened to the bedchamber.

"Oh, no!" he cried when he saw Webensenu.

Iaret nodded. "It's the poison. He has the same symptoms as the others. He collapsed in the courtyard as we were walking back from the chapel. One moment he was fine, the next moment he was like this."

Iaret heard a commotion outside the bedchamber.

"My Princess, the physician is here." The voice was of the guard posted just inside the sitting area.

"Let him in!" Iaret shouted.

The physician entered the bedchamber and immediately knelt next to Webensenu's bed. After feeling the prince's forehead, he asked, "How long as he been like this?"

Iaret relayed what happened when she and the prince left the chapel and entered the courtyard.

"And he exhibited no symptoms prior to that?"

"None that I saw," Iaret replied. "I was with him in the chapel for nearly an hour, but it just looked like he was praying."

"Three cases of the same malady," the physician said to himself. Turning to Iaret and Amenemipet, he said, "Help me search the body."

"What are we looking for?" Amenemipet asked.

"Anything that looks like a bite or a sting. It might help me discover what's causing this."

The physician, Iaret, and Amenemipet began looking closely at Webensenu's skin for any blemishes that looked unusual.

"Did the other two cases have any marks that looked like a bite or a sting?" Iaret asked.

"Yes," the physician replied. "Senebsen had a mark on her

upper arm, and the slave girl, Shayari, had one on her upper back just below the shoulder.

Iaret felt along the back of Webensenu's legs and felt a small welt on the calf muscle of his right leg. Lifting the leg, she saw the mark. "Is that what you mean?"

The physician looked at the back of Webensenu's leg and nodded. "That's the same mark as the others," he confirmed. "It looks like a scorpion sting. Given its location on his body, I think it's the most plausible answer. We'll have to watch him closely and hope that his body can fight the venom."

The physician stood. "I'll check back on him later."

When the physician left the bedchamber, Iaret looked up at Amenemipet and whispered, "This was no scorpion sting. It was Tiaa."

Webensenu lingered in his feverish state for two days before he finally slipped away in the middle of the night and crossed over to the netherworld.

Amenemipet sent a dispatch to Peru-nefer instructing Admiral Thuti to tell Pharaoh personally about the loss of his second-born son. Amenemipet also instructed the admiral to inform Pharaoh about the loss of his concubine, Senebsen, in spite of Tiaa's wishes that Pharaoh not be told about Senebsen's death. Amenemipet believed that the death of two people so close to Pharaoh should not be kept secret.

Webensenu's body was prepared for burial according to the rites and traditions for royal princes. Most of the court was content to accept the "scorpion sting" story, but Iaret, Amenemipet, and Kenamun knew that the story wasn't true.

Amenemipet increased the number of spies he had in the palace at Men-nefer. He gave them orders to kill any of Tiaa's spies that got in the way. Unfortunately, Tiaa gave her spies the same instructions about Amenemipet's spies.

Merytamon barged into Tiaa's apartment, pushing past the servants and guards who tried to keep her out.

"Where are you, Tiaa?" Merytamon shouted as she entered the sitting area.

"I'm right here," Tiaa said coolly. Her face looked sympathetic, but her voice had no warmth in it.

"You murdered my son!"

"I did nothing of the kind, Merytamon," Tiaa said smoothly, sitting down and offering Merytamon a seat.

Merytamon took a step forward. "Oh, you may not have done the deed yourself, but it was your hand that guided the assassin's act. First Senebsen and now my son. Prince Amenhotep is one step closer to the throne of Egypt; isn't that right? Isn't that why you had my son killed?"

Tiaa shook her head. "How many times do I have to say that I had nothing to do with Webensenu's death?"

"As many times as it takes to get the truth out of you."

Merytamon stormed out of Tiaa's apartment, but instead of returning to her own, she went looking for Amenemipet. She found him in his office on the other side of the palace.

"May I speak with you, Vizier?" she asked, standing in the doorway of his office.

Amenemipet gazed up at her before standing. "Yes, but not here. Follow me."

He led her to his private meeting room. Once inside, he said, "I'm truly sorry about your son, Great Lady."

"Thank you, Vizier." She hesitated for a moment, and then she said, "I need your help, Amenemipet."

"Anything, Great Lady."

"Tiaa killed my son. I know she did. Don't tell me you don't suspect her, too."

Amenemipet kept his face neutral, saying nothing.

Merytamon persisted. "I know you do. I confronted her this morning, but she denied it. I don't want to follow my son into the afterlife just yet, and I don't want my surviving sons to follow their brother yet either. It's not safe for us in the palace."

"What do you want me to do?" Amenemipet asked.

"I want to leave the palace, and I want to take my two

remaining sons with me. I need us to be someplace where Tiaa can't reach us."

Amenemipet leaned back and rubbed his face with his hands. "Waset is out of the question. Tiaa has spies there, and the priests at Karnak do her bidding. What about Peru-nefer? Pharaoh's personal palace and is well protected by soldiers and the Medjay guards. You could sail up there this afternoon, if you like. I can arrange for the royal barge to take you."

"I'd prefer something a bit less noticeable," Merytamon said. "I want to escape unseen, not announce to the kingdom where I am."

Amenemipet nodded. "Very well. I'll arrange for a fishing vessel and a contingent of guards to take you to the palace at Peru-nefer this afternoon, and I'll see to it that Tiaa is kept distracted while you're leaving. Her spies might see you leave, but I'll spread the word that you're going to Iunu to pray in the temples for your son."

"Thank you, Amenemipet." Merytamon stood to leave. "And please see to it that my son is interred in his father's tomb with all of the royal rites followed."

"You won't be there?" Amenemipet looked confused as he stood.

"No. I won't be anywhere that Tiaa is until Pharaoh returns or until Tiaa is dead."

Merytamon and her sons – the Princes Amenemopet and Aakheperure – left Men-nefer that afternoon in secret. Iaret kept Tiaa busy, but Tiaa's spies in the palace observed the departure. The spies also overheard Amenemipet inform the guards that Merytamon and the Princes were making a pilgrimage to Iunu, the spiritual center of northern Egypt, to pray for Prince Webensenu.

Admiral Thuti disembarked and walked across the beach where

Pharaoh was waiting on his war chariot. This was not the news he wanted to bring to Pharaoh, but he had his instructions from the Vizier.

Prisoners and plunder were already being loaded into the ships as he reached Pharaoh.

"I see that the campaign is going well, Great Pharaoh."

Pharaoh nodded. "Resistance is light, and the plunder is vast. We've captured over fifty thousand prisoners so far, and we're barely half way to the southern border of Canaan!"

Admiral Thuti nodded. "Pharaoh, I have a message from Amenemipet, and he instructed me to deliver it to you and you alone."

Pharaoh's pleased expression faded as he saw the grave expression on Admiral Thuti's face. He stepped off his war chariot and motioned for the admiral to follow him. When they were far enough away that they wouldn't be overheard, Admiral Thuti delivered his message.

"Your second-born son, Prince Webensenu, is dead, Great Pharaoh."

Pharaoh gaped at the admiral. "What? How?"

"The physician has declared that it was the result of a scorpion sting, but the Vizier, Amenemipet, suspects poison."

Pharaoh's expression turned dark. "Who poisoned my son?"

"The Vizier cannot prove who it was, but he has suspicions."

Pharaoh turned his face away and put a hand on the admiral's shoulder. "Thank you, Thuti."

"There's more, Great Pharaoh," the admiral said. "Your concubine, Senebsen, and the slave girl that was coupling with Prince Webensenu both died of the same malady. This is why the Vizier believes it was poison and why he's working hard to find who was responsible."

"Senebsen's dead, too?" Pharaoh cried out in grief.

Admiral Thuti stood there silently. After a moment, Pharaoh patted the admiral's shoulder and walked away without speaking.

"I'm truly sorry, Great Pharaoh," the admiral called after him.

General Ahmose, who had arrived on the beach a few moments earlier, walked up to Admiral Thuti.

"What's wrong?" the general asked. "Has something

happened?"

The admiral nodded. "I just had to inform Pharaoh that his second-born son is dead."

CHAPTER 10

Word of Prince Webensenu's death spread rapidly throughout the army encampment, as did the rumor that his death might have been an assassination. The thought that a member of the royal family had been murdered – especially the prince who was in line to be the next Pharaoh – enraged the Egyptian soldiers. The campaign in Canaan took on a completely new intensity after that, and the company commanders had to restrain their soldiers to prevent the slaughter of valuable prisoners.

As Pharaoh's army moved into southern Canaan, their progress became choked by all of the herds and flocks that they had captured. Prisoners were being taken back to Egypt by the navy, while flocks and herds traveled with the army.

"We need to slow our advance south so the navy can begin taking livestock back to Egypt," Pharaoh told General Ahmose and his company commanders one evening. "We cannot continue the campaign and manage all of these animals. Egypt needs beasts of burden, wool from sheep, and meat. We'll keep what we need to sustain the army and the prisoners we're taking, but the rest need to be taken back to Egypt as quickly as possible."

General Ahmose nodded. "I agree, Great Pharaoh. As much as the men want to complete the campaign and return home, they could use the rest. The settlements in southern Canaan now know that we're coming and what we're after. Resistance could stiffen, and the army needs to be rested to face it."

"Then it's settled," Pharaoh stated. "We'll set up a new

encampment at the next rendezvous site and let the navy begin taking the livestock back to Egypt. Is there anything else that we need to discuss?"

One of the company commanders cleared his throat.

"Yes?" Pharaoh asked.

"Great Pharaoh, we captured something unexpected in our last raid."

"What?"

"Hebrew prisoners, Great Pharaoh."

Pharaoh was shocked. "Hebrews? How is that possible? Moses led them to Midian in the south. What's he doing in Canaan?" *Is this my chance to finally take my revenge on Moses, or is this another trap set by his god?*

"Great Pharaoh, we haven't encountered Moses or the bulk of the Hebrews yet. As far as we know, they're still in Midian. This is a group of Hebrews who broke away from Moses and the others when Moses led the rest of them south through Mafkat."

"Why did they break off?" General Ahmose asked.

"Because they believe that their god promised them a homeland in Canaan. When the Hebrews were allowed to leave Egypt, many thought that Moses was leading them to that land, not to Midian, which is in the opposite direction. This group knew that they were close to Canaan and decided to come straight here instead of following Moses south. They were camped not far from here, and we captured all of them quite easily."

"How many?" Pharaoh asked.

"Thirty-six hundred including the women and children, Great Pharaoh."

Pharaoh roared with laughter. *They disobeyed Moses by not following him to Midian, and now they're going back to Egypt. I wonder if their god will send them another deliverer, or if returning to slavery is punishment for their waywardness.*

"I don't want them taken back to Goshen," Pharaoh said finally. "I don't plan to have any more issues with the Hebrews *or* their god. The men and boys are to be castrated so they cannot breed more of their race. The women and girls will be mated with Egyptians and slaves from other nations. I want all traces of these prisoners being Hebrew gone within a generation, and I want them spread out across central and southern Egypt. Any who defy us or cause any problems are to be executed on the spot. Understood? There will be no more Hebrew problems in Egypt!"

"Yes, Great Pharaoh!"

Pharaoh looked around. "Anything else?"

"Yes, Great Pharaoh," General Ahmose said. "The army is being watched."

"By whom?" *As if I don't already know.*

"Charioteers from the Hittites and Assyrians."

"How do you know?"

"I have scouts watching our rear flank, Great Pharaoh. The two groups of charioteers don't seem aware of each other. One watches us from the northeast, and the other watches us from the northwest."

They've undoubtedly reported back to their masters what we're doing here. If the Assyrians or Hittites were going to attack us, they'd have already done it. Perhaps our campaign is making them think twice about their assessment of our strength after the loss of our chariots at the Gulf of Reeds.

Pharaoh nodded. "Good. Keep watching them in case they're the lead elements of either army instead of just scouts. If one or both armies approach us from the north, we need to be ready."

"Yes, Great Pharaoh."

A servant escorted Sitamun into Tiaa's sitting area. Tiaa sat near the terrace and gestured toward a nearby chair. Sitamun sat down warily, never taking her eyes off Tiaa.

The two women regarded each other in silence.

"You sent for me, my Queen?" Sitamun finally asked.

"Yes, Sitamun. We have much to discuss."

Sitamun smiled, but there was no humor in her eyes. "I wondered how long it would take you to approach me, Tiaa. Now that Prince Webensenu is out of the way, only my son Thutmose stands between your son Amenhotep and the throne. What methods will you employ to remove the threat of my son from your plans?"

"You forget yourself, Sitamun," Tiaa snapped. "I am your queen!"

"No, you're my husband's royal wife... for the moment. He can replace you at any time. I, too, am his wife, so don't think for a moment that you're somehow superior to me! You were just first. Nothing else."

Tiaa tapped her fingers on the edge of her chair, and Sitamun was impressed at how well Tiaa controlled her anger.

"My, we are being direct this morning, aren't we?"

Sitamun sat expressionless, locking eyes with Tiaa. "Why waste time with pretense and games, Tiaa? I know what you're really after, so why don't you tell me why I'm here? You didn't ask me here to pass the time with pleasantries, so out with it. What do you want?"

"Your support, of course," Tiaa replied smoothly, but with an edge to her voice. "Your son is Pharaoh's oldest *surviving* son. My son is his second-oldest. I want my son to be the next Pharaoh. You can help me achieve that."

"By killing my son for you? Or by setting him up so one of your assassins can kill him?"

Tiaa smiled. "There *must* be another way to keep your son from becoming Pharaoh without doing either of those things, isn't there?"

"What, by convincing Thutmose to renounce his birthright? What good will that do? Pharaoh has already stated that he'll pick whichever of his sons will make the best Pharaoh. Thutmose can renounce his claim to the throne all he wants, but that won't change Pharaoh's decision."

Tiaa glared at Sitamun. "Well, I suggest you think of something. The palace already has the stench of death about it, and we don't want that to get worse, do we?"

"Not unless it's *your* death, Tiaa."

Tiaa laughed, but the sound made Sitamun shudder. "Something tells me that you'll never get to see my death, Sitamun."

"Because your priests and assassins will kill us all before long? Is that why Merytamon had to flee the palace with her two surviving sons?"

"Merytamon is in Iunu, praying for Prince Webensenu."

"Ha!" Sitamun spat out the word contemptuously. "She's in hiding from you, and I don't blame her. You had that slave girl murder her son, didn't you? The one who died right before he did? How heartless can you be, pretending to find him a wife while planning his death all along? Don't deny it!"

"Prove it, Sitamun." Tiaa's face contorted like a cobra about to strike.

"If I could prove it, your head would already be on a spike at the gates of Men-nefer, Tiaa."

Tiaa reached up and felt her head. Smiling, she said, "Since my head is still here, your accusations are pointless and insulting. Go. I have no desire to listen to your rantings any longer."

Sitamun stood, and Tiaa added, "Remember what I said, Sitamun. My son will be the next Pharaoh. Don't stand in my way, and don't let your son stand in my way. These are dangerous times, and we wouldn't want anything to happen to either of you, would we?"

Sitamun left Tiaa's apartment without saying a word. Once in the corridor, she hurried to find Amenemipet. *I need him to protect my son, and I need him to protect me. Tiaa has to be stopped, but I can't do it by myself.*

Amenemipet was furious when he heard that Tiaa had threatened Sitamun and Thutmose. He gave orders to the Captain of the Medjay Guards to triple the guards on Sitamun and Thutmose and to search thoroughly every person who tried to see them or enter their apartments. Amenemipet also instructed Kenamun to double their food tasters.

It's not enough, but it's all I can do until I can find out who else is involved in Tiaa's treason against Pharaoh.

Amenemipet and Kenamun sat across from their prisoner in Amenemipet's private meeting room. No one but the Medjay knew who the prisoner was or that he had been brought to the palace.

"Do you know why you're here?" Amenemipet asked.

116

"N-n-no," the prisoner stammered. "I don't even know where I am or who you are."

Amenemipet reached forward and removed the sack from the prisoner's head. "I am the Vizier of Egypt, and this is the Chief Steward of Pharaoh's household. You're here to answer for your interactions with certain nobles in the city who are unhappy with the current state of affairs."

Kaaper, the acolyte of Amenemhat, the High Priest of Amun from Karnak, squirmed nervously in his chair as he looked around the room.

"There is no escaping this room, Priest," Amenemipet stated flatly. "You will be here for as long as we want you to be, and you will leave only when we allow you to leave. Understood?"

Kaaper nodded.

Amenemipet crossed his arms. "Good. Now, what form of execution do you prefer? Burning? Beheading? Quartering? Being staked down in the western desert until the sun kills you? What's your preference?"

Kaaper's expression turned angry. "E-e-execution? B-b-by what right do you intend to execute a priest of the temple of Amun? You invite the wrath of the gods for even suggesting such a thing!"

"Pharaoh is the living god of Egypt," Amenemipet snapped. "You attempted to recruit nobles to turn against Pharaoh – something that we call treason around here. Not even Amun would defend a priest for treason against Pharaoh, or didn't they teach you that in the temple?"

Kaaper's face turned bright red.

"For your crimes," Amenemipet continued, "you will be executed in a manner consistent with your transgression, and your body will be desecrated, denying you any afterlife apart from what awaits you in the realm of demons. It's only because you *are* a priest that I'm giving you the choice of how you'll die."

Kaaper looked at both men. "Surely there's a way I can avoid being executed," he pleaded. "I'm just a priest. I follow the orders of my superiors."

"So you admit that your superiors instructed you to recruit nobles for a rebellion against Pharaoh?" Kenamun interjected.

Kaaper stared at Kenamun with his mouth agape and a look

of shock and terror on his face.

"So, you're more afraid of High Priest Amenemhat than of Pharaoh's wrath?" Amenemipet demanded. Looking at Kenamun, he added, "I think burning is best for this priest. I'll call the guards and have the execution proceed immediately..."

"Wait!" Kaaper licked his lips nervously. "Just wait. Yes, I'm afraid of High Priest Amenemhat, and yes, he had me meet with nobles throughout the city to recruit allies against Pharaoh. I know the name of every one who agreed to be his ally, and I can name the other priests who met with nobles here in Men-nefer. I can also find out who is meeting with the nobles in Waset and in the smaller cities along the Ar River."

Kenamun chuckled. "So you'd betray your High Priest just to stay alive?"

"Do you know how many priests of Amun there are in Egypt?" Kaaper asked. "Too many for me to ever be elevated to High Priest, or even a Senior Priest, for that matter. But if I can help you save Pharaoh and his family, perhaps Pharaoh's gratitude will be far greater than Amenemhat's. *He* only cares about serving Queen Tiaa, not taking care of the ones doing his dirty work."

"So the queen is behind the plots against Pharaoh?"

Kaaper stared at Amenemipet and then slumped in his chair. Looking down, he said, "The word of a single priest isn't proof. You'll need more if you're going to stop Amenemhat and the queen."

"Will you help us get that proof?" Kenamun asked.

"In exchange for my life? Yes."

"And you'll help us identify everyone involved in their conspiracy against Pharaoh, including the nobles who have allied themselves with Amenemhat and the queen?"

"Yes," Kaaper assured them. "But I want a guarantee that, if I help you, you'll ensure that I have an afterlife befitting one of Pharaoh's loyal servants."

Amenemipet nodded. "You work with us to stop the conspiracy and save Pharaoh and his children, and I'll see to it that you are rewarded handsomely in this world *and* in the next."

Kaaper relaxed. "Then we have a deal. What do you want to know first?"

"A priest told you all that?"

Iaret was surprised when Amenemipet and Kenamun finished telling her about their meeting with Kaaper. *I never thought one of Amenemhat's acolytes would turn on him.*

Amenemipet chuckled. "He didn't agree to help us because he was feeling generous, my Princess. He demanded a high price, but the information he shared was worth it."

"He even identified all of Amenemhat's spies in the palace, including some that I didn't suspect," Kenamun added. "I have my agents keeping an eye on them to see what they're up to."

"But we still don't have enough proof to arrest Amenemhat and Tiaa?" Iaret asked. "What more do we need?"

"We need to hear the two of them plotting against Pharaoh or one of his children directly, or we need to hear them instructing someone to carry out their plots, my Princess," Amenemipet said sadly. "It's the same with the nobles. Until they actually try to assassinate or overthrow Pharaoh, we can't move against them. There's no law against being angry at Pharaoh, only in acting on that anger."

"You know that Tiaa threatened my mother, right?" Iaret had met with Sitamun earlier in the day and knew what Tiaa had said.

Amenemipet nodded. "Your mother came to see me right after she left Tiaa's quarters. She's scared, but I don't know how to stop Tiaa with complete confidence. We thought that Prince Webensenu was safe, but she found a way to kill him anyway."

"And my brother?" Iaret asked. "Can you keep him safe?"

Amenemipet shrugged. "We've taken every precaution we can think of, but Tiaa's resourceful. She may still find a way that we haven't thought of."

Iaret looked grim. "Then maybe I need to suggest some ways to her."

"What do you mean?" Kenamun asked.

"If I can keep Tiaa focused on plans that we're already aware of and can prevent from working, it just might keep her from thinking about ways that we don't know about and can't prevent."

"Won't she get suspicious when all of your suggestions fail?"

Amenemipet asked.

"Possibly. Do you have a better idea?"

Amenemipet looked at Kenamun and both men shook their heads.

"Then let's come up with some ideas that we know we can prevent from working."

Merytamon looked around Pharaoh's study in the palace at Peru-nefer. She was the first of Pharaoh's wives ever to set foot in this particular palace, and she felt out of place, as if she were invading Pharaoh's privacy.

Her sons played in the garden under the watchful eyes of their Medjay guards. The study was on the far side of the palace away from anyone who might overhear her. Two men sat across from her, holding the bags of gold that she had just given them.

"Are you certain that you want to take this action, Great Lady?" one of the men asked. "After all, she *is* Pharaoh's royal wife."

"She's also the biggest threat to Pharaoh and his household," Merytamon stated flatly. "Doing this will save Pharaoh. Think of it as a service to the Kingdom, not just to me."

"When do you want it done?" the other man asked.

"Before Pharaoh returns from Canaan," Merytamon replied. "And I want her dead before she can move against any more of Pharaoh's children, wives, or concubines."

The two men nodded. "It won't be easy, Great Lady. There are ten of us, but we can't go up against the Medjay guards at the palace."

Merytamon snorted. "That's why you're being paid so much. You'll enter the palace as my personal servants. The token I've given you will give you access to anywhere inside the palace except for Pharaoh's personal apartments and the Vizier's office."

"And you don't care how it's done?"

Merytamon shook her head. "Try to make it look natural – a snake or scorpion, perhaps. But if all other means fail, stick a dagger in her heart, and make your escape any way you can."

"Yes, Great Lady."

Khaemtir, Pensekhmet, Sharek, Wadjmose and several other nobles sat around the courtyard of the same compound near the southern wall of Men-nefer where they had met with Kaaper and Amenemhat previously.

"I understand that you've been thinking about ideas to solve our problems," Amenemhat said.

There were nods from many of the nobles.

"Who wants to go first?" he asked.

Pensekhmet stood. "Before our firstborn were killed and the Hebrews were allowed to leave Egypt, there was a new temple to Ra being built. It was never completed, and some of the walls weren't shored up properly. Parts of them are about to topple. If we have Pharaoh make an inspection of the temple, and if one of the walls collapses and falls on top of him, he'd be dead, and our problems would be solved."

There were murmurs of approval around the courtyard.

"How hard would it be to make the wall fall at the right time?" Amenemhat asked.

"That part's easy," Pensekhmet replied. "The hard part is keeping them from collapsing before Pharaoh even gets there. I'll need to have supports put in place to hold up at least one section of wall. The supports can be rigged to pull away at the right moment, causing the wall to fall on Pharaoh. I'll only need about twenty men and two weeks to set everything up."

"Excellent." Amenemhat beamed. "Who else has a suggestion?"

Khaemtir stood. "Pensekhmet's plan is great if we want Pharaoh's death to look like an accident. But if we want it to look like an enemy is responsible, I suggest having archers shoot arrows over the courtyard wall outside Pharaoh's quarters in the palace. Whether he's in his bedchamber, lounging on the terrace, or sitting inside, the arrows should be able to find him and anyone with him."

"And how would you keep it from looking like we were

responsible?" Wadjmose asked.

"Good question," Khaemtir acknowledged. "First, we'd have the archers dressed in clothing typical of someone from one of the northern kingdoms – the Assyrians, the Hittites, or even the Mitanni. We also use bows and arrows from those kingdoms. Second, once the deed is done, we slit the throats of the archers and burn their bodies so they can't be identified. Only the bows and the arrows will remain, and they'll point away from us."

Amenemhat smiled. "An elegant plan, Khaemtir, thank you. Anyone else?"

One of the other nobles spoke up. "We could also use archers to shoot arrows at Pharaoh as he's going to and from the palace chapel each morning."

Amenemhat frowned at this suggestion. "I understand your suggestion, but Pharaoh usually goes to the chapel with his children. There's too much risk that archers would kill the princess and the princes. We're looking for ways to kill *Pharaoh*, not wipe out his entire bloodline."

"You're right. I hadn't considered that."

"What about poison?" Sharek asked, rising to his feet. "There are rumors all over the city that people inside the palace are being poisoned. Why not have Pharaoh poisoned, too?"

"It might work," Amenemhat admitted, "but the Vizier and the Chief Steward of Pharaoh's household have increased the guards and food tasters in the palace. It won't be all that easy to administer a poison when Pharaoh returns from Canaan. Still, it is a good idea and worth looking into."

Several other ideas were discussed over the course of the evening. Once the meeting was over and the nobles gone, Amenemhat turned toward his acolyte.

"They seem ready to begin a rebellion, don't they?"

"Yes, High Priest," Kaaper replied.

The two men left the compound and stepped onto the dark deserted street that ran along the city's south wall.

"By the way, where were you yesterday?" Amenemhat asked, regarding his acolyte closely as they walked. "I had people looking for you, but they couldn't find you."

"I... was meditating, High Priest. Just outside the city away from all the noise." *Does he know that the Medjay captured me*

and took me to the Vizier and the Chief Steward? Am I undone?
"What did you want to see me about? Is there something I can do
for you?"

Amenemhat hesitated, but then he said, "Yes. I need you to
go to Iunu for me in the morning."

"Why, High Priest?"

"I want you to meet with the priests up there and find out
how they're feeling about being ordered away from the port at
Peru-nefer. Pharaoh's decree that the priests are no longer to
collect port taxes must have hit them hard. I want to know if
they're angry enough to join us."

"Of course, High Priest. I'll take the first ship sailing north.
Is there anything else I can do for you?"

"One thing," Amenemhat replied. "Find out if Merytamon is
really in Iunu or not. If she's there, fine. If not, I want to know
where she is."

"Yes, High Priest."

CHAPTER 11

"That's the fifth settlement we've found abandoned, Great Pharaoh."

Pharaoh looked at the empty village in the distance where the general was pointing. "I'm not surprised that they decided to flee. They must know by now that we're approaching. It looks like they're heading southeast toward Shemesh-Edom and the river."

"That makes no sense," General Ahmose said. "They don't have enough boats to cross the river, and they don't have a Moses to part the waters for them, so if they're moving east, they're trapped."

"And it looks like the people from the other settlements are moving in the same direction. There may be an opportunity here."

General Ahmose agreed. "If the rest of the southern Canaanite tribes are massing at the river, we can end this campaign with a single stroke."

"Send word to all company commanders," Pharaoh ordered. "We're deploying southeast. And send scouts ahead and find out what's waiting for us at Shemesh-Edom."

"Yes, Great Pharaoh."

Pharaoh looked north. "Are we still being followed?"

"Yes, but they're falling farther and farther behind, Great Pharaoh. I think they're about to turn back and head for home. My scouts got close enough to the Hittite and Assyrian camps to hear them saying that they've seen all that they came to see."

Pharaoh chuckled softly. "Good."

Tiaa nuzzled Amenemhat's chest as they lay together in her bedchamber. She watched him sleeping in the low light. *I love being together with him. He's gentle with me, and what he lacks in forcefulness, he more than makes up for in stamina. I long for the day when I can have him all the time without worrying if Pharaoh will find out.*

She drifted in and out of sleep, enjoying the afterglow of a night filled with passion.

Tiaa woke with a start, feeling something at her feet. At first, she thought it was Amenemhat rubbing his leg against hers, but he was facing away from her, and the movement against her feet felt leathery.

She looked down and saw something moving underneath the sheet. It slowly moved along her bare leg as its path took it closer to her waist.

She heard a gentle hissing and knew immediately what it was. *A snake! In my bed! What do I do? If I call out, the Medjay guards in the corridor will rush in, I'll be caught with Amenemhat, and we'll both be executed. If I wake him, he could startle the snake, and it could bite one of us. If I move and try to get out of bed, it could bite me.*

Tiaa looked around, trying not to move anything but her head. She saw Amenemhat's clothes and his jeweled belt on the low table next to her, where he had deposited them earlier that night. Still attached to his belt was the ceremonial dagger that he kept with him at all times when he was away from the temple at Waset. She slowly reached for the dagger, trying not to disturb the snake.

The snake slithered closer to her stomach. Her hand reached the dagger's hilt and started to pull it free.

The snake slid up her belly and then back down just below her breast. She clutched the dagger's hilt tightly and raised it.

The snake had just about reached her shoulder when she struck. She brought the dagger down and pierced the snake's head through the sheet. Tiaa felt the snake struggle as the dagger went through its head and kept its jaws from opening.

Tiaa scooted out of the way, keeping her hand on the dagger and pressing the snake's head deeper into the bed. The tail of the snake twitched violently, causing Amenemhat to wake up.

"What the...!" He saw Tiaa standing naked, with the moonlight behind her, clutching his dagger and driving it deeper into the bed between them. He leaped out of bed and pulled back the sheet, revealing the cobra in its final death throes.

He reached for his dagger, and she let him take it. He grabbed the snake's tail with one hand and twisted the dagger so that the snake's head was upside down with the blade pointing toward the ceiling. Then he crouched down, put his knee on the snake's neck, and pulled the dagger free before using it to cut the snake's head off.

He stood and faced her. "It's over."

Tiaa came around the bed and fell into his arms. "Someone just tried to kill us!"

"Nonsense," he whispered. "It was just a snake. They get into the palace all the time. We find two or three in the temples daily."

"But this one was in my bed!" she hissed.

"Who would be trying to kill you?"

Tiaa snorted softly. "Take your pick. Pharaoh's other wives and concubines, his sisters, his brothers, his children... It could be any of them. If I had to guess, I'd say it was Sitamun."

"Why?"

"Because I threatened her a few days ago, and this is her way of getting back at me."

"She's a wife of Pharaoh, my darling. She wouldn't use a snake to do her work. She'd just drive a knife or spear through your heart. If her son is made Pharaoh's heir, she'd become the royal wife and be protected from any retribution."

"Then won't I be protected from retribution if I kill her first? After all, she's already tried to kill me. I only threatened to kill her, and it was a veiled threat at that."

"Remember the plan, my darling. We don't move openly against anyone. One slip-up and it's both of our heads. Be patient. The right opportunity to deal with Sitamun will present itself. First, you should find out for certain whether or not she's responsible. Don't kill her and let the real culprit go free."

"You think it's someone else?" Tiaa sounded unsure of herself.

"I think you shouldn't do anything until you know for certain who it was. Sitamun has reasons, but, as you pointed out, so do many others. Watch Sitamun closely. That's what my priests here in the palace are for. Find out if she's responsible, and, if so, plan her demise as quickly as possible."

Tiaa nodded and held him closely. "You're right."

"Of course I am."

Tiaa giggled. "Now get rid of that snake, and I'll show you how grateful I am."

"I see you've taken up a new interest, Sitamun. Snakes? Really? I thought you hated snakes."

Sitamun stared at Tiaa. They were sitting in the same chairs as the last time that Sitamun was in Tiaa's apartment in the harem of the palace. Tiaa looked furious. Sitamun looked confused.

"Of course I hate snakes, Tiaa. Everyone knows that. Why would you think I've suddenly developed an interest in snakes?"

"Because one got into my bed last night," Tiaa accused.

"And you think I put it there?" Sitamun scoffed. "First of all, the guards would have kept me from entering your apartment. Second, I would never touch a snake, let alone carry it into your apartment and release it in your bed. I'd be terrified that it would bite me."

"And you expect me to believe that?" Tiaa didn't hide her contempt.

"I don't care what you believe! I didn't do it, and no one did it on my instructions!"

"Who *else* has a reason to kill me?" Tiaa demanded.

Sitamun shrugged. "Oh, I don't know. The entire harem? How many of Pharaoh's wives and concubines have you threatened? How many of Pharaoh's brothers and sisters have you tried to corrupt? I think the real question is: Who *doesn't* have a reason to kill you?"

Tiaa glared at Sitamun. Sitamun rose and walked toward the

antechamber.

"I haven't dismissed you yet," Tiaa shouted.

"And I didn't ask for your permission," Sitamun countered. "Stay away from me and my sons, Tiaa. I didn't have anything to do with that snake, but I might do something if you try anything against me or my sons."

Sitamun disappeared into the corridor, leaving Tiaa fuming in her chair.

Iaret came to see Tiaa in her apartment later that day. She sat next to Tiaa just inside the terrace. "Do you remember asking me about Amenemipet's loyalty to my father?"

Tiaa nodded. "That was weeks ago."

"I know. I've been trying to get a sense of what he actually believes, and it's taken this long to figure out whether or not he'd support a change. I believe that he will."

Tiaa looked skeptical. "You're saying that he'd actually betray your father?"

"My father, yes. Egypt, no. It's like I said before, his loyalty is to the kingdom, not to any one particular ruler. Yes, according to the reports from Admiral Thuti, my father is having great success in Canaan, but Amenemipet believes that, if it weren't for my father's mistakes, there would have been no need for the Canaan campaign in the first place. He thinks that my father is just trying to reduce his losses, but he hasn't forgiven my father for the losses in the first place."

"And you're suggesting that I try to make an alliance with him to promote my son to be your father's heir and then to arrange Pharaoh's passage to the next world soon after?"

"Exactly."

Tiaa sat quietly for several moments. "I'll think about it. In the meantime, have you learned anything about who put the snake in my bed last night?"

Iaret shook her head. "I'm convinced that it's not my mother. She hates snakes and anything to do with snakes. Besides, if she were to move against you, she'd do it openly so there'd be no doubt that it was her. For a snake to just appear in your bed, it has to be someone else."

"Who? Merytamon? She's in seclusion at Iunu."

"That doesn't mean that she didn't hire someone to put the snake in your bed," Iaret noted. "If she blames you for the death of Prince Webensenu, there's no telling what she'd do to get even."

Tiaa sat back in her chair and stared absently at the far wall of her sitting area. Finally, she asked, "How could she have gotten someone into the palace? It's guarded more closely than ever before."

"Perhaps she's using someone already inside the palace," Iaret suggested.

Tiaa regarded Iaret. "If that's true, then no one in the palace can be trusted."

"You mean you *do* trust people in the palace? I don't."

"Why not?"

"How am I supposed to know whose side anyone is on anymore?" Iaret sounded exasperated. "Between your spies, Amenemipet's spies, Kenamun's spies, the Medjay guards, the soldiers, the priests, the servants, not to mention the others in the harem and my father's own siblings, I can't trust anyone."

Tiaa nodded. "Kenamun. I have to do something about him."

"What, kill the spymaster and the spies die, too?"

"Something like that. He watches me every moment of the day and night. I can't maneuver with him and his people around. And I need to get my people back into the kitchens before Pharaoh returns."

"Why?"

Tiaa flashed her cobra smile. "I'd rather Pharaoh die from something he ate than from a knife in his chest. Fewer questions and less scandal."

Iaret nodded. "Ah. I forgot that you'll have to answer to the priests should my father meet an untimely death."

Tiaa chuckled. "I'm not worried about the priests. I'm worried about the Medjay and the soldiers. They're the ones who will avenge Pharaoh if it looks like he was assassinated."

"Why don't you let me try to take care of Kenamun?" Iaret asked.

"You? I didn't think you wanted to get your hands dirty."

Iaret smiled demurely. "I told you that I'm here to help you in any way. If this will help, then I'm willing to do it. Besides, who would suspect me?"

"You might be right, my dear. Let me think about it. We'll talk again in a few days."

When Kaaper returned from Iunu, he immediately made his way to the house where Amenemhat was staying while in Men-nefer.

"What news from the temples in the north?" Amenemhat asked when Kaaper entered his courtyard and sat next to him.

"You were right about how angry the priests are, High Priest. Pharaoh banning them from the port has them furious and ready to rebel. I think we can count on them when the time comes."

Amenemhat nodded. "Good. And what about Merytamon?"

"I never saw her, but two priests of Ra told me that she's in seclusion in their temple along with her two remaining sons. She sees no one."

"She could be anywhere, then."

"If you choose not to believe the priests of Ra," Kaaper commented.

Amenemhat snorted. "You do remember that Pharaoh is the High Priest of Ra and the ruler of Iunu, right?"

Kaaper nodded. "But Pharaoh's not in Egypt right now, and he certainly wouldn't be in contact with his priests in Iunu while on a military campaign, would he?"

Amenemhat stared at Kaaper for a moment, and then he smiled. "Good point. A priest might lie on Pharaoh's orders, but not on the orders of one of his wives."

Kaaper relaxed. *He believes the story that Amenemipet told me to tell, and he doesn't appear to suspect that I was captured by Amenemipet and forced to become his agent. So far, so good.*

"Is there anything else I can do for you, High Priest?"

Amenemhat smiled. "No. Get some rest. You've done well. I'll be out all night, so you may stay here until morning. Tomorrow, go find Pensekhmet and tell him that I'd like to inspect the unfinished temple of Ra that he mentioned the other night."

"Yes, High Priest."

There was a strong breeze blowing off the Ar River and through the palace the next night. The sound of the curtains billowing made Tiaa sleepy.

I think I'll go to bed early.

She entered her bedchamber, pulled the curtain closed, and crawled into bed, pulling the sheet up to her chin. She was asleep a moment later.

She awoke to a faint tapping sound. She lay still, trying to figure out what it was. The sound seemed to come from all around.

She glanced at the floor and saw movement. Looking closer, she saw black shapes all around. Dozens. Hundreds. She looked on the other side of the bed and found the floor there was also covered with moving black shapes.

What are they?

Movement near her feet caught her attention. A few of the black shapes were now on her bed. Against the pale linen sheet, she finally recognized what they were. *Scorpions.*

She drew up her legs tightly against her chest. Sweat beaded her brow as she realized that there was no escape.

If I stay on the bed, they'll sting me. If I get out of bed, they'll sting me. What do I do?

Tiaa looked around and realized that she was alone. *Amenemhat isn't here tonight. He's meeting with some of the nobles again.*

"Guards! Help!"

She heard guards enter her apartment and cross the sitting area toward her bedchamber. When the curtain was pulled aside, she saw three guards standing there. Two were holding torches.

"My Queen…"

"Scorpions! Everywhere! They're on the floor and they're on my bed. DO SOMETHING!"

The two guards with torches leaned down and used the fire to clear a path to Tiaa's bed. The scorpions tried to swarm the guards from behind, but the third guard used his spear to push the scorpions back by laying it flat on the floor and swinging it from side to side, knocking the scorpions out of the way.

More guards and soldiers entered Tiaa's apartment. The soldiers used their shields to scoop up the scorpions and toss them into the courtyard.

The first two guards reached Tiaa's bed. One of the guards handed his torch to the other guard and scooped up Tiaa into his arms just as a particularly large scorpion was about to sting her thigh. The two guards retreated from the bedchamber – the guard with the two torches clearing the way as the other guard carried Tiaa to safety.

More guards, soldiers, and servants arrived. It took a while, but they finally got all of the scorpions out of Tiaa's bedchamber and into the courtyard, where the soldiers used their shields to crush the scorpions to death.

The servants and guards searched the rest of Tiaa's apartment while she sat on the far side of the sitting room with her legs pulled to her chest so her feet were nowhere near the floor.

Someone tried to kill me again. Someone got into my quarters unobserved and put hundreds of scorpions in here. I want the assassin caught, and I don't want it to happen again!

The Captain of the Medjay Guards arrived a few moments later. He crossed the sitting area to Tiaa and knelt before her. "My Queen, thank the gods that you're all right."

"No thanks to your men, Captain," Tiaa snapped. "Someone put several hundred scorpions in my bedchamber while I was asleep tonight. How did that happen?"

"I don't know, my Queen, but I'll find out. In the meantime, I'll post guards along your terrace and inside your apartment at all times. They won't be inside your bedchamber, but I'll have guards in your antechamber and here in the sitting area."

Tiaa nodded. *Amenemhat won't be able to visit me anymore until we find who's doing this, and I'll have to find somewhere else to have private conversations and to distill the poison from the castor seeds, but at least I'll be protected.*

"Your bedchamber is clear of all scorpions, my Queen," Tiaa's head maid said a moment later, as the guards, soldiers, and servants exited her bedchamber. "I've put fresh sheets on the bed."

"I'm not going back in there tonight," Tiaa stated. "Bring me

132

a sheet so I can wrap myself up in it. I'm staying right here with my guards."

"Yes, my Queen."

The head maid brought her a sheet and helped Tiaa get comfortable in the chair. The captain of the guards assigned six guards to stand post along the terrace just outside the curtains, and he placed two guards in the antechamber and four in the sitting area. One of the guards stood next to Tiaa for the rest of the night.

This is the second time that someone has tried to kill me. I thought Sitamun might have been responsible for the snake, but she hates scorpions even more than she hates snakes, and it would have taken several people to get that many scorpions in here so quickly. Who has the ability to get many people into this part of the palace without the guards seeing them? It would have to be someone with intimate knowledge of the palace. And there's only one person I can think of who it could be. I'll kill him. I'll see him dead at my feet. I'll show him what kind of woman he's dealing with, and then I'll deny him an afterlife so he'll be consigned to the realm of demons forever.

Tiaa spent the rest of the night plotting the demise of the person she thought was responsible for the assassination attempts against her. When the first rays of the morning sun reached the courtyard outside of Tiaa's apartment, Tiaa was still curled up in her chair. She hadn't slept since first discovering the scorpions in her bedchamber. Even though the servants, guards, and soldiers assured her that no scorpions remained, she was terrified to move. She kept seeing scorpions in the dark.

The morning sun chased away the shadows of the night and showed her that there were no scorpions left on her floor anywhere. Satisfied with her plans for vengeance, she relaxed and soon fell asleep.

"Scorpions?"

Amenemipet stared at the Captain of the Medjay Guards, who had just finished telling the Vizier and Kenamun about what had happened in Tiaa's quarters during the night.

"Yes, sir. Hundreds. Her bedchamber floor was covered in them, and they had started crawling onto her bed. If it weren't for the quick thinking of the guards who arrive first, she'd be dead."

Amenemipet glanced at Kenamun, who looked just as shocked as the Vizier. "First a snake and now scorpions. Someone really *is* trying to kill her. I thought the snake had just slithered onto the palace grounds, but there is no way that so many scorpions would be inside one room of the palace at the same time."

"We're taking steps to keep her safe, but it's clear that she has enemies here in the palace," the captain said.

"Do what you can, Captain," Amenemipet instructed. "Guards are to be with her at all times, even if she tries to dismiss them. Understood? She is never to be left alone."

"It will be done!"

The captain left Amenemipet and Kenamun alone. "Why not just let the assassin kill her?" Kenamun whispered.

"Because I don't like the idea of someone getting into the palace and killing a member of the royal family. If they can kill her, they can kill anyone, including Pharaoh. Besides. If we have guards with her all the time, she won't be able to plot against Pharaoh's wives, concubines, and sons as easily."

"It will also interfere with her sexual dalliances." Kenamun chuckled.

"That, too."

Kenamun stood to leave Amenemipet's office. When he reached the door, Amenemipet heard a loud thud. Looking up, he saw a knife stuck in the door next to where Kenamun was standing.

"It almost hit me!" Kenamun was shaking as Amenemipet jumped up and pulled Kenamun back into the office.

"Did you see who threw it?"

Kenamun leaned against the wall. "No, I didn't see anyone." He faced Amenemipet with his eyes open wide. "Someone just tried to kill me!"

CHAPTER 12

"Have you given any more thought to what we discussed last week? Tiaa asked.

Tiaa sat in her apartment across from Pharaoh's four younger sisters, the Princesses Beketamun, Iset, Meritamen, and Nebetiunet. Each was married to a noble who had lost slaves and the contents of their granaries, thanks to Pharaoh. The guards who normally filled Tiaa's apartment were all posted in the antechamber and on the terrace so Tiaa and the princesses wouldn't be disturbed.

"I've already spoken about it to my husband," Beketamun replied. "He has no interest in which of Pharaoh's sons becomes the next Pharaoh, but he doesn't want to be involved with any plot that would shorten Pharaoh's life. He owes his position to Pharaoh, and he doesn't believe that the next Pharaoh would be so generous."

"And what if he received guarantees that the next Pharaoh would be even more generous in return for his support?"

Beketamun stared at Tiaa. "How could you offer such guarantees unless you yourself became Pharaoh, which is impossible since you don't descend from the line of kings?"

Tiaa flashed an amused smile. "It's true that I can't be Pharaoh, but I could be regent, if Prince Amenhotep is named to be the next Pharaoh. As regent, I'd have the same powers as Pharaoh, and I'd be in a position to influence the next Pharaoh's generosity in your husband's favor."

"Is the same true for the rest of our husbands?" Nebetiunet asked.

"Of course," Tiaa said warmly.

"But how could our husbands move against Pharaoh?" Iset asked. "There are guards everywhere, watching everything. It would be suicide, and we all know the punishment for a move against Pharaoh. Torture, public execution and the defilement of our bodies to deny us an afterlife! Is it worth the risk?"

"I'm more worried about my brothers than I am about Pharaoh's wives and children," Meritamen interjected. "If Siamun and Menkheperre catch wind of a plot against Pharaoh, they might exploit it so one of them becomes the next Pharaoh, and that would almost guarantee that you and Pharaoh's children would all be entombed at the same time."

Tiaa frowned. *I hadn't considered that one of Pharaoh's brothers might take advantage of the situation for his own gain.* "Do you really think one of them might make a move for the throne?"

Meritamen nodded. "Their claim is at least as good as Pharaoh's surviving sons. They're not skilled in the arts of war, but they've held key posts in Egypt's government for years. They already know how to rule. The nobles might see them as the safer choice than untested, inexperienced sons and their squabbling mothers."

Tiaa's face flushed. "Squabbling?"

"Oh, come on, Tiaa." Nebetiunet sounded exasperated. "All of Men-nefer knows about your threats against Merytamon and Sitamun, and they know that Merytamon fled from Men-nefer with her sons to get away from you. Most of the nobles we know are disgusted with the plots and intrigues that are stinking up the palace these days, and they'll welcome any alternative to you and your son."

Tiaa stared at Pharaoh's sisters, trying to mask the doubt that she felt. *The nobles in the city are aware of what's going on? I had no idea. I thought that Amenemhat had the nobles under his sway. Has he failed me, or is he betraying me? Either way, I'd better find out before approaching anyone else to help me with my plans. I'd hate to think I've killed three people only to find out that the nobles are planning to kill all of Pharaoh's wives and sons in order to place one of his brothers on the throne.*

"You haven't mentioned Pharaoh's daughter, Tiaa," Iset commented. "Where does she stand in all of this intrigue?"

"She's with me," Tiaa stated confidently. *She's proven herself loyal to me, and I trust her.*

Iset looked at her sisters. "That's something to think about. Iaret is shrewd and cunning despite her young age. If she's chosen a side, she must think it's the best one, and she'll work diligently to help that side win."

The other sisters nodded slowly.

"We'll give it more thought, Tiaa, and speak with our husbands again," Beketamun said. "But in the meantime, you should begin thinking about Pharaoh's brothers and how you'll convince *them* to take your side. They can rally the nobles against you with little effort, and then all of your plans will be undone. Move against them, and the nobles and the rest of Pharaoh's family will turn on you faster than a viper can strike. If you can't make them your allies, you will fail."

Tiaa shivered as Beketamun's words reminded her of the snake that had found its way into her bed.

Pharaoh's sisters stood and left Tiaa's apartment.

Tiaa watched the guards return to their posts around her sitting room. *How could I have overlooked the possibility that Pharaoh's brothers might make a move for the throne? After all, my husband is a second son who only became Pharaoh because his older brother was killed in the same accident that killed his mother. Will all of my plans fail because I waited too long to ally with Pharaoh's siblings? Is it true that I can't move against them without risking my life and the life of my son? Where is Amenemhat? I need him now more than ever.*

At Princess Beketamun's request, Amenemipet, Iaret, and Kaaper met with Pharaoh's sisters and their husbands late that night at a compound owned by Beketamun's husband in the northeastern quarter of the city. Pharaoh's brothers and their wives were also there. Pharaoh's siblings and their spouses had secretly met together with Amenemipet and Iaret several times, and they all remained steadfast in their support for Pharaoh.

The sisters told everyone about their meeting with Tiaa. "She believes that you are her trusted ally," Iset said to Iaret.

Iaret smiled. "Good. As long as she doesn't suspect that I'm working against her, she'll continue to trust me, and I can continue to interfere with her plans."

"I think Tiaa is convinced that her plans need to be completely reworked after today," Beketamun said. "When we told her that our brothers pose the greatest threat to her and her son, I thought she was going to cry!"

"You did mention that it would be suicide to move against either of us, didn't you?" Pharaoh's brother Siamun asked. As the Overseer of the Seal and Overseer of the Gold-Land of Amun, he held a key position in Pharaoh's inner circle.

Beketamun chuckled. "Of course we did! We told her that the nobles would rise up against her if she moved against either of you."

"It's clear that she thought she had all of the nobles on her side," Meritamen added. "She has definitely been stirring them up against our brother and trying to ally with them to advance her plots for her son and herself."

"Do you want us to pretend to support her?" Nebetiunet asked. "Or at least pretend not to oppose her?"

Amenemipet nodded. "Absolutely. Don't give her a reason to move against any of you." He gestured toward Kaaper. "Kaaper has been meeting with the nobles in the city on behalf of Amenemhat, the High Priest of Amun, who is also Tiaa's lover. He knows the nobles who have refused to be part of Tiaa's and Amenemhat's plots. I think all of you should begin meeting with the loyal nobles and form a strong alliance of those ready to stand with Pharaoh. If this breaks out into open conflict, you'll need allies to protect your families and to protect Pharaoh."

"I wish we could just arrest her already," Siamun lamented. "There's more than enough evidence against her for treason."

"I know," Iaret said. "But until we know who else is actively involved in her plots against my father, we need to be patient. Once all of the conspirators are known, they'll be dealt with, believe me. But for now we need to watch and move carefully so she never suspects what *we're* planning."

The assassin crept toward Kenamun's quarters near the kitchens. He had previously missed the target with his dagger, and he was determined to finish the job this time.

He stopped, listening for any soldiers or servants nearby. The palace was quiet. He crept along, pausing at each corridor to make certain that no one saw him in the moonlight that bathed the palace floors in a pale blue light.

He was only a few steps from the entrance to Kenamun's apartment. He quietly drew his khopesh, a curved bronze sicklesword. Unlike the full-sized khopeshs used by Pharaoh's guards, his was a shorter version – easier to conceal but just as deadly.

He hefted the shortsword in his hand and moved toward the apartment entrance. The doorway he was staring at began spinning before everything went dark.

Kenamun stepped out of his antechamber accompanied by two Medjay guards. A servant followed, holding up a torch.

One of the Medjay guards bent down and wiped off the blade of his khopesh on the assassin's clothing before sheathing it.

"Where's his head?" Kenamun asked.

The guard walked over to where the head had landed and picked it up by the hair.

Kenamun studied the face for a moment and nodded. "That's one of the new spies that the queen smuggled into the palace. Now we know who's trying to kill me."

"Shall we go arrest her?" the guard asked.

Kenamun looked down at the headless body. "Not yet. But have someone dispose of the body and clean up this mess."

"Yes, sir."

Tiaa woke to the sound of wood clattering across the floor of her bedchamber. She sat up and felt the air move as something whizzed past her face. Whatever it was, it hit the far wall and fell to the floor, landing loudly.

Looking toward the sound, Tiaa recognized the arrow shaft lying on the floor. Two more arrows whizzed past her and hit the far wall of the bedchamber. Tiaa rolled onto the floor as several more arrows flew into her bedchamber through the terrace curtains.

There's more than one archer out there. Why aren't the guards on my terrace doing anything? They should be able to hear the arrows flying past them.

She heard shouts in her courtyard. Three of the Medjay who guarded her sitting area burst into her bedchamber with their shields facing the terrace. They stood shoulder to shoulder, creating a barrier with their shields.

"My Queen, stay behind us. We'll protect you."

Tiaa slid across the floor until she was behind the guards. She heard five arrows strike the shields, but the guards were uninjured. More arrows hit the shields, and Tiaa crouched behind the guards and moved with them to her sitting area. One arrow hit the shoulder of the guard in the lead, but he kept moving with the others to provide protection for their queen. Once they reached the sitting area, the guards stepped backwards away from the terrace, giving Tiaa protection until she could reach the stone wall that separated her antechamber from the sitting area.

More guards raced into the apartment and formed ranks to protect Tiaa as she backed out of her quarters toward the main corridor of the harem.

Tiaa heard more shouting in the courtyard as additional guards arrived to hunt down the archers. Tiaa sat in the antechamber next to one of the washing pools, surrounded by guards.

After quite a while, the Captain of the Medjay Guards entered Tiaa's apartment from the terrace. He talked quickly with the guards who had recovered the arrows fired at the queen, and then he approached Tiaa.

140

"We killed three of them, my Queen, but two got away." He held up one of their bows and two of the arrows. "These are not Egyptian or Nubian. From the markings, they look Babylonian, but bows and arrows from Babylon are easily available across the region."

"Did you recognize the men that you killed?" Tiaa was surprised that the bows and arrows were Babylonian. *Is someone avenging Shayari's death? She was a gift from the King of Babylon. Is this revenge for killing her?*

"No, my Queen. They were strangers."

"This is the third time that someone has tried to kill me, Captain, and the second time that your guards have saved my life."

"I'm grateful that the men were here to protect you, my Queen. Under the circumstances, you might want to sleep in other quarters until we can secure your courtyard and terrace from more archers."

Tiaa nodded, and a detachment of guards escorted her to one of the empty apartments further down the corridor.

Did my assassin kill Kenamun tonight? If so, will the attempts on my life end? Or is someone else responsible? If it's not Kenamun, did I send my assassin after an innocent man? And if my assassin failed, have I now made Kenamun my enemy? Could it be Pharaoh's brothers coming after me so I won't move against them? Who's trying to kill me?

"Babylonian?" Amenemipet asked when the Captain of the Medjay Guards made his report the next morning.

"Yes, Vizier. The bow and arrows had Babylonian markings."

"And there were five archers?"

"Yes. We killed three, but two escaped. No one recognizes the three we killed."

"And one of your guards beheaded the assassin who was sent to kill Kenamun, the Chief Steward?"

"Yes, Vizier. Kenamun recognized him as one of the queen's new spies."

Amenemipet shook his head. "This palace is supposed to be the safest place in Egypt. Now it's becoming a battlefield! Archers, snakes, scorpions, poison… it has to stop before Pharaoh returns."

"Yes, Vizier. My men can begin patrolling the palace at night, rather than just standing guard at specific posts, but we'll need soldiers to help secure the compound and surrounding streets. I would also post soldiers on top of the outer walls."

Amenemipet nodded. "I'll see to it. Thank you, Captain. If you think of anything else that will keep the royal family safe, please let me know."

"Yes, Vizier."

Amenemipet watched the captain leave his office. *Is it safe for Pharaoh to return to Men-nefer? Should I encourage him to remain in Peru-nefer until we can regain control of things down here? It's bad enough that Tiaa and Amenemhat are using assassination to advance their plots, but how many attempts will be made on Pharaoh once he returns from Canaan? Can I protect him from what's going on?*

At the end of Peret Pharmuthi, the fourth Month of Emergence, Senebsen's body had been mummified and prepared for burial according to the rites and customs of a royal concubine. She was entombed in one of the smaller chambers of Pharaoh's tomb, and the wall was sealed.

Pharaoh stood on the deck of his war chariot in the predawn stillness, looking down at the valley that ran along the riverbank. The sky grew lighter in the east, illuminating the sight below. Camped against the river at Shemesh-Edom were the Canaanite tribes that had been fleeing from the advancing Egyptian army.

Pharaoh and General Ahmose stared at all of the people massed alongside the river.

"How many are down there?" Pharaoh asked.

"At least twenty thousand, Great Pharaoh," the general replied. "What are your orders?"

"I'll take the chariots and swing around to approach them from the south. You lead the soldiers and archers to attack from the north and the west. We'll surround them, and if we're lucky and the gods are with us still, we'll capture them all. Can your men be in position to attack before midday?"

"Yes, Great Pharaoh!"

Pharaoh turned and gave orders to his chariot company commanders. Then he ordered his driver to lead the chariots to the southwest out of sight of the encamped Canaanites.

Pharaoh led his chariots around the Canaanite encampment and stopped when he was well south of Shemesh-Edom. He deployed his chariots in three ranks and ordered his charioteers to tend to their horses while they waited for the soldiers to move into position.

Shortly before midday, the charioteers mounted their chariots and prepared to advance. Pharaoh held his spear over his head and ordered his chariot driver to move northward.

Pharaoh's chariots followed him toward the Canaanite encampment. It took a while for the chariots to reach the Canaanites, and as soon as the encampment came into view, Pharaoh signaled for the second rank of chariots to move alongside the front rank, doubling the length of the line. The third rank spread out to twice its original length but remained behind the front rank.

Pharaoh signaled for the chariots to increase speed.

In the distance, he saw the Canaanites begin running to the north to get away from the advancing chariots. When he had just about reached the southern end of the encampment, his soldiers appeared on the ridge above the encampment, cutting off the escape of the terrified Canaanites.

Some of the Canaanites tried to form ranks and defend the encampment, but the Nubian archers to the north and the advancing chariots to the south made any sort of defense impossible. The Canaanites surrendered before Pharaoh's chariots reached them.

While the army marched the prisoners toward the coast, several companies of soldiers entered the encampment to see what plunder remained.

Pharaoh met with his company commanders that evening to review results of the day's action against the Canaanite tribes.

"Several caravans had taken refuge in the encampment, Great Pharaoh," one of the company commanders reported. "We've recovered all of the goods they were taking north to the Hittites. Weapons, fabrics, gold, silver, precious stones… it's an impressive amount of merchandise!"

"We captured twenty-five thousand prisoners, Great Pharaoh," one of the other company commanders reported. "They are all healthy, and there were no injuries among them. They're being moved to the coast so the navy can take them back to Egypt."

Pharaoh looked over to his chief scribe, Djehuty. In addition to the archers, soldiers, and charioteers, Pharaoh had dozens of scribes responsible for keeping a tally of the plunder and prisoners captured, as well as the bounties that were owed to each man on the campaign.

"What are the final tallies from this campaign, Djehuty?"

Djehuty stood and consulted his notes, which were written across dozens of pieces of papyrus. "Great Pharaoh, you have captured a total of 101,128 prisoners so far on this campaign. This includes Hebrews, Shasu, Kharu, Nagasuites and Neges, plus all of their family members, their property, their cattle, and their herds. You have captured weapons, chariots, gold, silver, precious stones, fabrics, jewelry, and other items that make this the richest campaign plunder in Egypt's history. No Pharaoh has ever returned from a campaign with so much, guaranteeing that your name will be remembered as the greatest Pharaoh who ever lived."

The company commanders cheered when Djehuty finished his report and sat back down.

"Do you have the bounties for each man calculated?" Pharaoh asked.

"Almost, Great Pharaoh. I will have it completed in two days' time, and I can review it with you then."

"Thank you, Djehuty."

Pharaoh looked at his company commanders. *They have done what no army has ever done, and our losses have been minimal. I am proud of each and every one of them.* "We've accomplished what we set out to accomplish. We have more than enough slaves to get us through the harvest season and begin the repairs that have been left unattended since the Hebrew calamities struck Egypt. We have taken enough plunder to refill the treasury, with enough left over to make every Egyptian soldier rich and to repay the loyal nobles for the grain that was seized from their granaries. I believe that there is nothing more to be gained from remaining in Canaan, so as soon as we have all of the prisoners loaded onboard our ships, I propose that we head for home."

It took a week to march the prisoners to the coast, where the navy waited to carry them to Egypt. It took several trips to transport all of the prisoners, flocks, herds, and plunder back to Egypt.

Pharaoh didn't want the bulk of his army sitting idly by in Canaan, so he ordered one of the three divisions to march for Egypt immediately, along with a third of the Nubian archers. Once the navy had finished transporting the prisoners, livestock, and plunder, it would sail along the coast and pick up the first division to complete its journey home. Pharaoh wanted more soldiers in Egypt to help acclimate the prisoners to their new role as slaves.

Once all of the prisoners had been loaded onto the ships, Pharaoh ordered the second division and another third of the Nubian archers to march for Egypt. General Ahmose accompanied the second division. The navy would pick up the second division once the first division was taken back to Egypt.

Pharaoh and the chariots remained behind with the third division and the last third of the Nubian archers until all of the livestock and plunder had been loaded onto the ships. Then he ordered his men to break camp and follow him. They'd march south and west until they reached the landing area where the navy would be waiting to sail them back to Egypt.

The campaign into Canaan was over, and Pharaoh was

anxious to return home to the triumphant welcome that would greet the conquering Pharaoh.

And I will find out who killed my son and deal with their treachery.

CHAPTER 13

Tiaa felt increasingly isolated and lonely. *Amenemhat can't get near the palace anymore, thanks to all of the extra guards that are protecting me. I miss his touch and the way he makes me feel, but right now I miss his advice and counsel most of all.*

Tiaa looked around the temporary quarters that had been her home in the harem for the past two weeks. *I miss my own apartment in the harem. I can't go near my seeds to create more poison, I can't have private conversations with Pharaoh's family, and the guards still don't know who tried to kill me. I might as well be in prison!*

She glanced over at the guards standing at their posts in her sitting area. *Damn that Amenemipet! He ordered the guards to never leave me. I have no privacy!*

Iaret's words rang in her head. *"...Amenemipet believes that, if it weren't for my father's mistakes, there would have been no need for the Canaan campaign in the first place. He thinks that my father is just trying to lessen his losses, but he hasn't forgiven my father for the losses in the first place."*

Tiaa shook her head in confusion. *What should I do? Iaret offered to set up a meeting with Amenemipet, and I never pursued it. She also offered to kill Kenamun for me, and I assigned my own assassins to do it instead. Now look at what's happening. I'm cut off from Amenemhat and the nobles he's meeting with, and my spies and Amenemipet's spies are killing each other here in the palace. Not a single assassination I've ordered has been carried out, thanks to Amenemipet's spies and all of the extra guards and soldiers patrolling the palace day and night. Kenamun still lives, but then again, so do I. I guess the situation works both ways, since there are still at least two assassins out there trying to kill me.*

Tiaa picked up a dispatch from Nubia and pretended to read it. *One thing's for certain. Until my spies and Amenemipet's spies stop killing each other, nothing can happen that will keep my plans moving forward. I need to meet with Amenemipet. We may not reach an agreement about the next Pharaoh, but we can at least call for a truce and stop the killing.*

Tiaa called for a servant and told him that she needed to see Amenemipet.

Iaret came to see Tiaa later that morning.

"How are you today?" She sat down across from Tiaa.

Tiaa glanced at the ever-present guards standing nearby. "Every day is a delight. Can't you tell?"

Iaret smiled. "I have something that might cheer you up."

She handed a piece of rolled papyrus to Tiaa. Tiaa unrolled it and stared at it. Then she looked up at Iaret. "How...?"

Iaret held up her hand. "An intermediary gave it to me and requested that I give it to you."

"Can this intermediary be trusted?"

Iaret nodded. "The sender thought so."

"And can messages be sent back the other way?"

Iaret cocked her head to one side. "Why would I set up a way to receive without also setting up a way to send? Of course messages can be sent back."

Tiaa read the papyrus closely. It was from Amenemhat, and even though the news wasn't what Tiaa had hoped for, she read the words as if they were caressing her skin the way her lover would in person. *He says that support from the nobles and the priests is lessening because of the prisoners and plunder coming back from Canaan. The pain of losing their firstborn is beginning to heal. He suggests that I build alliances for Prince Amenhotep, rather than take any more direct action against Pharaoh's other wives, his children, his siblings, or his officials. I guess it's more important than ever to meet with Amenemipet to stop the slaughter.*

Tiaa finished reading the papyrus, rolled it up tightly, and placed one end in the braziers next to her chair. The papyrus burned quickly, and Tiaa watched it turn to ash. *I don't need anyone accidently finding that note.*

Tiaa reached for a stylus and a sheet of blank papyrus so she could begin writing a message back to Amenemhat.

"Did you know that I'm meeting with Amenemipet this afternoon?" Tiaa asked while she was writing.

"No. Are you going to talk to him about the future or the present?"

"A little of both." *I have to stop the killing now, but I still have to secure my son's future as Pharaoh and my position as regent.*

Changing the subject, Tiaa said. "I'm certain you've noticed that the task you asked me to assign to you has still not been completed." *Kenamun still lives. I should have let you kill him.*

"I'm sure it can't be that easy." Iaret said respectfully "It's nearly impossible to get anywhere near his quarters, and he's surrounded by servants and guards all day. I can still handle it for you, but it'll take time."

"Time we don't have," Tiaa reminded her.

Iaret nodded. "Are you still certain that he's the right person?"

Tiaa frowned. "Not completely certain, but there are still good reasons to do it."

"Even with my father returning from Canaan soon?"

Tiaa's head shot up. "He's returning soon? What have you heard?"

"Amenemipet told me that the first third of the army has arrived at Peru-nefer, and that the other two thirds will arrive as soon as the fleet returns with them."

"So the campaign is over?"

"It is," Iaret confirmed. "Pharaoh captured over one hundred thousand prisoners, and Amenemipet says that the plunder is richer than has ever been brought back to Egypt by any Pharaoh in history."

Tiaa's shoulders slumped. *He'll be the most popular Pharaoh*

149

who ever lived. Have I waited too long? Will all of my plans have been wasted when Pharaoh returns in triumph? Perhaps Amenemhat is right that I need to be making allies instead of trying to assassinate everyone I identify as a threat.

Tiaa regarded Iaret. "Don't worry about the task you asked me to assign to you. I think that it'll no longer be necessary."

"Are you certain?"

"Yes. I may change my mind, but for now take no action. I want to see how things go with Amenemipet this afternoon."

"Very well."

Tiaa finished writing her note on the papyrus, rolled it up tightly, and handed it to Iaret. "Get this to my friend. He and I need to coordinate our actions more closely now that Pharaoh is returning."

Iaret took the papyrus. "I'll see to it that he gets it. And perhaps you'll trust me enough to start delivering these messages personally, rather than through intermediaries."

"Perhaps. One step at a time."

Iaret brought the papyrus to Amenemipet's private meeting room, where Kenamun and Kaaper were also waiting for her. She handed the papyrus to Amenemipet, who unrolled it and read it aloud.

When he was finished, he looked at Iaret with a wide grin on his face. "She never once suspected that the papyrus you handed her was not from Amenemhat?"

Iaret shook her head. "She's convinced that it was genuine. She even told me not to take any steps to assassinate Kenamun. Between the papyrus saying that support for an uprising is waning, and me telling her that my father is returning to Egypt, she's rethinking all of her plans."

"Brilliant!" Kenamun blurted out. "Does that mean I can start sleeping easier?"

"For now," Iaret said with a twinkle in her eye.

Amenemipet laughed. Reaching for a sheet of papyrus and a stylus, he asked, "So, what message do we want to take back to Amenemhat?"

"Something that will make him stop stirring up the nobles," Kenamun suggested.

"Something that will make him stop stirring up the priests," Kaaper said.

"Something that will cause him to question Tiaa's commitment to him," Iaret said. "If we can keep the two of them at odds with each other, it may keep them distracted enough for us to undo all of their plans."

"That's a tall order," Kaaper noted. "The High Priest has most of the priests and a substantial number of nobles between here and Waset ready to revolt."

"Let's see what we can do about that," Amenemipet commented as he started writing a new note for Kaaper to take to Amenemhat.

Knowing that Tiaa wanted to speak in private, Amenemipet arranged to meet with her in his private meeting room. Medjay guards stood outside, but they couldn't hear what was being discussed inside.

"You wanted to see me, my Queen?"

Tiaa nodded. "I have resisted meeting with you so far, Vizier, but Princess Iaret says that you're a man who can be trusted."

"She's too kind," Amenemipet said modestly.

"Perhaps. I also understand that Pharaoh is on his way back to Egypt."

"He is. The first division of his army has already disembarked at Peru-nefer, and the second division is on its way."

"If Pharaoh is as successful as you told Princess Iaret, then he'll return triumphantly and receive the adoration of the people."

"I believe that to be true, my Queen."

Tiaa leaned forward and lowered her voice. "Then all that remains for him to do is to settle the issue of the succession, and life in Egypt can truly return to normal."

Amenemipet didn't respond.

Tiaa continued. "Princess Iaret tells me that you've taken no position on who the next heir to the throne of Egypt should be."

Amenemipet nodded. "As I've told her many times, my loyalty is to Egypt, not to any one particular Pharaoh. After all, the Vizier does all of the work that Pharaoh is credited for doing. With the exception of military matters, the Vizier rules the kingdom. Whichever prince ascends to the throne needs to understand that and allow the Vizier to do his job. A good Vizier will make Pharaoh look like a great leader to his people, providing Pharaoh can also be successful in battle. The heir to the throne need only be trained in the arts of war and instructed to allow his Vizier to keep the wheels of government turning on his behalf. Any heir who understands that will have my support."

"Does that include regents?" Tiaa asked bluntly.

"Is Pharaoh going to be dying soon, my Queen? The princes would need a regent only if he were dead, and he's only twenty-nine years old, after all."

"I didn't say that, Vizier. I merely asked if you feel the same way about regents as you feel about Pharaohs."

Amenemipet sat quietly for a moment before nodding. "A regent is simply a temporary Pharaoh until the next Pharaoh is old enough to take power for himself. If a regent allows his or her generals and admirals to conduct the military campaigns as they see fit, and allows the Vizier to run the kingdom as he sees fit, then I would support that regent... in the event that Pharaoh is no longer with us."

Tiaa hid a smile. "Do you believe that our current Pharaoh is a good leader, or would you prefer to see a regent on the throne until whichever heir he names is ready to ascend the throne?"

"Be careful, my Queen," Amenemipet warned. "A lesser man might think you're talking treason."

"Not at all, Vizier. I'm just asking if our Pharaoh is someone that Egypt still needs to be Pharaoh. Yes, he's had great success in Canaan, by all accounts, but why did he have to invade Canaan in the first place? To make up for his mishandling of the Hebrew affair. And let's not forget that he's only bringing back one hundred thousand prisoners, but he lost two million Hebrews. Hardly an impressive showing when you compare it to Egypt's losses. In your judgment, should a man who bungled the Hebrew affair so badly be allowed to remain Pharaoh?"

"Perhaps. Perhaps not. The choice of regent plays into that

decision, my Queen. It will most likely be the mother of the designated heir, since that person will be the royal wife. Unless the prince's mother is dead, in which case the regent will be the Vizier of Egypt, by tradition."

Tiaa gaped at Amenemipet. *The Vizier as regent? I had forgotten about that. So is that what Amenemipet is playing at? Becoming the regent himself?* "Would you make a move against the royal wife in order to become regent?"

Amenemipet answered slowly. "Again, it depends on the choice of regent. There have been co-regencies in the past. A royal wife who was smart enough to allow the Vizier to rule from behind the throne would make an excellent co-regent. A royal wife who didn't would be an obstacle to the Vizier doing his job and would have to be dealt with."

Leaning forward, Amenemipet asked, "What kind of regent would *you* be, my Queen? An excellent co-regent, or an obstacle to the Vizier of Egypt?"

Tiaa reached out and rested her hand on Amenemipet's arm. "I would be the kind of regent who would let you rule in my name, Vizier."

A faint smile appeared on Amenemipet's face. "Then you would have my support to be regent, should Pharaoh no longer be with us after he chooses *your* son to be his heir. But the *circumstances* of you becoming regent have me concerned."

"What do you mean?" Tiaa demanded.

"I don't like all this bloodshed in the palace. This is supposed to be the safest place in Egypt, but your spies and my spies have taken to killing each other in the hallways, someone is trying to kill you, you're trying to kill the Chief Steward, at least four people have been poisoned... The murders have to stop, my Queen. No more princes killed, no more concubines or wives killed, no more officials or servants killed. Let Pharaoh choose from his surviving sons, and should Pharaoh's reign meet an untimely end, let no man be able to say that it was murder. We have too many enemies in the world who would look at an assassination of Pharaoh as an invitation to invade. We're not strong enough yet to defend against an invasion. That's what the real purpose of the campaign into Canaan was about – preventing an invasion. The prisoners and plunder are just the spoils of war. We need a stable Egypt for any transition of power to go unexploited by the Hittites, Assyrians, Babylonians, or Mitanni. Remember what happened when Pharaoh ascended his father's throne?"

Tiaa nodded.

Amenemipet regarded her for a moment. "That's the price of my support, my Queen."

"May I have time to think about what you've said?"

"Of course, my Queen. But don't take too long. Pharaoh will be home soon, and depending on what happens when he returns, all friendships, agreements, or alliances may be broken."

Tiaa blanched but said nothing. After she left Amenemipet's private meeting room, Amenemipet chuckled to himself. *It was almost too easy. If this doesn't get her to rethink all of her plans, nothing will. I need to find Princess Iaret and let her know how the conversation went. She'll be pleased to know that her ideas seem to be working.*

Pharaoh saw his fleet approaching the beach where his division had camped for the night.

There's a welcome sight. If we can load the chariots and horses quickly, we'll be sailing home no later than tomorrow.

He looked around the encampment. The early morning sun cast long shadows along the beach, and the breeze felt cool on his face. *It will be good to be home, but what awaits me there? I've lost two sons and a concubine that I know of. What other intrigue will I face? How many nobles will rebel against me because of the Hebrews and the grain I seized? Will the priests rise up against me because I took their grain and their tax revenue? Will my wives come after me to secure their sons as my next heir? Will any of them attempt to become regent by eliminating me?*

Pharaoh saw the first of his ships reach the beach. He recognized Admiral Thuti and walked toward him. *Military campaigns are straightforward. You see the enemy, you attack the enemy, you defeat the enemy. Palace intrigue is not for me. You don't know who the enemy is, what they're willing to do, or why. I'm anxious to be home, but I'm not anxious to be plunged into all that nonsense I left behind so many weeks ago.*

Admiral Thuti stood at attention when Pharaoh reached him. "Good morning, Great Pharaoh!"

"Good morning, Admiral."

"Shall we begin loading your chariots?"

Pharaoh nodded.

"Very well."

Pharaoh watched the admiral return to the ship to issue the orders. *Why do I feel like the real battle of my life lies before me instead of behind me?*

Amenemhat read the papyrus that he thought was from Tiaa and crumpled it in anger.

"Princess Iaret gave you this?" he demanded.

"Yes, High Priest," Kaaper replied. "She's the one who took your message to the queen."

"Did you read it?"

"No, High Priest. Of course not."

Amenemhat stared at the crumpled papyrus. *I don't understand. I told her that the priests and nobles are ready to move against Pharaoh and declare her son as Pharaoh and her as regent, and she tells me she doesn't want the nobles and priests involved because it'll make Egypt appear weak to its enemies. What's happening at the palace that made her abandon our plans? Has she found another lover who is trying to usurp power that should rightfully be mine? Has someone discovered our plans and is using that knowledge against her? Has my role in her plans been discovered, and is this her way of protecting me? I must see her. I must speak with her if I'm going to understand what's going on here.*

"Is there any way I can get into the palace?" Amenemhat asked.

Kaaper shook his head. "No, High Priest. *I* can't even get onto the palace grounds. I meet the princess in the bazaar to exchange messages. The palace guards don't let anyone in who hasn't been approved by the Vizier or Pharaoh, and the guards have specific instructions not to let any priests into the palace under any circumstances."

"Why is that?"

"From what the princess told me, the Vizier believes that the priests can no longer be trusted after Pharaoh seized the temple grain and stopped the priests from stealing the import and export taxes at Peru-nefer."

"They weren't stealing the taxes," Amenemhat snapped. "They were taking tribute for the gods to protect the ships and their merchandise."

Kaaper held up his hands. "Those were her words, High Priest, not mine."

Amenemhat nodded. "I'm sorry, Kaaper. I'm not angry with you; I'm just frustrated. I need to see the queen."

"I don't know how you can, but when I meet with the princess tomorrow, perhaps we can find a way to make it happen."

Amenemhat's face brightened up. "I appreciate that, Kaaper. I know it won't be easy, but I'll do anything to see her."

"I'll see what I can do, High Priest. It might take time to arrange something, but I'll try."

Pharaoh stood on the prow of the lead ship as Peru-nefer came into view.

Home at last. I think I'll spend a few days here before returning to Men-nefer. I want to know what's going on in the palace before I have to deal with that nonsense. General Ahmose will still be in Peru-nefer. I'll send for Amenemipet so we can plan for my return to the capital. Perhaps if I treat this like a military campaign, I'll be better prepared for what lies ahead.

CHAPTER 14

Pharaoh disembarked as soon as his ship docked at Peru-nefer. General Ahmose, who had arrived several days earlier, welcomed him to Peru-nefer, and the two men waited for Admiral Thuti to join them.

"Is everything ready for the ceremony?" Pharaoh asked General Ahmose.

"Yes, Great Pharaoh. Once the rest of the men have disembarked, we can begin."

Pharaoh was pleased. The victory ceremony, which would give thanks to the gods for the success of the campaign, was an important ritual, and Pharaoh wanted it performed in Peru-nefer before the army redeployed to its various barracks across Egypt.

"And the bounties?" Pharaoh asked, referring to the share of the spoils that the army had earned.

"Ready to be paid, Great Pharaoh. As you instructed, each man will receive the same bounty, regardless of whether they were on the campaign or remained here to defend Egypt."

Pharaoh watched with satisfaction as his soldiers helped unload the chariots and the horses.

General Ahmose cleared his throat. "Great Pharaoh, I must inform you that your third wife, the Lady Merytamon, and her two surviving sons, are currently living in your palace here."

Pharaoh turned away from the harbor to look at his general. "Why? None of my wives has ever been to my palace here."

"I don't know, Great Pharaoh, but she has dispatches from

Amenemipet that she claims will explain everything."

Pharaoh nodded. "I'll see her after the ceremony." *Are things so bad in Men-nefer that one of my wives had to flee the palace with her sons, or is this just her way of grieving for the death of Webensenu?*

Once all of the men, chariots, horses, and supplies had been unloaded from the ships, the men gathered in the staging area where Pharaoh had spoken to them just before they loaded the ships to begin the campaign into Canaan. Across the front of the staging area, where Pharaoh stood, were statues of the gods to whom Pharaoh would present the offerings.

The victory ceremony was a solemn affair involving making offerings from the plunder taken from Canaan to each of the gods being given credit for the success of the military expedition. There were priests on hand to help present the offerings to the gods and take the offerings back to the temples once the ceremony was over, but Pharaoh served as the chief priest for the ceremony. Pharaoh bestowed the blessings and offerings to each god, and the men chanted the prescribed response.

Pharaoh picked up the woven basket holding a jewel-encrusted gold statue captured from the Kharu. "This gift is for Ra, ruler of the Gods of Egypt, the everlasting sun who lights our way through life and into the afterlife," Pharaoh stood in front of the statue of Ra. A priest took the basket and placed it at the feet of the statue.

"For Ra." The men intoned.

Pharaoh picked up the woven basket carrying the next offering and stood in front of the statue of Osiris. "This gift is for Osiris, ruler of the netherworld who welcomes our honored dead."

"For Osiris."

One by one, Pharaoh selected a woven basket containing an offering from the plunder of Canaan, which included weapons, gold, silver, statues, clothing, food, and other captured items. He then stood in front of the statue of the god, and gave the blessing. A priest took the basket from Pharaoh and placed the offering at the feet of the statue of the god.

"This gift is for Isis, wife of Osiris and mother of Horus, for her protection of the army during our victorious campaign."

"For Isis."

"This gift is for Horus, son of Osiris and Isis, protector of Pharaoh and herald of Ra."

"For Horus."

"This gift is for Ptah, the patron god of Men-nefer."

"For Ptah."

"This gift is for Amun, the patron god of Waset and the protector of Egypt."

"For Amun."

"This gift is for Hathor, the goddess of foreign lands who held back the gods of the Canaanite tribes so that we could have our victory."

"For Hathor."

"This gift is for Anhur and Montu, the gods of war who gave us the strength to defeat all opposition and return home in glory."

"For Anhur and Montu."

"This gift is for Khnum, the god who gives life to the gods and man through the Ar River."

"To Khnum."

"This gift is for Neper, Nepit, and Renenutet, the gods and goddesses of agriculture and grain who will oversee the prisoners we have brought back to Egypt as they tend to our fields and produce the food we eat."

"To Neper, Nepit, and Renenutet."

Pharaoh lowered his arms and knelt. The men knelt and remained silent. "And my life is the gift to Sekhmet, concubine of Ptah and my protector in battle," he whispered. "And to Maat, I offer to build a new temple at Men-nefer. All I ask of you is a return to order, justice, and truth when I reach Men-nefer and take up the rule of Egypt once more."

Pharaoh stood, signaling that the ceremony was concluded. He dismissed the men with his thanks, and the men lined up to receive the bounty that they had earned during the campaign.

When Pharaoh reached his palace at Peru-nefer, Merytamon was waiting for him, along with the Princes Amenemopet and Aakheperure. Pharaoh greeted his sons warmly and then told them to wait in the garden while he spoke with their mother.

"Why are you here, Merytamon?" he inquired once they were alone.

Merytamon held up the dispatches from Amenemipet. "These will—"

Pharaoh cut her off. "I'll read those later. Talk to me, Merytamon. Tell me what has happened and what's going on."

Pharaoh gestured toward a bench near the terrace and sat next to Merytamon, whose eyes filled with tears.

"Your son, Webensenu, is dead, my Husband."

"I know." Pharaoh put his hand on hers. "I received a message from Amenemipet that he and Senebsen had died suddenly—"

"It was Tiaa!" Merytamon spat. "She killed our son! And she killed your concubine. She would have killed me if I remained in Men-nefer, which is why Amenemipet helped me escape. Everyone in the palace thinks I'm in Iunu, praying for Webensenu, but I've been here in the one place no one would look for me."

Pharaoh nodded. *That's true. I have never brought one of my wives or concubines here, and I've only brought three of my sons here once. This is my private sanctuary, and no one – particularly Tiaa – would think to look here for one of my wives.*

"She's mad with ambition, Husband," Merytamon continued. "She wants her son, Prince Amenhotep, to be the next Pharaoh. She killed our son because he was a threat, being the oldest after her firstborn died. Sitamun's son, Prince Thutmose, is the only surviving threat, and he'll be the next to die if she has her way."

"I know about—"

"There's more, Husband," Merytamon interrupted. "She's been trying to get your brothers and sisters to back her son as the next Pharaoh and to offer their support for her becoming regent."

"Regent? But I'm not dead!"

"Not yet, Husband, but if you pick Prince Amenhotep to be your heir, you'll be dead by her hand within a season. And if you pick any of your sons *other* than Prince Amenhotep to be your heir, she'll kill you and your other sons until only she and Prince Amenhotep remain. He'll be named Pharaoh by default, and she'll be named regent since she's still your royal wife."

Is this true, or is Merytamon so grief-stricken that she sees threats where there are none? "No one would stand for that!"

"That's not all, Husband. The High Priest of Amun from Karnak is stirring up the nobles and the other priests against you. He has them so angry that they'll support anyone who replaces you on the throne. And what's worse, your daughter by Sitamun, Princess Iaret, is helping Tiaa destroy the rest of your family."

Pharaoh chuckled.

"You think that's funny?" Merytamon sounded shocked.

Pharaoh shook his head. "Yes. If you believe that my daughter is helping Tiaa, then no one suspects what she's really doing."

"You mean she's only pretending to be helping Tiaa?"

Pharaoh saw understanding flash across Merytamon's face.

"She's your spy, isn't she?"

Pharaoh nodded. "I asked her to get as close to Tiaa as she could."

"Then why is our son dead?" There was anger in Merytamon's voice.

"I don't know. I can only guess that Iaret didn't know anything about how our son would be killed."

"Well, it won't be easy for Tiaa to kill anyone else, that's for certain."

"What do you mean?" Pharaoh demanded.

"The palace is like a fortress now. The Medjay guards are everywhere, soldiers patrol the grounds, and Amenemipet's spies and Tiaa's spies are killing each other in the corridors. Why even my own assass..."

Merytamon bit her lower lip and fell silent. She looked at her hands and fidgeted with her rings as if they were suddenly too tight. Pharaoh regarded her and saw a guilty look on her face.

"Your own... what? What have you done, Merytamon?"

Merytamon avoided his gaze and didn't answer.

"Look at me, and answer my question," Pharaoh commanded gently.

"I did the only thing I could do, Husband. I decided that, if my sons and I were to live, then she had to die. I hired assassins to kill her, but they've failed in every attempt. There are just too many guards around her day and night."

Pharaoh put his arm around her shoulder. "There's no need for you to do that. Between Amenemipet, Kenamun, and Iaret, Tiaa's being watched very closely. If she tries to harm anyone else, she'll get caught."

Merytamon stared at her husband. "But you're Pharaoh! Your word is law. You could have her killed right now if you wanted."

"Yes, but I don't know who is helping her. If she's dead, her plots against me don't end there. I need to know who she's conspiring with if I'm ever going to be safe."

"It could be too late by then, Husband."

"I know," Pharaoh admitted. "But for now she believes that I don't know what she's planning. If I can keep her believing that, then perhaps she'll let her guard down, and I can discover who else is involved."

"And what about our son, Webensenu?"

"I have other sons to protect, too, Merytamon. Besides, can you prove that she's behind Webensenu's death? Did you hear her give the order? Believing and proving are two different things."

Merytamon shook her head. "She threatened his life, but I didn't see her do anything. In fact, she had started looking for a wife for him, and she assigned a slave girl to instruct him in the art of coupling."

Pharaoh didn't know that. "Could the slave girl have killed Webensenu?"

"We'll never know, Husband. She died just before our son did... of the same malady that took him and Senebsen. The physician thinks it was a scorpion sting, but I know it was poison."

Pharaoh sat silently next to his third wife for a while. Then he picked up the dispatches she had brought from Amenemipet.

Pharaoh read each of the dispatches carefully. When he had finished, he shouted for a servant. The servant appeared a moment later, and Pharaoh commanded, "Send a ship to Men-nefer and fetch Amenemipet. I need him here as quickly as possible."

"Yes, Great Pharaoh."

Turning to his wife, Pharaoh said, "I'll find out what

happened to our son. And when I do, I promise you that the person or persons responsible will pay dearly for what they've done."

At the end of Shemu Pachons, the first Month of Harvest, while Pharaoh was still at Peru-nefer, Prince Webensenu's funerary rites and mummification were completed, and the prince of Egypt's sarcophagus was entombed in the same chamber of Pharaoh's tomb as Prince Thutmose. The stone wall was resealed, and guards were posted to prevent the princes' bodies and treasures from being desecrated by robbers.

A few days later, Tiaa walked along the terrace at the end of the harem's main corridor, enjoying the morning breeze. She saw Iaret approaching from her own quarters, and Tiaa waited for Pharaoh's daughter to join her.

"Good morning, my Queen," Iaret said.

"Good morning, Princess," Tiaa replied.

Tiaa and Iaret walked together along the terrace, exchanging pleasantries for a few moments. No one saw Iaret pass the rolled papyrus to Tiaa.

"Well, I must be going, Princess," Tiaa said.

"Enjoy your day, my Queen," Iaret responded.

Tiaa headed back to her temporary apartment. Once she was seated in her sitting area, she unrolled the papyrus anxiously and read it.

Her excited expression fell as she finished reading Amenemhat's note. *This isn't the news I was expecting. The priests are angry with Pharaoh, but they refuse to join with the priests of Amun out of fear of their own gods. Each temple has a different plan, and they refuse to coordinate their efforts with the other temples. At least two of the temples want Pharaoh's entire bloodline wiped out and a new dynasty ushered into power. That means that they'd kill my son! That means that they'd kill me! If each temple is allowed to act on its own against Pharaoh, all of my plans will fail. Amenemhat needs to calm them all down so no temple makes a move against Pharaoh or the rest of his family. I need to send instructions immediately to Amenemhat before he accidently unleashes the temples on us and destroys Egypt in the process. And I'd better have another conversation with the Vizier. Maybe it's time to form an alliance with him. He might know a way to stop the priests from rising up and ruining everything.*

Tiaa reached for a sheet of papyrus and a stylus to write a reply to her lover.

When she was done, she called for a servant.

"Yes, my Queen?" the servant said, bowing low.

"I need to see the Vizier as quickly as possible."

"I'm sorry, my Queen. The Vizier has left the palace."

"Where is he?" Tiaa demanded.

"He sailed for Peru-nefer this morning on Pharaoh's orders, my Queen."

"Pharaoh is back in Egypt?"

"Yes, my Queen."

Tiaa was shocked that no one had informed her. "Then tell Princess Iaret that I need to see her."

"Yes, my Queen."

Tiaa picked up the stylus and added a few more lines to the papyrus, letting Amenemhat know that Pharaoh was in Egypt.

Things are moving too fast and getting out of control. If I'm not careful, all of my plans will crumble around me.

Princess Iaret entered Tiaa's sitting area a short while later.

"You wanted to see me, my Queen?"

"I've just been informed that your father is back in Egypt, Princess."

Iaret's face lit up. "Is he on his way to Men-nefer?"

"Not yet. He's in Peru-nefer. Amenemipet sailed at first light to meet him there. I'm certain that they'll discuss his victorious homecoming."

Tiaa handed the papyrus to Iaret. "As quickly as you can," She whispered.

Iaret nodded. "Will that be all, my Queen?"

"Yes, thank you, Princess."

Tiaa watched Iaret leave. *Of course, Pharaoh's homecoming*

does provide an interesting opportunity. He'll be exposed as he rides through the city. If an Assyrian or Hittite arrow should find him and kill him while he's in the procession to the palace, then, as royal wife, I could step in as regent, kill Prince Thutmose, and declare my son Amenhotep as the next Pharaoh. The people will demand war with the Assyrians or the Hittites, and the kingdom will rally around me in our time of mourning. I won't need the priests or the nobles to support this plan. I can become regent without owing anyone anything.

Tiaa smiled. *I like this plan! Now all I have to do is find an assassin who has a bow and arrows from one of the northern kingdoms. And I have to arrange for the assassin to kill Pharaoh without the Medjay guards or the soldiers finding out. I can't reach out to Amenemhat for help with this; what does he know about hiring archers to be assassins? And with Amenemipet in Peru-nefer, who can I turn to for help?*

Tiaa thought about it for several moments. *Princess Iaret! She has proven herself a loyal friend, and she has professed her loyalty to me and her willingness to betray her father. Now it's time to see if she told the truth. But how can I ask her to do this without being overheard?*

Tiaa remembered Amenemipet's private office. *That's perfect. I'll ask her to meet me there later today. Now I just need to figure out how to kill Prince Thutmose once his father is dead.*

Iaret and Kaaper met in Amenemipet's private office as soon as Iaret left Tiaa's quarters.

"I think the queen isn't very happy with your master," Iaret said once she finished reading the papyrus.

"Then the plan is working?" Kaaper asked.

"It's working perfectly. Only a few lines need to be changed, and it's ready to be delivered to the High Priest of Amun."

Iaret rewrote Tiaa's note. Once she was finished, she handed it to Kaaper to read. When he was finished, he nodded and rolled up the papyrus.

"I'll take this to the High Priest immediately."

"Thank you, Kaaper. With any luck, the alliance between the queen and your master will fracture and crumble soon."

Iaret watched Kaaper leave Amenemipet's private office. *I hope he can be trusted. If he's willing to betray Amenemhat for the promise of reward, would he betray us for the promise of more reward? But what choice do we have? We need someone to spy on Amenemhat, and Kaaper's willing to be that spy. If Amenemipet trusts him, I guess I should, too.*

Amenemipet watched the banks of the Ar River pass by as the ship sailed north from Men-nefer to Peru-nefer. *Thank the gods that Pharaoh has returned safely to Egypt.*

As the sun rose higher in the sky, the ship sailed past the last inhabited settlements along the river before reaching the fertile delta region to the north. Amenemipet turned to the person standing next to him, who wore a heavy shroud to cover his face and features.

"We've passed the last settlement until we reach the delta. No one will see you."

The man pulled the shroud back, revealing his face and bald head. "I'm taking a huge risk, Vizier."

"You worry too much, Priest."

Mery, one of the senior priests at the temple of Amun in Karnak, shook his head. "Amenemhat has spies everywhere. If he knew that I was meeting with you, he'd have me killed immediately."

"He's not going to find out," Amenemipet assured him. "The men on this ship are Pharaoh's men, and none of them has seen your face. No one will see your face when we get to Peru-nefer either."

"Do you think Pharaoh remembers me?"

"He certainly remembers your mother, Hunayt," Amenemipet assured him. "She was his chief nurse in the children's palace. And he knows that your father was the first prophet of Min of Koptos. Trust me, there is no one he'd rather elevate to be the next High Priest of Amun at Karnak than you. If you help us expose what Amenemhat is plotting, stop his plans from succeeding, and bring him down, the post is yours."

Mery nodded. "Just know that I'm not doing this for a promotion. What Amenemhat is doing is wrong, and he needs to be stopped. If Pharaoh chooses to be generous to those who helped, that's his right."

Amenemipet smiled. "Well spoken, Priest."

They watched the Ar River banks continue to glide by in silence.

"I need an archer," Tiaa said when she and Iaret were alone in Amenemipet's private office later that day. "One who has access to weapons from either the Assyrians or the Hittites."

"An archer?" Iaret was intrigued. "What do you need an archer for? Aren't there too many guards inside the palace and soldiers outside for an archer to hit its intended victim?"

"The victim won't be inside the palace," Tiaa said quietly. "He'll be riding through the streets of Men-nefer between the docks and the palace."

"As part of the victory procession?"

Tiaa nodded. "The archer must hit his victim with one shot, because he won't get a second one. And he must use a bow and arrow from one of the northern kingdoms to deflect suspicion from me and place it on whoever has been trying to kill me."

Iaret smiled. "Very clever. But it won't be cheap. The streets will be lined with soldiers."

"I'll pay any price. I just need you to find someone willing to do the job."

"I'll see what I can do. Who's the intended victim?"

Tiaa regarded Iaret carefully before answering. *Prove your loyalty to me, daughter of Pharaoh. Do this, and I'll reward you handsomely. Fail or betray me, and you'll feel the strike of my cobra ring before you know what happened.*

"Your father."

CHAPTER 15

Squads of soldiers entered the city of Iunu to summon the High Priests of the temples there to appear before Pharaoh. Even though the city was dominated by the Temple of Ra, many of the other gods had small temples or chapels within the city walls. Two ships of Pharaoh's navy waited at Iunu's harbor to escort the two dozen High Priests and their soldier escorts to Pharaoh's palace at Peru-nefer.

The High Priests weren't accustomed to being summoned in this manner, and they stood in small groups around the decks, speculating about the summons and what awaited them when they reached Peru-nefer.

When they arrived, Pharaoh met them in the courtyard of his palace. He offered them no greeting, and he barely acknowledged their bows of supplication. The High Priests glanced at each other, looking apprehensive.

"What do you call it when someone boards a ship and steals from it?" Pharaoh demanded.

"Piracy, Great Pharaoh," the High Priest of Ra answered.

"And what is the penalty for piracy in Egypt?"

"Death, Great Pharaoh," the High Priest of Osiris responded.

"That's right," Pharaoh snapped. "And what do you call it when someone boards a ship in *my* name, demands the payment of a tax, and then fails to turn over that tax to *my* treasury?"

The faces of the High Priests blanched, but no one uttered a sound.

Pharaoh glared at each of them and finally shouted, "You call it *piracy!* Neither my father nor I decreed that priests were to collect import and export taxes, and even if we had, that money should have been turned over to us and not kept in your temples for yourselves. That's piracy, and it's what each of you is guilty of. You and your priests have been engaging in piracy here for ten years. By your own admission, the penalty for these acts is death. You are all, therefore, condemned to death along with your priests. I will appoint new priests to tend to your temples and to the gods, but your lives are forfeit."

"You can't do that!" the High Priest of Isis blurted out.

"I am Pharaoh, and I am the acknowledged ruler of Iunu. Your lives belong to me and to me alone. I most certainly can and will do that!"

The High Priests prostrated themselves on the ground at Pharaoh's feet. "Please, Great Pharaoh! Allow us to make amends."

"Amends for your acts of piracy, or amends for your acts of treason against me?" Pharaoh demanded.

"T-t-t-treason?" The High Priest of Ra looked like he was about to faint.

"You've been plotting against me ever since I expelled your priests from the port and seized your granaries to feed my people. Don't deny it. Do you think I don't know what goes on in Egypt? Do you think that your *living god* is so impotent as to be unaware when his chief priests are plotting to overthrow him? Do you think my royal wife will save you from my wrath?"

The chief priests remained prostrate and silent.

"Give me one good reason why I shouldn't have your heads removed this very day."

The High Priest of Ra looked up at Pharaoh. "Great Pharaoh, show us mercy, and we will be your loyal servants for life."

"I already expected that of you, and you betrayed me," Pharaoh growled.

"Yes, but we can tell you who has been plotting against you."

"As my priests, you should do that anyway."

The elderly High Priest of Amun from Iunu spoke up. "Great Pharaoh, we can help stop the nobles who are plotting against you. We can help unravel their plots and keep an eye on them for you so you'll know who is truly loyal and who is simply waiting for a chance to strike."

Pharaoh smiled. "Now *that* is a good reason. Do you all swear to do this for me?"

The High Priests all swore that they would.

"Good. Because if you don't, or if I find that even one of your priests is still speaking out against me, or if any priest of your order in any part of my kingdom attempts any action against me, or if I even *suspect* that you or your priests are disloyal to me, then I will execute every priest, acolyte, and servant in your temple and appoint new ones to take over your duties. And I will desecrate your bodies so you will have no afterlife except in the realm of demons. Am I clear?"

"Yes, Great Pharaoh," the High Priests intoned nervously.

"Good. Get up. You may consider the taxes you stole from me as compensation for the grain I took. Now I want to hear everything about this conspiracy against me."

When the High Priests were escorted from the palace and back to the ships waiting to return them to Iunu, Amenemipet and Mery left their hiding place and joined Pharaoh in the courtyard.

"Masterfully handled, Great Pharaoh," Amenemipet said.

"Thank you, Amenemipet." Turning to Mery, Pharaoh said, "And thank you, Priest. If it hadn't been for the information you provided, I'd never have gotten them to reveal the plot and the chief conspirators. Now the priests of Iunu are working *for me* against the conspirators."

"My pleasure, Great Pharaoh." Mery bowed.

Pharaoh gestured for the two men to sit. "I still need to deal with the conspirators in Karnak, Waset, and possibly Nubia. Securing Egypt from Men-nefer to the Middle Sea is not enough. I need all of Egypt secure before I'll feel safe."

"You have enough evidence against Tiaa and Amenemhat to arrest them for treason, Great Pharaoh," Amenemipet pointed out. "Why wait any longer?"

"Because we must be certain that we know all of the

conspirators first," Pharaoh insisted. "If we arrest the two of them, and another conspirator takes their place, my sons and I will never be safe, because we won't know who is plotting against us."

Amenemipet nodded. "Speaking of sons, are you any closer to deciding on who you will name as your heir?"

"Well, it can't be Prince Amenhotep, for obvious reasons."

"Does that mean it will be Prince Thutmose?"

Pharaoh shrugged. "He's been my preferred choice even before the death of Prince Webensenu. He's the oldest of my surviving sons, and he has the best chance of becoming a great Pharaoh when he comes of age."

"I think he's a good choice," Amenemipet said. "That will also make Sitamun your new royal wife. Tiaa will not take the news calmly."

"That's why I cannot announce my decision until I'm ready to move against her," Pharaoh stated. "She has to be in the custody of my guards when she learns of my choice, so she cannot strike against me or my sons."

"Very wise, Great Pharaoh."

A servant entered the courtyard and announced the arrival of General Ahmose and Admiral Thuti.

"Show them in," Pharaoh instructed.

Turning to Amenemipet, Pharaoh said, "Now we can plan for my return to Men-nefer."

Amenemipet, Mery, General Ahmose, and Admiral Thuti remained in Peru-nefer with Pharaoh for several days, planning for Pharaoh's triumphant return to Men-nefer.

On the third day, a messenger arrived from Men-nefer with a dispatch for Pharaoh. Pharaoh read it and then handed it to Amenemipet. "It's from my daughter. Tiaa is looking for an assassin archer to kill me during the procession from the port of Men-nefer to the palace. She wants to make it look like the assassin is either Assyrian or Hittite, so the people will demand war, and no one will notice her eliminating my other sons so Prince Amenhotep will become Pharaoh with her as regent."

General Ahmose leaped to his feet. "Great Pharaoh, this has gone on long enough! She must be arrested for treason before one of her plots actually kills you!"

Pharaoh nodded. "I know, General. I wanted to make sure we identified all of the conspirators first, but I'm not so sure that we have that luxury anymore."

"Can we move against Tiaa and Amenemhat the day of your return to Men-nefer?" Amenemipet asked. "If Princess Iaret is supposed to arrange for the assassin, then Tiaa will believe that an assassin is ready to strike. We'll know there won't be any assassin waiting to kill you. I've been keeping Amenemhat out of the palace, but if I allow him to enter that day, we can take him and Tiaa at the same time. The priests in the north are now under control, so that just leaves Waset, Karnak, and the nobles that Amenemhat has corrupted. Kaaper has given us the names of the disloyal nobles in Men-nefer, and as soon as he gets us the names of the ones in Waset and the smaller towns along the Ar River, then we can move on them all at the same time. And if Mery here can give us the names of the priests in Karnak who are actively plotting treason, we'll have all of the conspirators' names. We can deal with them all quickly and publicly."

"I have those names, Great Pharaoh," Mery said.

Pharaoh regarded Amenemipet for a while, thinking about the suggestion. *I'd like to get the intrigue and plotting over with quickly. Egypt needs time to finish rebuilding after what Moses and his god did to us. A power struggle serves no purpose.*

"All right," Pharaoh agreed. "Let's push my return to Men-nefer back to give us enough time to plan this carefully. I want it to go as smoothly as the campaign in Canaan."

"Yes, Great Pharaoh," Amenemipet responded. "And if anyone asks why you're staying in Peru-nefer so long?"

"Tell them that, since my last return to Men-nefer followed a humiliating defeat, I want this return to Men-nefer to be glorious – more glorious than any other Pharaoh's return to his capital, as befitting how successful the campaign in Canaan was. I want my people to remember this return so that the previous one can disappear from Egypt's memory altogether."

"Yes, Great Pharaoh." Amenemipet smiled. "And don't worry about what the people of Egypt will remember. *This* return is what will be carved on the walls of your palaces, temples and tombs. There will be no permanent record of your return from Mafkat anywhere in your kingdom. I'll see to that myself."

Pharaoh flashed a grateful smile. "Thank you, Amenemipet."

Two days later, five great barges glided up to the docks at Peru-nefer. The barges bore the flag of the Hittites. Their emissary came ashore and was escorted to the palace.

Pharaoh met the emissary wearing his full armor and his khepresh war crown, rather than his state crown, which was in Men-nefer. "What news from your master the Emperor of the Hittites?"

"Great Pharaoh, live forever!" the emissary began. "Son of Ra, Amenhotep II, divine ruler of Iunu, ruler of rulers, a panther who rages in every foreign land and in this land forever. My master, Muwatalli I, sends his fraternal greeting and his congratulations on your successful campaign in Canaan. As a token of his loyalty to you and to Egypt, he has sent five full barges of tribute – triple the amount that he would normally send to you each year. In addition to gold, silver, jewels, and goods, he sends women for your harem, livestock for your fields, and grain for your people, to replace what was lost from last year's harvest."

Pharaoh was impressed. "And what does your master want in return for such generosity?"

"Only your friendship, Great Pharaoh. He wishes to restore all agreements between our two kingdoms, and he pledges himself to your side."

Pharaoh nodded to the emissary.

"Would you care to inspect our tribute, Great Pharaoh?"

"Certainly," Pharaoh said to the emissary.

Pharaoh gestured to the Captain of the Medjay Guards. Several detachments of guards had left the palace to inspect the barges before Pharaoh arrived, in case this was a Hittite trick.

Pharaoh followed the emissary to the docks. He was met by the Captain of the Medjay Guards, who confirmed that it was safe for Pharaoh to board the barges.

Most of the barges contained food – grains and livestock – but the fifth barge was filled mostly with gold, silver, and jewels. The women for his harem were all quite beautiful, and according to the emissary, all highborn daughters of the Hittite empire.

When Pharaoh was finished inspecting the barges, he said to the emissary, "Please convey to your master my deep gratitude for his generous gift, which I willingly accept. If your barges could sail the tribute upriver to Men-nefer, I'd like the people of my capital to see the generosity of our friends in the Hittite Empire."

"It will be done, Great Pharaoh."

The next day, six barges glided up to the docks at Peru-nefer. From the design of these barges, Pharaoh knew that they were from Arzawa, but they flew the flag of the Assyrians. The Assyrian emissary carried similar letters of friendship and pledges of fidelity from Ashur-nadin-ahhe I, Emperor of Assyria, to Pharaoh and to Egypt.

The barges that carried the Assyrian tribute contained the same items as the Hittites had sent, only more of everything, including weapons. Pharaoh accepted the tribute and, again, asked the emissary to take the tribute to Men-nefer.

Seven barges arrived the next day from Agum III, the King of Babylon.

As Pharaoh inspected the barges, he whispered to Amenemipet, "It would appear that the campaign in Canaan served its purpose. Our friends to the north seem determined to outdo each other in begging for our friendship. The Babylonians must have paid a fortune to acquire all of these barges since they have no direct access to the Middle Sea."

"Your victory is complete, Great Pharaoh. We've heard from all of the northern kingdoms except for one: the Mitanni."

Ten barges arrived the next day from Artatama I, the Emperor of the Mitanni. In addition to a vast tribute, the Mitanni emissary also brought Pharaoh an unusual request.

"Great Pharaoh, for years our two kingdoms have been friendly rivals. My master wishes to change that. There is a growing threat in the northern region: the Hittites. They are encroaching on their neighbors, attempting to expand their borders through conflict and annexation. They threaten to destabilize the region. My master wishes to form a formal alliance with Egypt to stand against the Hittites and their expansion. He wishes to enter into negotiations for a permanent peace and permanent alliance between our two great kingdoms for our mutual benefit and protection."

Pharaoh was shocked. Egypt had never entered into such an agreement, but he saw the wisdom of it. And since the Mitanni were the farthest away of all of the northern kingdoms, they posed the least threat to Egypt.

"Tell your master that I look forward to beginning those negotiations, and tell him that his gratitude overwhelms me."

Once all of the barges had sailed south to Men-nefer, Pharaoh and Amenemipet reviewed the dispatches left behind by the four emissaries of the northern kingdoms.

"Did you notice that each of the four rulers offered to deliver next year's tribute in person?" Amenemipet asked.

Pharaoh chucked. "I'm just grateful that there *will* be tribute next year. We can use it to buy more slaves to replace our losses."

"The Mitanni offer was interesting. Do you think they're serious about a peace treaty with us?"

Pharaoh shrugged. "I have no idea. It's never been done before, but that's no reason to turn them down. Let's see where the negotiations go. There's no harm in having the conversation, is there?"

"No, Great Pharaoh."

"I have found an archer, my Queen," Iaret whispered to Tiaa as they walked together through the palace.

"He is able to disguise himself as Assyrian or Hittite?"

"Hittite," Iaret answered.

"I want to see him," Tiaa said.

"There's no way I can bring him to the palace unseen," Iaret protested. "If he's seen now and captured or killed after… he does what he's being paid to do, they'll know you and I were behind it. No, you must never meet him, and he must never come to the palace."

Tiaa glared at Iaret's insolence, but then nodded. "You're right. Make certain he's ready when the time comes. I understand that the date for Pharaoh's return has changed again."

"I heard that, too. Something about tribute from the Assyrians, Babylonians, Hittites, and Mitanni arriving first."

"Your father's campaign in Canaan seems to have been a complete success," Tiaa noted. "His success will be carved on every building in Egypt."

Iaret giggled. "Along with the dedication of his tomb and the elevation of your son as the next Pharaoh?"

"We'll see," Tiaa said, smiling. "By the way, how much does the archer want?"

Iaret told her the amount.

"You're joking!"

"No, I'm not. He won't take any less. He says it's going to be next to impossible to escape after it's done, and he wants his family taken care of."

"Oh, they'll be taken care of, all right," Tiaa stated. "Just not the way that he wants them to be. See to it."

"Yes, my Queen."

Amenemhat read the dispatches from the priests in Iunu with a mixture of shock and rage.

He slammed his fists on the table, picked up the stone bowl next to him, and flung it at the wall, watching it shatter into little pieces across the floor.

Kaaper rushed in. "High Priest, is everything all right?"

Amenemhat glared at his acolyte. "NO! Do I look like everything is all right?"

Kaaper cowered from Amenemhat's rant. "I-I-I'm sorry, High Priest. Forgive the intrusion."

He turned to flee from Amenemhat's presence, but the High Priest called him back. "Wait, Kaaper. Sit down."

Amenemhat handed him the dispatches from the priests at Iunu. "Read them."

Kaaper read the dispatches carefully. When he was done, he stared at Amenemhat. "What happened?"

"Pharaoh. That's what happened. They were ready to rise up against him, and he threatened to kill them all for piracy."

"Piracy? How could he accuse them of that?" Kaaper asked.

"Because by boarding ships at Peru-nefer and demanding that the captains pay a tax without a decree from Pharaoh allowing them to collect taxes, and by keeping the tax money at the temples and not sending the money to Pharaoh's treasury, they committed acts of piracy under the law. Pharaoh threatened to execute them all unless they swore to stop participating in any rebellions against him."

"Execute them all?! Can Pharaoh do that?"

Amenemhat nodded. "He can in Iunu. He might even be able to do it in Karnak, although I'd have to look into that."

"So we have no allies left in the north?"

"Not among the priests," Amenemhat replied. "All we have are the nobles, and I hope they're enough."

Amenemhat rummaged through the papers on the table and pulled out a sheet of papyrus. He rolled it up and handed it to Kaaper. "This is for the queen. She needs to get it no later than tomorrow."

"Yes, High Priest. I'll make certain that it gets there."

Kaaper was almost to the hallway when Amenemhat shouted, "Wait!" Kaaper turned and faced Amenemhat.

"After you deliver that to the queen, take a ship to Waset. I need the final list of nobles who have agreed to support us. And meet with Sennefer, the Mayor of Waset. He's the Overseer of the Granaries and Fields, Gardens, and Cattle of Amun, so he knows how much grain Pharaoh seized from Waset and Karnak. He may be the son of Amenemipet's half-brother, but his loyalty should be to Amun and Egypt. I need him to be with us if we're to take control of Waset when the time comes to move against Pharaoh."

"Yes, High Priest."

When Kaaper left with the note, Amenemhat tossed the dispatches from the priests into the brazier next to him.

I have to see Tiaa before Pharaoh returns. She must know what's going on, and we have to rethink our plans if we're to salvage the situation. Even if I have to tunnel into the palace, I will be with her again soon.

CHAPTER 16

Kaaper strolled through the bazaar on his way to the port at Men-nefer. The bazaar, the largest marketplace in northern Egypt, was an open part of the city that surrounded the great obelisk celebrating Thutmose III's military campaigns. The bazaar was filled with tents, booths, and wagons laden with goods for sale. It could easily take days to see all that was being sold there, and sellers had almost everything that someone would want to buy, including food, weapons, livestock, cloth, wooden beams and lumber, jewelry, rugs, tents, and slaves. Goods from all around the Middle Sea were available for purchase, and those gifted in the art of haggling could usually get a good price for whatever they came to buy. A thousand different smells arose from the bazaar on any given day. Two great avenues ran along either side of the bazaar – one to the north and one to the south.

Kaaper bumped into a young woman who was walking in the other direction. "A thousand pardons, my lady," he said, bowing to the woman. He slipped his rolled papyrus into her hand and took the folded papyrus that she handed him.

"All is forgiven." The woman hid the rolled papyrus in the folds of her dress.

Kaaper continued to the port, where a ship was waiting to take him to Waset. *I need to get to Waset and back as soon as possible. Once I've learned the identities of the nobles in the south who are conspiring with Amenemhat, I can take the list to Pharaoh and Amenemipet. Then they'll know who all the traitors are, and*

I'll have done my duty and can receive my reward.

As he approached the port, he saw his ship. He boarded it, and the crew immediately got underway. To ensure a safe journey, Kaaper said a prayer to the gods and goddesses of the Ar River and the winds. A strong wind blew south as the ship left the harbor, which helped the ship make good time as it sailed upriver toward Waset.

He unfolded the papyrus that Princess Iaret had given him and read it. *If you get the list of nobles in Waset who are plotting against Pharaoh, get a copy of that list to the garrison commander at Waset and a copy to Amenemipet.*

Kaaper tore up the note and threw it over the side of the ship into the river. Closing his eyes, he offered one more prayer.

Great Horus, give me speed on my way. I cannot fly like the falcon, but you can bring the wind that will make this ship speed along the great river. Help me fulfill my tasks.

Iaret unrolled the papyrus once she was alone in Amenemipet's private office. She giggled when she read the High Priest's note.

Amenemhat knows that the northern priests have abandoned him, and he believes that Tiaa has abandoned him as well, preferring to carry out her own plots rather than working together to bring down my father. Well, that much is true. Ah, he sent Kaaper south to Waset to gather the final list of nobles who are disloyal to my father. Good. Oh, how sweet. He still pledges his undying love to Tiaa. I wonder how Tiaa will react when she reads that he sent Kaaper to Waset to tell the nobles that there is no longer a conspiracy against Pharaoh, and that he is abandoning her because he no longer believes that she loves him. That should fracture their alliance once and for all.

Iaret grabbed a sheet of papyrus and a stylus so she could begin writing a different note for Tiaa to read.

Pharaoh, Amenemipet, General Ahmose, Admiral Thuti, and Mery read through the plans for capturing all of the conspirators in league with Tiaa and Amenemhat. They had spent more than a week working out the details of a campaign that involved soldiers in Karnak, Waset, Men-nefer, and many of the smaller cities and villages along the Ar River.

"I see that we still don't have all of the names of the traitorous nobles south of Men-nefer," General Ahmose noted.

Amenemipet nodded. "Once we have them, it will be forwarded to the garrison commander at the Waset barracks. We do have all of the names from Men-nefer and can forward that list to the soldiers at any time."

"We do have the names of all of Amenemhat's priests who are involved," Mery pointed out. "As well as the priests from the other temples who support Amenemhat against Pharaoh."

"What about the route through Men-nefer when Pharaoh arrives at the port?" Admiral Thuti asked.

Amenemipet pointed to the map of Men-nefer on the table. "We'll let it be known that the route will go along the south side of the bazaar, and then the morning of Pharaoh's arrival, the soldiers will take position along the north side of the bazaar, which will ensure that any assassins waiting on the rooftops will be in the wrong position to strike. It will also keep Tiaa from learning that Princess Iaret never did actually hire an archer to kill her father. The Princess can use the excuse that the archer was in the wrong place when the route was changed and couldn't move positions unseen."

"What about the banquet?" General Ahmose asked. "Tiaa will be there, and as royal wife, she will have a duty to perform. She will also sit next to you at your table."

"I am concerned about her trying to poison me," Pharaoh admitted. "How will we prevent her from doing that?"

"There will be two tasters, Great Pharaoh," Amenemipet said, making a notation in the corner of one of the pages. "One will taste your food when it is plated, and the other one will taste your feed when it is served to you."

"Will the taster hand the offering to me or will Tiaa?" Pharaoh asked.

Amenemipet looked uncomfortable. "By tradition, she will

181

hand the offering to you."

"Can't we arrest her before she touches the offering?" General Ahmose asked. "Why take the chance that she'll tamper with it, or worse yet, stab Pharaoh when he accepts it?"

"I'll have my armor on and the khepresh war crown," Pharaoh said. "I don't remove the armor and put on the traditional crown of Upper and Lower Egypt and the wesekh collar until after her offering to me. I should be able to avoid any attempt by her to stab me."

"I still don't like it," the general stated. "Only the soldiers and the Medjay guards will have swords, but most of the men will have daggers to use on their food. If the disloyal priests and nobles strike at the same time, you could be killed before my soldiers can react."

"Then make certain that your soldiers are deployed so they can intercept anyone approaching me or my sons," Pharaoh snapped. "The whole point of the banquet is to have all of the conspirators in one place at one time so we don't have to tear the city apart looking for them. Your men will have to be ready for anything. If you're that worried, then double the number of soldiers at the banquet. And I want soldiers and archers in the guardrooms inside the palace's pylon towers in case there's any attempt by the conspirators to seize the palace."

"Yes, Great Pharaoh. I'm understandably cautious. This is your life we are talking about."

"Yes, and if our plan works, the banquet will be the last time that my life is in danger for quite a while. Just make sure your men are ready to carry out their part."

General Ahmose nodded.

Amenemipet looked around the room. "If there are no other changes to the plan, I'll return to Men-nefer this afternoon and start making preparations for Pharaoh's arrival, the procession, and the banquet at the palace."

"Make certain that all of the conspirators in Men-nefer are there at the banquet," Pharaoh reminded him. "And work with the garrison and the Captain of the Medjay Guards to coordinate security."

"Yes, Great Pharaoh. Will Merytamon and your sons be returning to Men-nefer with me?"

Pharaoh shook his head. "No, they'll return when I do. Tiaa still thinks they're in Iunu, and if Merytamon returns with you, then Tiaa will know that they were in Peru-nefer and have talked to me about what's going on in the palace. I prefer for Tiaa to think that I'm ignorant of her plots and schemes."

"Yes, Great Pharaoh. When I return to Men-nefer, I'll have the royal barge sent up here for your return."

"Thank, you, Amenemipet."

"When should I leave Peru-nefer?" Mery asked. "I feel like I should return to Karnak before I'm missed."

"You may return any time," Pharaoh said. "But be certain that you're with the soldiers from the garrison at Waset before they start rounding up the conspirators. I don't want you taken by mistake."

"Yes, Great Pharaoh."

A tear rolled down Tiaa's cheek when she read the papyrus note from Amenemhat that Iaret had just given her. She quickly wiped the tear away before any of her guards saw it.

He has rejected and abandoned me. I'm truly on my own now. I'll miss his touch, but there are other men here in the palace that can satisfy my needs. It's a good thing that Iaret is still loyal to me. Her archer should end Pharaoh's reign when he returns to Men-nefer, but what if he misses? In those few seconds while the arrow is in flight, any number of things can happen to keep the arrow from finding its mark. What do I do then?

Tiaa thought about the banquet that would normally be held to celebrate Pharaoh's return. *If the banquet actually happens, it's my duty as royal wife to bring the offering of beer to the living god of Egypt. I'm sure that Amenemipet will have tasters on hand to protect Pharaoh, but I'm the one who will hand the bowl to him. My cobra ring can pierce his hand when he takes the bowl from me. With a large enough dose of poison, he'll die within a day or two, giving me time to remove Prince Thutmose from the line of succession. Then my son will be named Pharaoh, and I'll be regent. I don't need nobles and priests to help me. This I can do all* on my own. Then I'll marry Pharaoh's daughter to a foreign prince and be free to rule Egypt however I want.*

Tiaa started writing a reply to Amenemhat, but then she crumpled the papyrus and threw it into the brazier. *Why bother? I don't need him anymore.*

Kaaper's ship arrived back in Men-nefer two weeks after he left for Waset. The winds allowed him to reach Waset faster than anticipated, and the swift current of the Ar River made the return trip equally fast.

He had two copies of the list of nobles who were ready to take control of Waset and the cities along the Ar River. The first copy, which was incomplete, was for Amenemhat. The second copy was the complete list, and it was for Amenemipet if he were back in Men-nefer. Kaaper had already given a copy of the complete list to the garrison commander at Waset.

I don't mind taking the ship to Peru-nefer, but if I'm gone for that long, Amenemhat will suspect something. No, it's better if I can give the list to Amenemipet here and let him get it to Pharaoh in Peru-nefer.

Kaaper disembarked as soon as the ship was tied up to the dock. *If I take the list to Amenemhat first, I might not be able to get the copy to Amenemipet until tomorrow at the earliest. Or Amenemhat could send me somewhere else, and I'd never get to deliver the list. But if I go to the palace first, I might be seen, and Amenemhat could demand to know what I was doing there. I could always say that I was checking to see if Princess Iaret had a message for the High Priest, and I wanted to deliver the message and the list of names at the same time. I think I could make him believe that story.*

Kaaper pulled his cowl over his head and headed for the palace. When he arrived, he was escorted into Amenemipet's private office.

"What do you have for me?" Amenemipet asked.

"The list of nobles in the south that you've been waiting for," Kaaper replied, handing over the list. "I've already given a copy to the garrison commander at Waset."

Amenemipet's face lit up as he reached for the list. He read the names on the list with a mixture of emotions. When he was finished, he said, "This is great work, Kaaper. Thank you! I noticed that Sennefer, the Mayor of Waset, is not on this list. Do you know where he stands?"

Kaaper nodded. "I spoke with him myself. He is loyal to Pharaoh, and he refuses to be part of any plot to overthrow Pharaoh or influence the choice of heir."

Amenemipet nodded. Holding up the list, he said, "I'm grateful for this. We're laying a trap for the conspirators on the day that Pharaoh returns to Men-nefer. I want you to be there when we snare them all. Check in with me every few days so I can keep you informed about the plans."

"I will," Kaaper said, standing. "Thank you, Vizier."

Amenemipet nodded and handed Kaaper a pouch filled with coins.

Kaaper took the pouch and left the palace. He headed for the house where Amenemhat stayed when he was in Men-nefer. When he arrived, Amenemhat glared at him impatiently.

"Your ship docked more than an hour ago. Where have you been?" he demanded.

"I wanted to see if there was a message for you from the queen before I brought you the list of names from Waset."

Kaaper handed the list to Amenemhat.

"Was there a message for me?"

Kaaper shook his head. "No, High Priest. There was no message."

Amenemhat looked ill. "I don't understand. There has been no response since you left for Waset. What could have happened?"

Kaaper remained silent, knowing better than to interject his thoughts into Amenemhat's problems with the queen.

Amenemhat glanced at the list of names that Kaaper had brought. He nodded absently and stared out the window.

After several moments had passed, Kaaper cleared his throat. "Is there anything else you need me to do, High Priest?"

"What? No... no, thank you, Kaaper. I'll send for you if I need you."

"Yes, High Priest." Kaaper left Amenemhat to his thoughts.

I wonder how Amenemhat will react when he discovers that none of his actual messages made it to the queen, and none of her actual messages made it to him. I imagine he'll be furious. I only hope that he doesn't find out before the soldiers capture him.

Iaret stopped by Tiaa's quarters to visit the queen. Tiaa had moved back into her old apartment, and so far, there had been no further attempts on her life.

Tiaa and Iaret exchanged pleasantries for a few moments before Iaret lowered her voice to a whisper.

"The archer is ready, my Queen."

"He knows where to be and what to do?" Tiaa asked.

Iaret nodded. "As long as Pharaoh doesn't change his route through the city. I talked to Amenemipet when he returned from Peru-nefer, and he told me that the procession will take the avenue that runs along the south side of the bazaar. Pharaoh will be the most exposed there, so the archer will be waiting on top of one of the buildings along that route. He should have a clear shot, and his escape will be easier because of the people who will be in the bazaar to see the procession."

Tiaa nodded. "You have done well, my dear. Everything is ready. Now we must wait for Pharaoh's return."

"Yes, my Queen."

Khaemtir, Pensekhmet, Sharek, Wadjmose and several other nobles sat around the courtyard of the same compound near the southern wall of Men-nefer where they had met with Kaaper and Amenemhat originally.

"Has anyone heard when Pharaoh is returning to Men-nefer?" Pensekhmet asked.

"It should be some time in the next week or two," Wadjmose replied.

"What's taking him so long?" Khaemtir demanded. "He's

been back in Egypt for a month at least. Why the delay?"

"Amenemhat told me that Pharaoh wants to return to Men-nefer in the most glorious way possible," Sharek answered. "He wants the people to forget about his return to Men-nefer after the disaster at the Southern Sea against the Hebrews."

"Has Amenemhat given us our instructions yet?" Khaemtir asked.

Sharek shook his head. "Only to say that we're to attend the banquet at the palace that night and be ready to strike when he gives the signal. I don't know what the signal will be, but I assume he'll let us know before then."

"I heard a rumor that Pharaoh is going to pay us for the grain that he seized," Pensekhmet mentioned. "He's going to use some of the plunder from Canaan to repay us for our losses."

Wadjmose's eyes flew open wide. "I hadn't heard that. That changes everything, doesn't it?"

"No!" Sharek spat. "Why would you think that paying us for our grain changes anything? We're still without our grain. And our firstborn are still dead. Is he going to replace them for us? And what about our slaves? Is he going to give us some of the Canaanites to replace our Hebrews?"

"Oh, for the love of the gods, Sharek!" Wadjmose exclaimed. "How many times do we have to talk about this? *You* didn't lose any Hebrews. The Hebrews working in your fields weren't *yours*! They just happened to be assigned to your fields at the time that Pharaoh allowed them to leave – fields that had already been destroyed by their god, by the way."

"That doesn't matter," Sharek snapped. "My son is dead, my fields still need to be tended to, and I need slaves to do it with. What am I supposed to do? Use the money Pharaoh gives me to buy slaves?"

Khaemtir stared at Sharek with his mouth open. "That sounds like a perfect idea to me. Buy your own slaves instead of borrowing Pharaoh's. Then if Pharaoh ever sets his own slaves free again, you won't be affected."

Sharek threw up his hands in exasperation. "That's not the point!"

"Then what *is* the point?" Khaemtir demanded. "Or are you just angry at Pharaoh, and nothing anyone says will make you think differently?"

Pensekhmet interjected, "I don't think bickering among ourselves is going to help anything. We're committed to the High Priest's plan to take control of Egypt and name Prince Amenhotep as the new Pharaoh with Queen Tiaa as regent. What Pharaoh does or doesn't do with the plunder from Canaan doesn't change that, right?"

Pensekhmet looked around the courtyard. The other nobles slowly nodded their heads. Pensekhmet stared at Sharek until Sharek finally nodded. "Good. Then let's stop talking about anything else until *after* the deed is done, all right?"

"Is there any chance that the people will rise up with us against Pharaoh?" Khaemtir asked.

"I don't think so," Wadjmose replied. "They blame the *Hebrews* for the calamities that plagued Egypt, including the loss of their firstborn. In fact, most now believe that the Hebrew presence in Egypt was the *true* calamity. They see Pharaoh as the savior who chased the Hebrews out of Egypt, distributed his own grain to feed the people, and made war against Canaan to bring fresh slaves to serve Egypt and her people. He's more popular than ever."

The nobles sat silently, absorbing what Wadjmose had shared.

"Then is there any reason to think that they won't rise up against *us* if we overthrow Pharaoh?" Khaemtir asked.

"If we control the army, they won't rise up," Sharek declared.

"But we don't control the army," Pensekhmet pointed out.

Sharek nodded. "The queen will as soon as she's declared regent."

"Then we should make certain that we kill Pharaoh's generals and commanders at the same time that we kill Pharaoh," Khaemtir suggested. "Otherwise, the army could go against us, and we'd all be killed for our efforts."

"I agree," Sharek said. The other nobles nodded, and the rest of their conversations focused on the plan to seize control of Mennefer and the military on Amenemhat's orders.

Amenemhat stood in the shadows outside the palace wall, close to the harem's courtyard where Tiaa's apartment was located. He watched the soldiers and guards patrolling outside the walls and on top of the walls. He had never seen so many guards and soldiers around the palace before.

For hours, he watched the patrols, looking for a weakness in their pattern, a gap in their posts, anything that he could exploit to get into the palace and back out again unseen. There was nothing that he could use.

They've blocked all of the ways that I used to sneak in and out, and there's never a moment when soldiers or guards don't have every bit of the wall in sight. There are torches all along the palace walls, plus the patrols are carrying torches. And even if I did get over the wall, there's no telling how many guards and soldiers are waiting inside. I'll never get inside the palace unless the gods themselves carry me in.

Amenemhat watched the patrols for a while longer before slipping down a side street and heading back to his lodgings in the city.

Somehow I have to get inside. I must speak with Tiaa and let her know what I've done. The priests and nobles are ready to rise up and seize power in her name. But I have to make sure that she knows this so she doesn't do something on her own that puts my priests and the nobles in jeopardy.

Amenemhat continued walking along the dark and deserted streets of the city. *If she comes to the bazaar to welcome Pharaoh when he returns, I might be able to get close enough to her to speak with her for a moment. But if she waits for him at the palace, I'll never get to see her unless I'm allowed to attend the banquet, and then it'll be too late to coordinate anything.*

He saw his lodgings looming in front of him. *I'll see if Kaaper can get a message to her saying that I'll meet her in the bazaar before Pharaoh arrives in Men-nefer. If she meets me there, I'll know we're still in this together. If not, I'll know she has abandoned me and is pursuing her own plans.*

CHAPTER 17

The garrison commander of the army barracks at Waset led several squads of soldiers to the riverbank. This was one of the more dangerous assignments he'd ever been given, but he did Pharaoh's bidding without question.

Near the riverbanks between the city and the ferries that went to Karnak on the opposite bank, lay a number of large pens surrounded by stone walls that were twice the height of a man. When the Hebrew slaves built Waset and Karnak, these pens were used to keep crocodiles away from the workers moving the great blocks of stone from the barges to the building sites. Now they were empty, but that was about to change.

One of the squad leaders approached the garrison commander. "How many crocodiles do we need to move into the pens?"

"Several dozen at least," the garrison commander replied.

"So many…"

The garrison commander regarded the squad leader. "I don't mind clearing the riverbank of crocodiles, but wrangling them into the pens is something else altogether. The pens must be filled with crocodiles before the garrison can move against the priests and nobles plotting against Pharaoh. We're going to lose men today if we're not careful. The problem won't be finding the crocodiles, it'll be creeping up on them from behind so they don't attack."

"Yes, Commander."

The garrison commander ordered his men to move toward the

riverbank. The men had ropes and leather straps at the ready.

One of the larger and strongest soldiers in the garrison scoffed at the idea of a crocodile getting the better of him. He waded confidently into the water and quickly threw a rope around the legs of a nearby crocodile. But as he started dragging the crocodile back to shore, he didn't see the two crocodiles along the edge of the papyrus reeds. They lunged at him at the same time. One grabbed the soldier's arm while the other went for the soldier's leg. The soldier screamed in pain just before he disappeared below the surface of the river, never to be seen again.

The squads on the shore watched in horror as the crocodiles dragged the soldier underwater. Three soldiers rushed forward to save their comrade, but it was too late. They retreated from the water and waited with the rest of the soldiers on the riverbank.

When the garrison commander gave the order for them to get to work, the soldiers cautiously approached the papyrus reeds growing along the riverbanks, where dozens of crocodiles could be seen staying cool in the shallow water. Several more soldiers were injured or killed trying to capture the first few crocodiles, but the men learned quickly. They threw the leather straps around the crocodiles' snouts first so they couldn't bite, and then the soldiers threw ropes around the crocodiles' midsection just behind their front legs to drag the reptiles to the pens.

The crocodiles thrashed violently as they were being restrained and dragged from the river, but the soldiers worked together and forced the reptiles towards the pens.

Getting the crocodiles into the pens proved even more difficult. The soldiers tried to use ropes to haul the crocodiles up and over the walls, but the reptiles proved to be too energetic and heavy to be lifted that high. Finally, the garrison commander ordered the men to remove a section of the walls and drag the crocodiles into the pens. Several soldiers held the ropes around each crocodile to keep the beasts away from the openings until the pens were filled.

Once the men were ready to close up the walls, soldiers entered the pens through the openings to cut off the leather straps around the crocodiles' snouts, while soldiers on top of the walls held the ropes tightly so the crocodiles couldn't bite the soldiers in the pens. Once all of the straps had been removed, the soldiers scrambled back out of the pens. The walls of the pens were closed, and the soldiers on top of the walls pulled the ropes free to release the crocodiles.

Liberated from the straps and ropes, the crocodiles thrashed about, looking for a way out and back to the river. The soldiers poured buckets of river water into the pens to keep the crocodiles cool.

"Do we feed them?" one of the soldiers asked the garrison commander.

The garrison commander smiled grimly. "No. They'll be getting all the food they can eat in the next day or so."

Similar measures were taken at Men-nefer for Pharaoh's arrival. In addition to the crocodile pens, squads of soldiers took up posts around the city in preparation for moving against the conspirators.

Both the northern and southern ports at Men-nefer were going to be used for Pharaoh's arrival. The Nubian archers, foot soldiers, and chariots were to disembark at the southern port and secure the riverfront all the way to the northern port, where Pharaoh's fleet would dock. The archers and foot soldiers would lead the procession, followed by hundreds of captured prisoners and pallets of plunder from Canaan. Pharaoh, General Ahmose, and Admiral Thuti would lead the chariots at the end of the procession through the city to the palace. Once the procession had reached the palace, the prisoners would be marched back to the port and sailed to Goshen, but the soldiers would deploy throughout the city to prevent any uprisings.

Amenemipet personally oversaw all of the preparations for Pharaoh's homecoming. Kenamun stood next to him, watching the crocodile pens being filled.

"Crocodile pens? Is it really necessary to put them all in pens just to make it safer for the soldiers when they line up across the riverfront?"

Amenemipet shook his head. "That's not why we're putting crocodiles in the pens. It's just what we're telling people who ask so no one will suspect the real reason."

Kenamun looked confused. "You mean it's not to make it safer for when Pharaoh disembarks for the procession?"

Amenemipet looked grim. "Of course not. Yes, it will make it safer for the soldiers, but that's not the reason. The pens are for the executions after the soldiers seize the conspirators."

"You mean you're going to throw the nobles and priests into crocodile pens... to be eaten?"

Amenemipet looked at Kenamun and saw the horror in his eyes. "Not all of them. The pens are for the children of the conspirators. The adults will be beheaded after watching the fate of their children, and then their bodies will be cast into the eastern desert to deny them an afterlife."

"And Pharaoh agreed to this? I thought that he was going to use some of the Canaanite plunder to repay the nobles for their grain as a way to convince them to abandon their plots against him."

Amenemipet shook his head. "Only loyal nobles will be repaid. Would you ever trust a noble whose loyalty could be bought so easily? What if someone came along and offered them *more* money? We'd have to go through all of this again. Pharaoh knows that he has to end this conspiracy decisively. If he's seen as weak or too merciful, he'll be facing plots against him for the rest of his reign. No, he must be ruthless so those who survive will know the fate that awaits traitors. It will discourage others from plotting treason in the future. This is as much for his heir as it is for himself."

"And Pharaoh is okay with killing innocent children this way?"

"No," Amenemipet replied. "But he knows he has no choice. Treason has to be punished in the most severe way possible, and no pharaoh has ever allowed the family of a traitor to survive. He's using the same methods that pharaohs before him have used, even though he personally finds it distasteful and cruel."

Kenamun shuddered. "I understand. I just didn't think he'd choose a method that was so gruesome."

"Gruesome ways are the ones that are remembered," Amenemipet pointed out.

"And what of Tiaa and Amenemhat?"

"I don't know what Pharaoh has planned for them,"

Amenemipet admitted. "But I'm sure it will be unpleasant."

Amenemhat was dozing when Kaaper burst into his sleeping chamber.

"High Priest, I bring news!"

What the... what does this fool acolyte want now? Amenemhat sat up in bed and glared at Kaaper. "Haven't I told you not to enter without knocking?"

"Yes, High Priest," Kaaper said hurriedly, "but I bring news."

"What is it?" Amenemhat grumbled.

"You are invited to participate in Pharaoh's homecoming festivities at the palace! The High Priests from Iunu will be there, and Pharaoh has extended the invitation to any of the High Priests from Karnak who can be here in time!"

Amenemhat leaped out of bed. "How many priests can accompany me?"

"Five, High Priest."

I've been looking for ways into the palace for weeks now, and Pharaoh himself solves my problem by inviting me inside. If I arrive early, I can meet with the queen and finalize our plans to seize power. There's still hope!

"Perfect," Amenemhat said. "Absolutely perfect. Go to the nobles, and make certain that they all attend the festivities as well. My priests will be ready to carry out their instructions, and by the end of the banquet, Egypt will have a new ruler."

"Yes, High Priest! Who are you going to take to the palace with you?"

"Don't worry, Kaaper," Amenemhat assured him. "You'll be one of them. You've earned the right to be there when Pharaoh is overthrown."

"Thank you, High Priest!"

Amenemhat looked at his acolyte. "Now go; you have your instructions."

Kaaper left Amenemhat's sleeping chamber.

He's a good acolyte, but he's too eager to please. In ten or fifteen years, once he's matured a bit, he'll be ready for greater responsibilities. I'll keep an eye on him until them. He's still useful, even if it's just as an errand boy.

Wadjmose, one of the nobles conspiring against Pharaoh, watched the preparations for Pharaoh's homecoming taking place along the riverfront. He paid particular attention to the crocodile pens near the southern port.

I don't care what the soldiers are saying, those pens are for executions, not to keep the soldiers along the riverfront safe. My father saw it done before during Hatshepsut's reign, when she ordered all newborn Hebrew males killed. Pharaoh must know about the plots against him, and if they have three pens like this ready for executions, he knows who the conspirators are.

Wadjmose walked toward the southern port in the late afternoon sun. *Pharaoh has laid a trap for all of us. I knew that the High Priest of Amun would lead us to ruin. It's one thing to be angry at Pharaoh, but to actively plot his demise is quite another. It's treason, and I'm guilty of it.*

He approached three ships that were tied up next to each other. "I'm looking for passage south for myself and my family," he said to the captains.

"How many passengers?" one of the captains asked.

"Ten," Wadjmose replied. "That includes three servants, plus our personal items."

"How far south are you going?" another captain asked.

"Nubia."

"This is the wrong season to make it all the way to Nubia by ship," the third captain commented. "Any of us could get you well south of Waset, but you'd have to make the rest of your journey overland."

"When do you want to leave?" the first captain interrupted.

"Tomorrow."

The first two captains shook their heads and walked back to their ships.

The third captain asked, "Can you be ready to leave at

dawn?"

Wadjmose nodded.

The third captain named his price, and Wadjmose agreed.

"I'll see you at dawn, then," the third captain confirmed.

Wadjmose made his way through the city to his home, noticing how many soldiers were patrolling the city. The sun was setting in the west when he arrived. He called his family and servants together into the courtyard.

"We're leaving Men-nefer at dawn tomorrow. Pack light – only what you need. We have to take as much of our gold and silver as we can carry."

"What's going on, Father?" Wadjmose's son asked.

"There's a plot against Pharaoh, and Pharaoh believes that I'm part of it. We have to get out of the city before he returns."

"Why does he think you're part of it?" Wadjmose's wife demanded.

"Because most of the noble families in the city are part of it, and Pharaoh is coming after all of us to make an example of us. Have you seen how many soldiers are in the city lately? And I saw the crocodile pens where he's going to execute the prisoners. We can't stay here."

"Where are we going?" Wadjmose's oldest daughter asked.

"Nubia. Possibly even Kush or Ethiopia."

"Will we ever return here, Father?" his son asked.

"I don't know. We'll worry about that later. I have passage booked for all ten of us at dawn tomorrow. Go and pack."

His family and the servants obeyed. Wadjmose went to the locked chamber in the center of the house where he kept his family's wealth. He counted out the price that the captain had demanded and placed those coins into a leather pouch. Then he began distributing the gold coins and bars into leather pouches that would be hidden inside his families' and servants' traveling bags with their clothes. He picked up the pouches to make certain that they weren't too heavy, and then he put them aside.

I'm leaving most of my wealth behind. Pharaoh will seize it, but I'd rather he have my gold than my life and the lives of my family.

He took the pouches to his family members and the servants and instructed them to wrap their clothes around the bags so that the pouches wouldn't be found if the bags were searched. Then he joined his wife and packed his own clothes.

"Were you part of a conspiracy against Pharaoh?" Wadjmose's wife asked when they were alone.

Wadjmose nodded. "There were a number of us who used to meet and complain about the situation in Egypt after that Moses fellow arrived. Then the High Priest of Amun met with us and told us that there was a conspiracy underway to overthrow Pharaoh and replace him with someone who would lead Egypt back to its former glory. We believed him, but lately I've had my doubts about what we were doing. I finally decided that I couldn't go through with it, but when I saw the soldiers preparing Pharaoh's return to Men-nefer, I knew that we had to get out of the city."

"Why did you join in a conspiracy like that?" she demanded.

"Because I felt trapped. If I said 'yes,' and the plot failed, I could be killed. But if I said 'no,' and the plot succeeded, I could be also be killed. I didn't know what to do, so I said 'yes' and kept my eyes open to see if the plot might actually succeed. At first I thought it would, but now I think that Pharaoh knows exactly what's happening, meaning that the plot will fail. This is all I could think of to keep you safe."

His wife nodded and patted his arm. "Then we'll leave the city with you and go south. Hopefully one day we can return."

"Hopefully."

An hour before dawn, he led his family and the servants toward the port through the dark and deserted streets of the city.

They were stopped by a patrol of soldiers who demanded to know where they were going.

"We're visiting family members in Waset, and our ship leaves at dawn," he explained.

The soldiers let them pass, and Wadjmose walked faster through the streets, wanting to reach the docks before another patrol happened upon him and his family.

They reached the southern port just as the eastern sky began to lighten. "Right on time," the captain of their ship noted.

Wadjmose handed over the pouch of coins to pay for his family's passage.

"Take your family on board," the captain said. After giving his crew orders to get underway, the captain said, "There seems to be a lot of you traveling south all of a sudden."

"What do you mean?" Wadjmose asked as he boarded the ship.

"Them other two captains you met left hours ago with families like yours. Something going on in Nubia that you all wanna get to?"

Who else has fled the city? "Something like that," Wadjmose replied.

"Well, we'll get you as close as we can as quick as we can," the captain said as he climbed on board.

Wadjmose stored his belongings with his family's bags and came back on deck. The ship was already south of Men-nefer, and Wadjmose saw the white walls of the city gleam in the morning sun. *I may never see the white walls of Men-nefer again, but at least I'll live through Pharaoh's homecoming. Damn all priests!*

Pharaoh's barge glided up the Ar River, surrounded by the ships of his navy. The fleet was an impressive sight. Ships filled with soldiers, chariots, horses, prisoners, and plunder filled the river from riverbank to riverbank.

Pharaoh sat on the raised platform in the center of the royal barge. A large cloth stretched between twelve poles along the gunwales of the barge provided shade for Pharaoh and anyone joining him on the platform.

Merytamon and her two sons sat with him, along with Admiral Thuti and General Ahmose.

Merytamon and her sons listened silently as Pharaoh finally told them what would be happening at the homecoming celebration when they reached Men-nefer.

"So *this* is why you had me order my assassins to stop trying to kill Tiaa." Merytamon sounded shocked. "I had no idea that your plans were so intricate."

"Now you see why I couldn't move against Tiaa immediately?" Pharaoh asked. "First, I had to know who all the conspirators were, or none of us would ever be safe. Tomorrow night at the banquet, I'll name Prince Thutmose as my heir. When I do, my soldiers will arrest Tiaa and every priest, noble, official, and servant that she and Amenemhat have convinced to join with them."

"What about outside Men-nefer?" Merytamon asked.

"The soldiers will start arresting the priests, nobles, officials, and servants in Waset and the other cities along the Ar River that morning. Their executions should be finished before the banquet begins at the palace."

"And what about Prince Amenhotep?" one of the princes asked. "Will he be killed along with his mother?"

Pharaoh regarded his sons. "I will speak with Amenhotep in private. If he knew about his mother's plans, then yes, he will be killed. But if he knew nothing about her plans, then he'll be spared. I've lost enough sons. I'm not going to lose another one unless there's no choice. I won't hold the crimes of his mother against him unless he's a willing participant."

"Are you worried that Tiaa and Amenemhat might move against you at the banquet?" Merytamon asked.

Pharaoh nodded. "I expect them to. The question that remains is: who will move first? Will she strike me down before I give the order to have her arrested, or will I have her arrested along with her conspirators before they can overthrow me?"

"Aren't you worried, Father?" the other prince asked.

Pharaoh grinned. "A bit, but it's also like a game. And you know how much I like to plan and win games."

Merytamon and her sons fell silent as the fleet continued south toward Men-nefer.

Iaret gave Hannu – her personal guard – a kiss on his cheek as he finished getting dressed.

"You were wonderful," she said dreamily as she reached for her clothes.

"It's a pleasure to serve, my Princess," Hannu intoned.

Iaret giggled. "Will you be guarding me tomorrow when Pharaoh returns?"

Hannu shook his head. "I've been assigned the kitchens to

make certain that no one tampers with the food. But I'll be back the next day."

Iaret straightened her clothing, quickly brushed her long black hair, and put on her seshed – a gold circlet with the uraeus design at the front – on her head.

"Now you look like a princess again." Hannu smiled.

Iaret pouted. "And what do I look like when we're coupling?"

"A goddess, my Princess."

"Good answer! Why don't you come find me after the banquet? That is, unless you're too tired."

Hannu put his arms around Iaret and pulled her close. "I'll never be too tired for you, my Princess."

She kissed him again and then said, "You'd better get back to your post before the captain notices that you're not there."

"Yes, my Princess."

CHAPTER 18

Amenemhat approached the palace on the morning that Pharaoh was expected to return to Men-nefer. Soldiers stopped him as he approached the avenue of sphinxes flanking the main entrance of the palace.

"What business do you have here?" one of the guards demanded.

"I'm the High Priest of Amun," Amenemhat stated arrogantly.

"Okay, what business do you have here, High Priest of Amun?" the guard asked contemptuously.

"There are rites to Amun which must be performed before Pharaoh enters the palace. I'm here to perform those rites."

One of the other guards spoke up. "We already have a High Priest of Amun here. He arrived with the High Priests of Ra, Osiris, Isis, and several of the other gods."

Ah, the High Priests from Iunu are here already. Amenemhat drew himself up to make himself appear taller. "Those are the High Priests from Iunu. I'm the High Priest from Karnak. I was summoned to join them."

The first guard glanced at the second guard. "Go check it out."

The second guard turned and ran down the avenue of sphinxes. Amenemhat stood there staring at the remaining guards. *They have to let me in. I must see the queen.*

Several other dignitaries from Peru-nefer, Iunu, and other

cities and towns around Egypt approached the guards and were allowed to enter the palace. Amenemhat grew increasingly annoyed, but he was also concerned that he'd be denied entrance.

The second guard finally returned and whispered to the first guard. "It seems that the High Priests from Iunu didn't know that you were in Men-nefer, but they say that you're welcome to join them in blessing the palace. You may enter, but you may only be in the courtyards, throne room, banquet hall, and the other public areas. If you attempt to enter any of the corridors that lead to the apartments of the royal family or the harem, or if you attempt to enter the kitchens and storerooms, you will be arrested. Do you understand?"

"I understand." Amenemhat tried to sound grateful, but he was seething at the way he had been treated.

The guards stepped aside, and Amenemhat strode down the avenue of sphinxes and entered the palace.

Khaemtir, Pensekhmet, and Sharek met at the bazaar to welcome Pharaoh as he rode through the streets of Men-nefer. They would then follow the procession to the palace and participate in the homecoming banquet to commemorate Pharaoh's victory in Canaan. Their wives would join them at the palace later – before the banquet began.

"Has anyone seen Wadjmose this morning?" Khaemtir asked, looking around the bazaar.

Sharek shook his head. "No, I haven't seen him in a couple of days."

"I went by his house last night," Pensekhmet mentioned. "No one was there, not even the servants. It was deserted."

"Where could he be?" Sharek asked.

Khaemtir looked at his two friends and realized the truth. "He has fled from the city, and he took his family and servants with him."

"What?" Sharek sounded enraged.

Khaemtir continued. "I knew he had doubts about the plan, and I know of several other noble families who have fled the city in the last couple of days. The compound next to mine has been deserted for days. They left their livestock behind and their gates open. They're obviously not planning on returning."

"Wadjmose's gates were open when I got there!" Pensekhmet exclaimed. "Where did he go?"

Khaemtir shrugged. "Nubia? Kush? Ethiopia? Or they could have sailed north and gone to Canaan or one of the northern kingdoms."

"Do you think that he betrayed us before he left?" Pensekhmet asked.

Khaemtir shook his head. "If he had, we'd be dead already. No, he just fled. He must not believe that the plan will succeed."

"But it will succeed, right?" Pensekhmet asked nervously.

"Of course it will," Sharek stated confidently. "Everything is ready. Tonight, we'll make history!"

Khaemtir looked at his two co-conspirators. *I hope you're right, my friend. One thing is for certain. History will be made tonight. But will it be our successful overthrow of Pharaoh, or will it be our executions for treason?*

Amenemhat tried to avoid the guards and soldiers patrolling the corridors and terraces, but the deeper into the palace he went, the harder it became.

They have all of the secret ways blocked. I can't get to the harem from the inside or from the outside. Even if I made it to the roof, I couldn't lower myself into her apartment unseen. How will I see the queen if every way from here to her is impassable?

The ships of Pharaoh's navy reached the southern port of Mennefer and began unloading the archers, soldiers, and chariots that would line the riverfront and escort Pharaoh into his capital city. The archers and soldiers deployed carefully along the riverfront, making certain not to disturb the few remaining crocodiles sunning themselves among the papyrus reeds.

Once the chariots had been unloaded and the horses harnessed, the charioteers positioned themselves along the river road that connected the two ports.

Meanwhile, at the northern port of the city, prisoners and pallets of plunder taken during the campaign were unloaded. A gilded chariot captured from one of the Canaanite cities was unloaded for Pharaoh to use during the procession. It was larger than the Egyptian chariots, and the gold and silver covering its exterior gleamed in the midday sun.

As Pharaoh's barge approached the northern port, several detachments of soldiers left the riverfront and marched through the streets of Men-nefer to clear the way to the palace for the procession and to post guards along the route to keep the streets cleared.

When the soldiers reached the bazaar, an overturned wagon blocked the route that followed the avenue on the south side of the bazaar. Rather than clear that route, the soldiers immediately deployed along the avenue that ran along the north side of the bazaar. This was part of the plan all along, but the presence of the overturned wagon made it look like a last-moment change, so Princess Iaret would have a way to explain why her archer failed to complete his task.

From high atop the palace's north pylon tower, one of priests serving as Tiaa's spy witnessed the soldiers deploying along the north side of the bazaar. The spy turned and descended the stairs inside the tower, being careful not to alert the guards in the guardrooms that he was there.

Amenemhat searched for any way to reach the harem, but there seemed to be no way to get there unseen. He heard footsteps behind him and ducked into the shadows behind a nearby pillar so he wouldn't be spotted.

Peering from the shadows, he recognized one of his priests approaching. This priest served as one of the queen's spies in the palace. Amenemhat stepped out from behind the pillar.

204

"High Priest!" The spy immediately recognized Amenemhat. "What are you doing in the palace?"

"I'm trying to see the queen," Amenemhat whispered, looking around to make certain that no one saw them talking.

"I'm heading there myself. Pharaoh's route through the city was changed at the last moment. I need to tell her that the assassin is in the wrong place."

Amenemhat was confused. "What assassin?"

"The archer that Princess Iaret paid to kill her father. He's on a rooftop along the south side of the bazaar, but the procession route was moved. The archer will never be able to hit his target from where he's positioned."

Amenemhat's mind raced. *Tiaa really has abandoned our plans. But if her assassin can't kill Pharaoh, then maybe OUR plans will still work.* "Can you get me into the queen's apartment?"

"Not dressed as a priest."

Amenemhat heard guards approaching, and he pulled the spy into the shadows of the pillar. As the guards passed, he whispered his instructions to the spy.

The spy stepped out of the shadows and raced after the guards. He reached the last guard and tapped him on his shoulder. The guard turned around to face the priest.

"Forgive me, but I need some help. Can you follow me?"

The guard looked back at the rest of his squad, which was rounding a corner ahead and was soon out of sight. He nodded.

The spy led the guard back to the pillar where Amenemhat was waiting. As the guard passed the pillar, Amenemhat crept up from behind and hit the guard on the back of his head with the hilt of the jeweled dagger. The guard fell to the floor with a loud thud.

"Help me get his clothes off," Amenemhat hissed as he dragged the guard into the shadows.

A few moments later, Amenemhat, disguised as a guard, escorted his spy to the harem.

When they reached the entrance to the harem, the spy said, "I have urgent news for the queen."

The guards allowed the spy and Amenemhat to pass.

Amenemhat followed the spy into the antechamber of Tiaa's apartment. It was the first time that he had been in her apartment since the night when the cobra interrupted their time together.

A guard motioned for the spy and Amenemhat to enter the sitting area.

"What do you want?" Tiaa demanded.

"My Queen," the spy began, "Pharaoh's procession route through the city has changed. He'll be going along the north side of the bazaar instead of the south side."

"That means that Princess Iaret's plan won't work," Tiaa grumbled. "Find the princess, and bring her to me."

"Yes, my Queen," the spy intoned. He left Tiaa's apartment, but Amenemhat remained where he was, gazing longingly at her.

Tiaa saw him standing there and demanded, "What are you still doing here?"

"Waiting for you to command me, my Queen."

Recognition flashed across her face, but she didn't move toward him. "Actually, I could use your help over here," she said, gesturing toward the room where she had processed the castor seeds into poison.

"Certainly, my Queen."

Tiaa led him into the room and pulled the heavy curtain over the entrance to muffle their voices. Amenemhat took her in his arms and kissed her passionately.

"What are you doing here?" she whispered.

"I've been trying to get into the palace for weeks to see you. Why did you abandon our plans? I had everything arranged."

"What do you mean, 'abandoned our plans'? Your notes said that the plans had fallen apart and I was on my own."

"I never wrote that to you!"

"Well it's what the notes that I received said."

Amenemhat saw the confusion on Tiaa's face. Then the truth came to him. "Someone has intercepted our notes and changed them so we'd turn on each other!"

"But who?" Tiaa hissed.

"It can't be Kaaper," Amenemhat said. "He's been carrying dispatches for me all over Egypt, and they've all been correct. Who does Kaaper give the notes to here in the palace?"

"Princess Iaret," Tiaa replied, "but I trust…"

Tiaa fell silent, and Amenemhat saw that she was concentrating on a thought. Her eyes opened wide and she looked up at him.

"The Princess!" she said. "It was her all along! She's been intercepting our notes. She's the one who arranged for the archer today. I'll bet that the procession route was changed on her instructions so she'd have a reason why her assassin failed. She has been pretending to be my ally, when all along she has been working against me!"

"What are you going to do about her?" Amenemhat asked.

Tiaa shook her head. "I can't do anything until after the banquet." Tiaa gestured toward the poison on the table. "That's when I'm going to kill Pharaoh myself. Once he's dead, I can have her disposed of."

"But you can't let her remain free until then," Amenemhat pointed out. "If she's working against you, she could thwart your plans for tonight, and we'd both get executed for treason."

Tiaa nodded. "I'll have her arrested." She reached for the leather pouch on the table and carefully took out the two rings. She placed the cobra ring on the table and held the ring that Shayari used to kill Prince Webensenu. "I'll say that she used this to kill her brother. The guards will take her somewhere until after the banquet, but instead of Pharaoh decreeing her fate, it will be me as Regent of Egypt."

The Nubian archers led the procession from the northern port to the palace. The people of Men-nefer lined the streets and rooftops to cheer the triumphant return of Pharaoh and his army.

Behind the archers marched the foot soldiers – the tips of their spears glinting in the sunlight. The people waved and cheered as they passed.

Thousands of prisoners taken from Canaan marched in chains behind the foot soldiers. No Hebrew prisoners were part of the procession, though. Pharaoh didn't want the people to be concerned that more calamities might be visited upon Egypt if there were still Hebrews present in the kingdom. No mention had been made that thirty-six hundred Hebrews had been captured. The males had already been castrated, and all of the Hebrews had been sent south to Nubia to work in the mines.

Behind the prisoners, servants used long poles to carry on their shoulders the pallets of plunder taken during the campaign. It was only a small part of the total plunder taken, but it showed the people how successful the campaign had been.

Pharaoh, riding on the captured gilded chariot, followed the pallets of plunder. He wore his armor and his khepresh war crown. The gold disks and the uraeus on the khepresh caught the sunlight, making it look like Pharaoh was bathed in light, as befitting the living god of Egypt. The crowds cheered loudly as he passed.

General Ahmose and Admiral Thuti followed Pharaoh on their chariots, and Merytamon and her two sons rode on Pharaoh's war chariot between the general and the admiral. The rest of the chariots followed at the end of the procession.

Once the procession reached the palace, the prisoners were taken along a different route back to the port to be returned to Goshen. The chariots, archers, and soldiers broke off at the avenue of sphinxes to take positions around the palace. The pallets of plunder were taken into the palace to be put on display for the guests attending the banquet that night.

Pharaoh, General Ahmose, Admiral Thuti, and Merytamon and her sons rode through the avenue of sphinxes to the entrance of the palace. Amenemipet, Kenamun, and several members of Pharaoh's family waited for Pharaoh at the entrance.

Amenemipet bowed low. "Welcome home, Great Pharaoh. Your triumphant return is an inspiration to us all."

Princess Iaret rushed along the corridor that led to the front courtyard of the palace. She wanted to be there with the other members of Pharaoh's family to welcome her father back to his palace. Her sheath dress restricted her movements, making it hard to run faster, but she resisted the urge to pull the dress up above her knees. *This is one of those times that I envy the servant girls and their shorter skirts.*

She was about to enter the courtyard when Tiaa's spy called out to her.

"My Princess, the queen commanded me to find you."

Iaret stopped and turned toward the spy. "What does she need?"

"I don't know, my Princess. I only know I was told to find you and bring you to her."

Iaret looked at where her family had gathered with the Vizier and the Chief Steward. She sighed heavily. "Oh, very well. Take me to her."

Iaret followed the spy to Tiaa's apartment. When she entered the sitting area, she saw Tiaa sitting near the terrace. Six guards stood along the walls.

"You sent for me, my Queen?"

Tiaa's face looked like a cobra that had just eaten a very large rat. "Yes, my dear. I have some disturbing news."

"What is it, my Queen?"

"The procession route through the city was changed at the last moment. It went north of the bazaar instead of south."

Iaret pretended to be shocked. "But that means that... my agent was in the wrong place!"

"Yes." Tiaa's voice sounded too smooth for Iaret's liking.

"What do we do now?"

"*We?*" Tiaa stood. "*We* do nothing. Fortunately, I have a back-up plan."

Tiaa raised her hand, and Amenemhat entered the sitting area from the terrace. He had changed back into his High Priest's robes, and his jeweled dagger glinted in the light given off by the braziers around the queen's apartment.

How did he get in here? If they've talked, then they know that I changed the contents of their notes. Iaret began slowly moving back toward the antechamber.

"Don't, Princess," Tiaa said coldly. "You are undone. Guards!"

Three of the guards rushed forward. Two grabbed Iaret by her arms while one put his hand over her mouth. Iaret recognized them as guards that had been assigned to Prince Webensenu's quarters.

Tiaa walked toward her and held up the ring that Shayari used to kill Prince Webensenu. "She killed her half-brother and used this ring to administer the poison. She planned to use it again tonight to kill her own father, but I had her apartment searched and took the ring before she could use it."

"What do we do with her?" one of the guards asked.

"Pharaoh has to decree her fate, but he won't be available until after the banquet," Tiaa said. "We need to put her somewhere so she can't harm anyone. The granaries of the palace are currently empty, aren't they? Lock her in one of those."

The guards began pulling Iaret toward the antechamber.

"And don't let her out unless it's on my orders," Tiaa called after them. "No one is to see her or talk to her until Pharaoh passes judgment on her."

"Yes, my Queen."

CHAPTER 19

Pharaoh pulled his fourth-born son, Prince Amenhotep, aside for a quiet conversation.

"How much are you aware of what's been going on in the palace while I've been away?" Pharaoh asked.

Prince Amenhotep seemed confused. "What do you mean, Father? Are you talking about the deaths of Webensenu and Senebsen?"

"I'm talking about your mother's attempts to have you named the next Pharaoh," Pharaoh answered bluntly.

"Me? The next Pharaoh? But Webensenu and Thutmose are older than I am."

"And now Webensenu is dead," Pharaoh pointed out.

Prince Amenhotep stared at his father. "You mean my mother was behind that? I thought it was a scorpion sting."

Pharaoh shook his head. "No, it was poison. Your mother has proven that she'll kill anyone to make you the next Pharaoh with her as regent."

"Why would she be regent? You're still Pharaoh."

Pharaoh regarded his son silently.

Prince Amenhotep scratched his head, and then his eyes went wide and his jaw dropped. "She'd kill you to become regent?"

Pharaoh nodded.

Prince Amenhotep dropped to his knees and took his father's hands. "Father, I had no idea that my mother was plotting against you. I would never agree to be part of anything that would hurt you! I don't want to be Pharaoh unless you want me to be, and I would never want my brothers to be killed just to improve my position."

Pharaoh smiled at his son. "I believe you. There are things that are going to happen tonight. Things that will affect you and your mother. Things that must be done. You cannot mention anything that we've talked about to anyone, understand? Especially your mother."

Prince Amenhotep nodded. "I understand, Father. Is mother going to be punished for what she did?"

Pharaoh nodded.

"Am I in trouble, too?"

"No, as long as you didn't know about her plans and as long as you don't tell her anything that we've talked about."

"I swear to the gods that I won't say a word to her."

Iaret put up quite a struggle as she was dragged toward the granaries behind the palace, but she was no match for three guards.

I have to warn Amenemipet and my father. If Tiaa's keeping me locked up until after the banquet, then that must be when she and Amenemhat are planning to strike. Where is Hannu? Is he in the kitchens yet? I need him to find me before Tiaa can kill my father!

The guards reached the granaries. One of the guards released Iaret's arm and opened the granary door. Iaret grabbed the hand covering her mouth, pulled it down, and shouted at the top of her voice. "Help me!"

The guards shoved her through the open granary door and slammed it closed behind her. One inserted the locking bolt on the door, and they took their posts around the granary to keep anyone from trying to free her from her temporary prison.

Amenemhat listened to Tiaa explain her plans as they sat in the room where she kept the castor seeds and the poison.

"I'm impressed," he said finally. "You have everything worked out to deal with Pharaoh and his sons. The nobles are ready to deal with the military leaders, and my priests will move against the civil leaders across Egypt to ensure that the government is loyal to you alone. But what about Amenemipet? Is he on your side or Pharaoh's?"

Tiaa shrugged. "I truly don't know. I'd like to keep him, but he could prove to be too much of a threat." Tiaa leaned over and patted Amenemhat's knee. "Besides, you'll make an excellent Vizier, don't you think?"

"Me? Vizier?"

"There's no one else I'd rather have helping me rule Egypt, and you can't do that as High Priest," Tiaa pointed out.

Amenemhat smiled. "Vizier. I like the sound of that."

"I knew you would."

Tiaa finished putting a large dose of the poison on the spike of her cobra ring, which would guarantee that death would come much more quickly. She held it up so Amenemhat could look at it. "This will be the instrument of our destiny tonight."

Amenemhat looked at the ring and nodded. "It's amazing how something so small can change the course of history."

"When it's wielded by the right hand," Tiaa purred.

"Will you wear your khepresh war crown tonight, Great Pharaoh?" Amenemipet asked when he was alone with Pharaoh in the royal apartment late that afternoon, "Or will you wear the traditional crown of Upper and Lower Egypt?"

"The war crown," Pharaoh decided. "This is the celebration of a military campaign, after all."

Amenemipet nodded. "Did you speak with Prince Amenhotep?"

Pharaoh nodded. "He says that he knew nothing about Tiaa's plots. I believe him."

"Good," Amenemipet said. "The soldiers will begin rounding up the families of the nobles on the list as soon as the banquet begins. It'll be a couple of days before we find out how things went in Waset, but word has already arrived that conspirators from some of the cities south of here have been arrested and executed."

Pharaoh nodded. "Where is Iaret? I thought she'd be there with my family to greet me when I arrived. I haven't seen her at all today."

Amenemipet shrugged. "I haven't seen her, either."

"Find her," Pharaoh ordered. "I want her to accompany me to the banquet."

"Yes, Great Pharaoh."

Amenemipet left the royal apartment and headed for the harem. When he reached Iaret's apartment, it was empty, except for the guards posted there.

"Have you seen the Princess?" he asked them.

"No Vizier," one of the guards said. "She left before Pharaoh arrived at the palace."

"Where could she be?" Amenemipet asked himself.

"You should ask Hannu," one of the other guards suggested. "He always seems to know where the Princess is."

The other guards snickered softly.

"Who is Hannu?" Amenemipet demanded.

"Vizier, he's one of the guards assigned to the Princess," the first guard said.

"Why isn't he here?" Amenemipet asked.

"I think the captain posted him to the kitchens tonight to make certain that no one tampers with the food."

"And where is the captain?"

"He should be in the courtyard outside the banquet hall, Vizier."

Amenemipet nodded and left Iaret's apartments. He strode across the palace, through the banquet hall, and into the courtyard where most of invited guests had already arrived and were taking their seats for the banquet.

Amenemipet scanned the crowd for several moments before finally finding the Captain of the Medjay Guards. He made his way through the throng of guests to reach the captain.

"Vizier! Is there something that you need?" the captain asked when Amenemipet reached him.

"Princess Iaret is missing, and Pharaoh wants her found

214

before the banquet begins. I understand that there's a guard named Hannu who is particularly close to her. I need you and him to help me find her."

"Of course, Vizier! This way."

The captain led Amenemipet to the kitchens, which was a whirlwind of last-moment activity as the cooks and servants worked at a feverish pace to have everything ready on time. The captain looked around for a few moments before pointing to a guard standing near the food tasters.

"That's Hannu, Vizier."

Amenemipet and the captain approached Hannu, who snapped to attention when he saw them.

"Have you seen Princess Iaret?" Amenemipet demanded.

"No, Vizier. Not since this morning. Why?"

"She's missing," the captain said. "Pharaoh wants her found before the banquet starts. Come with us."

"Yes, sir!" Hannu signaled for one of the other guards to take his post, and he followed Amenemipet and the captain out of the kitchens and into the corridor that ran along the banquet hall.

"Okay," Amenemipet said once they were away from the noise of the kitchen. "She's not in her quarters, and she wasn't at the palace entrance to welcome Pharaoh home. Where else could she be?"

"She spends a lot of time with the queen," Hannu suggested. "Have you tried her apartment?"

I was right there earlier. "No. Let's go."

Tiaa and Amenemhat arrived at the banquet hall together. Pharaoh's sons, concubines, and other wives had already arrived and were seated near Pharaoh's table. Pharaoh's siblings and their families were also already seated at the tables across from Pharaoh's. Amenemhat left Tiaa to join the other High Priests along the far wall. Kaaper stood and offered him a seat, which Amenemhat accepted with a smile.

Tiaa crossed the banquet hall floor and stood on the opposite end from Pharaoh's table. Ordinarily, she would be wearing a seshed on her head like the other women of the royal family, but since this was an important ceremonial occasion, she wore the crown reserved for the most important ceremonies and events. It was called the royal vulture crown, and it consisted of gold falcon wings spread round her head adorned by a uraeus. The gold wings caught the light from the braziers, making the wings look like they were on fire.

By tradition, Pharaoh entered the banquet hall last and stood behind his table. Tiaa's part of the ceremony was to take a bowl of beer, carry it across the floor, and kneel before her husband, handing him the bowl as a welcoming gift to the living god of Egypt. Then she and Pharaoh would sit at Pharaoh's table, and the banquet would begin.

But when he takes the bowl from my hand, my cobra ring will strike him down. Then I'll use the ring to strike down Prince Thutmose, and Amenemhat's nobles and priests will make their move. I'll be regent by this time tomorrow. There should be enough poison on the ring to kill both Pharaoh and Prince Thutmose before tomorrow night.

Amenemipet entered Tiaa's apartment in the harem. The guards snapped to attention when they saw the Vizier followed by their captain.

"Have you seen Princess Iaret?" Amenemipet demanded.

"Yes, Vizier," one of the guards responded. "The Queen had her arrested for attempting to murder Pharaoh and for murdering her half-brother, Prince Webensenu."

"You fools!" Amenemipet shouted. "The Queen is the assassin! Princess Iaret has been working with her father to stop the Queen."

"I'm sorry, Vizier," the first guard said, clearly shaken by Amenemipet words. "We didn't know."

"Where did the Queen have her taken?" the captain demanded.

"The granaries behind the palace."

Amenemipet, the captain, and Hannu ran out of the queen's

apartment.

Pharaoh paced impatiently in his royal apartment. Amenemipet and Iaret were supposed to meet him there, but they hadn't arrived yet. Pharaoh was alone, apart from the ever-present guards. He glanced toward the terrace and noticed that the sun had already set. *The banquet is supposed to be starting now. I don't want to be there without my daughter, but I can't keep the entire court waiting.*

Pharaoh placed the blue war crown on his head and looked at his reflection in the flat polished bronze disk on the wall. Then he turned and left the royal apartment, accompanied by four of his Medjay guards.

He strode to the other side of the palace until he reached the banquet hall. He peeked through the curtains, trying to make certain that no one saw him. *My family is all there except for Iaret. Where is she?* He noticed that Tiaa was on the opposite side of the hall, standing next to the taster who was ready to hand her Pharaoh's offering. *Tiaa's ready to perform her part of the welcoming ceremony. I'll give Iaret another few moments, and then I'll have to start without her.*

Amenemipet, the captain, and Hannu reached the granaries and saw three guards on duty.

"Where is Princess Iaret?" Amenemipet demanded.

"She's being held prisoner by order of the queen until Pharaoh is ready to pass judgement on her for murdering her half-brother and attempting to murder Pharaoh."

"Release her," Amenemipet ordered.

"I cannot," the guard stated. "My orders come from the queen."

"Release her," the captain stated, stepping forward.

"I'm sorry, Captain. My orders come for the queen."

"And my orders come from Pharaoh himself," Amenemipet growled. "Release her."

"Pharaoh wants to pass judgment on her before the banquet?" The guard hesitated, sounding confused.

Amenemipet threw up his hands in anger. "Pharaoh knows that it's *the queen* who's trying to kill him. The queen, and not the princess, is also responsible for poisoning Prince Webensenu."

The guard shook his head. "No. The queen showed us the ring that the princess used to kill the prince."

"And where did the queen get this ring?" the captain demanded.

"From Princess Iaret's quarters, Captain."

"Did you see the ring in the princess' quarters?"

The guard hesitated. "No, Captain. The queen already had the ring when Princess Iaret entered the queen's apartment."

"That's because the ring was never in the princess' apartment," Amenemipet snapped. "It had been in the queen's possession all the time."

The guard hesitated again, and Hannu drew his sword. "Release the princess, or I swear to all of the gods that I'll have your head right here."

The guard gestured to the two men standing in front of the granary where they had imprisoned the princess earlier. "Release her."

The men removed the locking bolt and opened the door. Hannu stepped forward and helped Iaret out.

She hugged him tightly. "Thank you," she whispered. "I knew you'd find me."

Amenemipet heard trumpets sounding on the other side of the palace. "The banquet's starting!"

"Tiaa has a ring shaped like a cobra that has a spike on the bottom like the one she used to kill Prince Webensenu," Iaret said. "If she's wearing it tonight, she plans to poison Pharaoh and probably Prince Thutmose."

"We have to stop her," Amenemipet said. Turning to the three guards who had imprisoned the princess, he said, "You three, come with us."

Amenemipet, Iaret, Hannu, the captain, and the three guards raced across the palace to the banquet hall.

Tiaa walked across the banquet hall slowly, making certain not to spill a drop of the beer in the carved wooden bowl that she carried. Her cobra ring glinted in the light from the braziers around the hall as she held the ring away from the side of the bowl. There was enough poison on the ring's spike to kill both Pharaoh and Prince Thutmose, and she didn't want any of the poison getting on the bowl instead.

She saw the taster standing to Pharaoh's side, ready to sample the beer before allowing Pharaoh to drink from the bowl. *Your tasters won't save you tonight, my Husband. The poison's not in the bowl; it's on my ring. And when you're dead, and the tasters are still alive, no one will be able to say that it was poison that killed you.*

Pharaoh stood in front of his table. The light from the braziers around the hall and the courtyard danced in the evening breeze, surrounding him with a golden glow as he waited for Tiaa to complete her part of the welcoming ceremony.

Tiaa had almost reached the place where she was to kneel before Pharaoh when she saw movement out of the corner of her eye. She glanced to her right and saw Amenemipet, the Captain of the Medjay Guards, and four guards enter the banquet hall.

You're too late Vizier. You're all too late.

Tiaa lowered herself to her knees and held the bowl up toward Pharaoh.

Pharaoh took a step forward to accept the bowl from his royal wife. The taster stepped forward as well.

Tiaa shifted her hand as his moved around the bowl. She moved the cobra ring into position, and...

Someone slammed into her from her right. The bowl tipped over, spilling its contents onto the floor. Tiaa's cobra ring missed Pharaoh's hand and embedded itself into the side of the bowl as Tiaa fell over onto the stone floor.

Her shoulder hit the floor hard, and her crown fell forward, covering her face. But in a flash she rolled into a crouching position and pulled the crown off her head. She saw Pharaoh standing in front of her. *I can still reach him.* She dropped her crown onto the floor and held out her hand to strike with the cobra ring again.

"No!"

Tiaa turned toward the voice and saw Princess Iaret diving toward her. *How is she here? She's supposed to be locked up in the granaries!*

The princess struck Tiaa, knocking her down again. She saw Pharaoh and the taster step back as the Captain of the Medjay Guards and four other guards moved between her and Pharaoh.

Tiaa felt tugging at her finger and saw Iaret's hands trying to pull off the cobra ring.

"Get away, Father," Tiaa heard the princess shouting. "Her cobra ring has poison on it."

Tiaa struggled to keep the ring on her finger. She tried to press the spike into the princess' hand, but the princess grabbed the top of the ring by the cobra's hood and began forcing the spike toward Tiaa's palm. Tiaa straightened her hand to keep the spike away, and when she did, the ring slipped off her hand and skidded across the floor.

Tiaa punched the princess in the shoulder and tried to reach for the ring, but one of the Medjay guards kicked it out of the way and reached down to drag Tiaa to her feet. The three other guards raced forward to surround Tiaa while the first guard reached down to help Princess Iaret to her feet.

Tiaa, breathless from her struggle with Iaret, glared at Pharaoh and his daughter.

"You have failed, Tiaa," Pharaoh growled.

Amenemhat saw the ring skid across the floor and stop a short distance in front of him. He leaped to his feet and reached for the ring.

"Don't let him reach the ring!" he heard someone shout. Two arms wrapped themselves around his waist, keeping him from moving forward.

He saw the guards around the hall hesitate, and he twisted

around to see who was holding him back.

"Kaaper!"

Seeing his acolyte betray him caused Amenemhat to snap. He drew his dagger and slashed it across Kaaper's chest. Kaaper fell backward, releasing Amenemhat. Blood covered Kaaper's chest by the time he hit the floor.

Amenemhat turned to retrieve the ring, but one of the Medjay guards had already recovered it. Amenemhat raised his dagger at the guard and took a step forward.

"Now!" cried Amenemipet.

Soldiers poured into the banquet hall and the courtyard. Several soldiers grabbed Amenemhat's arms and wrestled the dagger from his hand. Nobles and their wives from around the courtyard were seized and hauled away.

Tiaa was dragged from the banquet hall kicking and screaming at the soldiers, who didn't care if they hurt her. They took her to the granary where Princess Iaret had been held prisoner, and they threw her in. They locked the granary and took their posts so that no one could free the former Queen of Egypt. They had orders to keep her locked in the granary until it was time to carry out her execution.

Once all of the conspirators had been removed from the banquet, Pharaoh looked around the hall and the courtyard.

"People of Egypt," he began, "a conspiracy has been uncovered, and tonight the conspirators have been apprehended. My royal wife, along with the High Priest of Amun at Karnak, have conspired to kill me and my oldest surviving son so that my fourth-born son would be named Pharaoh, and my royal wife named regent. There were conspirators here in Men-nefer, in Waset, and in many of the other cities across Egypt. But they have failed and will all receive the retribution they deserve. We're here to give thanks to those who prevented the conspiracy from succeeding and for the success of our military campaign in Canaan.

"Before we continue with the banquet, I have two

announcements. First, I have chosen my heir. My third-born son, Prince Thutmose, shall be Pharaoh after me. His mother, Sitamun, is now my royal wife, and will have the title of Queen of Egypt from this day forward."

Pharaoh gestured for Prince Thutmose, Princess Iaret, and Sitamun to join him at his table. "Tomorrow, the conspirators will be dealt with harshly, as is fitting for anyone plotting to kill a Pharaoh. But tonight is a time for celebration."

Princess Iaret recovered Tiaa's crown and handed it to her father. Pharaoh accepted it and placed it on Sitamun's head. Sitamun beamed as she sat next to her husband.

Pharaoh nodded to Kenamun, and servants entered the hall and the courtyard with trays of food and drink.

Pharaoh leaned over to his daughter and whispered, "Thank you for saving my life."

"You're welcome, Father," she replied softly. "You're welcome."

Iaret glanced over her shoulder. Hannu stood behind her, protecting her as always. She smiled at him. His face remained neutral, but he winked at her quickly so no one would notice.

CHAPTER 20

After the banquet was over, Pharaoh met with Amenemipet, General Ahmose, and Admiral Thuti. Princess Iaret, the Captain of the Medjay Guards, and the Men-nefer garrison commander were there, too.

"Where are the conspirators?" Pharaoh asked.

"Your wife is locked in the palace granaries, Great Pharaoh, but the rest are all locked up at the city barracks," the garrison commander answered. "Their families were taken there as soon as the banquet began."

"Did we get all of them?" Amenemipet asked.

The garrison commander shook his head. "It seems that a few fled the city during the last few days. I've sent word to Waset and Nubia to be on the lookout for them."

"What do you want done with the prisoners, Great Pharaoh?" General Ahmose asked.

"None of the conspirators shall have an afterlife," Pharaoh replied. "Their names are to be stricken from all records, and their bodies defiled. All of the priests, other than Amenemhat, the High Priest of Amun, are to be beheaded immediately and their bodies cast into the western desert. I want the priests' heads stuck on pikes along the riverbank."

"And the nobles and their families?"

Pharaoh hesitated. *I know what's expected of me, and I've used extreme methods to vanquish my enemies. I've just never had to order the death of the innocent before. But I can't leave any members of a traitor's family alive. No pharaoh has ever done that without one of those family members trying to avenge the traitor's death. The children must die, and it has to be done in a way that discourages future acts of treason. I wish it could be otherwise; I wish there were an alternative. But if I appear weak in the face of such treachery, then there will be conspiracies against me and my sons for the rest of my reign. I have no choice.* "The children of the nobles are to be fed to the crocodiles in the pens while their parents watch. Then behead the parents. Dump their bodies in the desert and stick their heads on pikes along the river with the priests'. If any of the children survive the pens, have them beheaded."

"What about the High Priest of Amun and Tiaa?" Amenemipet asked.

"I have something special in mind for Amenemhat," Pharaoh said. Then he turned to his daughter. "But I want Princess Iaret to name Tiaa's fate."

"Why me, Father?" she asked.

"Because you knew her plans and her nature better than anyone. I don't think anyone could decree a more fitting fate for her than you could."

Iaret thought about it for a few moments. Then she smiled. "I know just the thing."

The executions of the priests took place at sunrise the next morning. All of Amenemhat's and Tiaa's spies in the palace were executed first. Hundreds of heads lined the riverfront by the time the nobles and their families were dragged to the crocodile pens near the riverfront.

The nobles and their wives watched in horror as their children were hauled to the top of the scaffolds along the walls of the pens and thrown to the crocodiles waiting inside. The screams of their children could still be heard as the executioners beheaded their parents, sticking the heads on pikes and throwing the bodies on flat wagons to be carried deep into the desert.

Pharaoh and all of his surviving sons watched the executions from a platform that had been set up between the crocodile pens and the city walls. The sounds of the screams tore at his heart, but he stood expressionless as the executions were carried out. His sons did the same, although Pharaoh knew that they were each deeply affected by what they heard and saw that day.

Once the executions of the nobles were finished, Pharaoh's guards escorted him and his sons to the city's west gate. There was one more execution to oversee with the princes.

Amenemhat was brought to the western gates of the city. Ropes were tied around his chest. Two chariots approached from the barracks and stopped in front of Pharaoh, who stood a short distance away with his sons. Amenemhat's ropes were secured to the back of one of the chariots.

"Your orders, Great Pharaoh?" the lead charioteer asked.

"Drag the body into the deep desert. Behead him and leave the body out there. But bring the head back. I want it sent to Waset and mounted on the wall, facing his temple in Karnak as a warning to the other High Priests down there."

"Yes, Great Pharaoh."

"Great Pharaoh, I beg of you. Don't—" Amenemhat's voice was cut off by Pharaoh's fist. Pharaoh struck the High Priest so hard on the side of his mouth that his knees buckled. Two guards had to grab Amenemhat by the arms to keep him from falling into the sand. The High Priest whimpered softly but said nothing more.

"Put a bag over his head, and get him out of my sight," Pharaoh snarled.

One of the charioteers pulled a leather sack over the High Priest's head so that man's features would survive being dragged. Then the driver of the lead chariot snapped his whip, and the chariot raced away, pulling Amenemhat forward and dragging him behind it. The second chariot followed, keeping far enough back so that the horses didn't trample the former High Priest.

Tiaa was tied up, and a bag was placed over her head. She was led out of the granary and tossed into the back of a wagon. She bounced around as the horse-drawn wagon made its way through the city to the southern port of Men-nefer, where Pharaoh's barge waited.

She heard the water lapping against the side of the barge and smelled the water as she was chained to the deck of the barge. Her hood remained in place except when she was fed and given water to drink. Guards surrounded her at all times, and she was not allowed to speak.

She had no consciousness of the passage of time, but it seemed like days before she heard the voices of many people in the distance. *We must be approaching a city, but which one? Perunefer? Waset? Where are they taking me?* The barge came to a stop, and she was unchained from the deck, led from the barge, and put in the back of another wagon. She heard someone shouting orders, and soon the wagon set off. The voices of the many people faded behind her, and the sun mercilessly made the timbers of the wagon uncomfortably hot. *Am I being taken into the desert?*

When the wagon finally stopped, she was roughly pulled out of the wagon and half-dragged down a series of steps and ramps.

The bag was removed from her head, and the ropes binding her wrists were cut loose. She looked around. "Where am I?" she demanded, rubbing her wrists to get the circulation flowing again.

"Don't you recognize this place?" she heard Princess Iaret ask.

Tiaa looked at the princess, who was standing next to a wall that had recently been opened by stonemasons.

"Should I?" Tiaa asked with as much contempt as she could manage.

Iaret gestured toward the open wall. "This is where Senebsen is entombed." Pointing toward the wall to her left, she added, "And this is where your firstborn son and Prince Webensenu are entombed."

Tiaa blanched. "I'm in Pharaoh's tomb in the Valley of the Kings? Why am I here?"

"You wanted to be Pharaoh, didn't you?" Iaret's voice sounded ice-cold. "Oh, I know you would have borne the title of Regent, but you'd be as close to being a Pharaoh as anyone without royal blood could hope to be, right? It only seems fitting that your life ends here in the tomb of a Pharaoh."

Iaret gestured for the guards to push Tiaa through the opening into the tomb where Senebsen's sarcophagus had been placed. Once Tiaa was inside the chamber, the stonemasons began closing up the wall again.

Tiaa looked around. In addition to the sarcophagus, there was a small oil lamp on the floor. "You're not actually going to seal me up in here to die, are you?"

"Why not?" Iaret asked. "You were ready to kill anyone who got in your way. How is this any different?"

The stonemasons worked quickly, and soon there was only one small opening left in the wall.

"Surely there's another way," Tiaa begged as the stonemasons prepared to seal her in the tomb forever.

Iaret held up her hand, and the stonemasons stopped. Iaret reached into a leather pouch at her waist and withdrew Tiaa's cobra ring.

"I imagine there's still enough poison on the spike to kill you in a couple of days. It'll be painful, but at least it will be better than dying after days of thirst and starvation in total darkness."

"Total darkness?" Tiaa didn't understand.

"There's only enough oil in that lamp to last for a few hours," Iaret pointed out. "When it goes out, your body will be entombed in darkness until the end of time. And when you finally die, the realm of demons awaits you."

Iaret tossed the cobra ring through the opening. It landed at Tiaa's feet. "Goodbye, Tiaa. May the gods treat you as you treated those around you."

The stonemasons placed the final stone in place and sealed Tiaa into her tomb.

Tiaa screamed and pounded on the wall, but she couldn't hear anything on the other side.

I'm trapped. I'm going to die in here. She looked down and picked up the cobra ring. *Do I take my own poison, or do I starve to death?*

She sat down in the corner of the room next to the oil lamp. *What do I do? Oh, gods, what do I do?*

The oil lamp began to sputter. *She lied to me. There aren't hours of oil left, there are only moments left.*

A moment later, Tiaa discovered what total darkness was. She cried for what seemed like hours, but all she heard were the echoes of her own voice – mocking her and her plight.

She only had two options left, and they both led to the same end. *Fast or slow. Those are my choices.*

She made her decision. *Amenemhat, I love you.* She pressed the spike of the cobra ring into the palm of her hand.

Princess Iaret rode in the front of the wagon between Hannu and the driver. She giggled as they left the site of Pharaoh's tomb behind them and rode through the Valley of the Kings past its many tombs and funerary temples.

"What's so funny, my Princess?" Hannu inquired as they reached the main road leading back to Waset.

"I'll bet that Tiaa has tried to poison herself with her ring by now. I wonder how long it will take for her to realize that there *is* no poison on that ring."

"What?"

Iaret smiled. "I had all of the poison removed from the spike of her cobra ring. She can stab herself a hundred times with that spike, and the worst that will happen to her is that she'll bleed a little."

"So she'll die a slow death, sealed in a dark tomb with no way out? That's diabolical, my Princess."

"But it is a fitting end for her, don't you think? Alone in that tomb until she dies of thirst or starves to death, she'll have time to think about what she did to my father's family and what she tried to do to Egypt."

Hannu nodded slowly. "It's still a terrible way to die, my Princess. I hope I never do anything to earn your wrath!"

Iaret patted Hannu on his knee. "Keep protecting me and taking care of my *other* needs, and you'll never have cause to worry about me becoming angry with you. Exhausted perhaps, but never angry."

Iaret started giggling again, and Hannu laughed with her. The wagon and Iaret's escorts increased speed to return the princess to the royal barge before nightfall, which waited at the port of Waset to take her back to Men-nefer.

Pharaoh had dinner with his family when Iaret returned from Waset.

"Is it finally over, Father?" Prince Thutmose asked.

Pharaoh nodded. "With the exception of a few conspirators who fled south, everyone plotting against us has been caught and dealt with. I know the executions seemed harsh – especially using crocodiles on the children – but the worst thing that a Pharaoh of Egypt can do is appear weak in the face of a conspiracy like this one. The executions will be remembered for years, which should deter anyone from plotting or attempting to murder a Pharaoh and his family."

Pharaoh looked at Prince Amenhotep, knowing that the young prince privately mourned the loss of his mother. The prince understood the reasons why she had to die. There was a touch of sadness around the young prince's eyes, but he gave no other indication that he was mad or upset with what had happened. Pharaoh had promised that he would not strike Tiaa's name from the memory of Egypt like Thutmose III did with Moses and Hatshepsut, and that pleased the young prince.

"What happened to Kaaper?" Iaret asked.

"He died of his wounds," Pharaoh replied. "I've ordered that he be buried with full funerary rites in the royal tombs for his service to us. Amenemhat's successor, Mery, will oversee the rites."

"What will you do now, my Husband?" Sitamun asked.

"I need to finish my father's work and have the names of Moses and Hatshepsut stricken from Egypt. Then I'll build terraces and temples to commemorate my victories in Canaan. After that, we'll continue to rebuild from the Hebrew calamities that plagued us so terribly. I inherited a great kingdom from my father. I intend to make my kingdom even more glorious before I pass it to the next Pharaoh of Egypt."

Amenhotep II reigned for another twenty-seven years (thirty-seven years in total). During that time, Egypt remained one of the most powerful empires in the world.

The harvest following the campaign in Canaan was bountiful, and Egypt never again came so close to starvation as it did following the plagues unleashed by Moses and his god.

Peace negotiations continued with the Mitanni until after Amenhotep II's death and were finally concluded by his successor, Thutmose IV. It was the first such alliance in Egyptian history.

The remainder of Amenhotep II's reign was one of the longest periods of peace in the history of the kingdom. This allowed Pharaoh to pursue an aggressive building program, leaving his mark on nearly every major architectural site across Egypt.

And it should be noted that, in spite of the loss of the Hebrew slaves, the kingdom inherited by Thutmose IV upon his father's death was richer and more powerful than the one Amenhotep II inherited from his father.

The End

ABOUT THE AUTHOR

Award-winning author and publisher William Speir was born in 1962 in Birmingham, Alabama. He attended the University of Alabama, and graduated from the University of Alabama at Birmingham in 1984. He spent over 25 years in corporate America, serving as a management consultant, leader, IT executive, and HR/Payroll executive for top tier consulting firms and Fortune 100 companies.

During William's corporate career, he published several articles on leadership and the human impact of organizational changes and technology changes.

His first experience with book publishing was with a series of ten textbooks he authored about field artillery in the 19th century. These textbooks were later consolidated into a single volume and re-published in 2015 as *Muzzle-Loading Artillery for Reenactors*.

In addition to his artillery manual, William has published 15 novels, including an 8-book action-adventure series (*The Knights of the Saltire Series*), five historical novels (*King's Ransom, The Saga of Asbjorn Thorleikson, Nicaea – The Rise of the Imperial Church, Arthur, King,* and *The Besieged Pharaoh*), one fantasy novel (*The Kingstone of Airmid*), and one science fiction novel (*The Olympium of Bacchus 12*).

William is a 5-time Royal Palm Literary Award winner: 2014 Second Place Unpublished Historical Fiction for *King's Ransom*, 2015 Second Place Unpublished Historical Fiction for *The Saga of Asbjorn Thorleikson*, 2017 Second Place Published Historical Fiction for *Arthur, King*, 2017 First Place Published Historical Fiction for *Nicaea – The Rise of the Imperial Church*, and 2017 First Place Published Science Fiction for *The Olympium of Bacchus 12*.

For more information about William Speir, please visit his website at WilliamSpeir.com.

Progressive Rising Phoenix Press is an independent publisher. We offer wholesale discounts and multiple binding options with no minimum purchases for schools, libraries, book clubs, and retail vendors. We also offer rewards for libraries, schools, independent book stores, and book clubs. Please visit our website to see our updated catalogue of titles and our wholesale discount page at:

www.ProgressiveRisingPhoenix.com

www.ingramcontent.com/pod-product-compliance
Lightning Source LLC
Chambersburg PA
CBHW032035240626
47154CB00003B/924